# The SECOND TREE from the CORNER

# Books by E. B. White

Poems and Sketches of E. B. White

Essays of E. B. White

Letters of E. B. White

The Trumpet of the Swan

The Points of My Compass

The Second Tree from the Corner

Charlotte's Web

Here Is New York

The Wild Flag

Stuart Little

One Man's Meat

The Fox of Peapack

Quo Vadimus?

Farewell to Model T

Every Day Is Saturday

The Lady Is Cold


An E. B. White Reader
    edited by William W. Watt and Robert W. Bradford

The Elements of Style
    William Strunk, Jr. (revised and enlarged by E. B. White)

A Subtreasury of American Humor
    co-edited with Katharine S. White

Is Sex Necessary?
    with James Thurber

# The Second Tree from the Corner

# E·B· White

WITH AN INTRODUCTION BY

E. B. WHITE

Harper & Row, Publishers, New York
Cambridge, Philadelphia, San Francisco, London
Mexico City, São Paulo, Singapore, Sydney

A hardcover edition of this book was published in 1984 by Harper & Row, Publishers.

First PERENNIAL LIBRARY edition published 1989.

*Designed by Daniel F. Bradley*

Library of Congress Cataloging in Publication Data

White, E. B. (Elwyn Brooks), 1899-
    The second tree from the corner.

    "Perennial Library."

    I. Title.
PS3545.H5187S4  1989    818'.5209    84-47609
ISBN 0-06-091516-1 (pbk.)

89  90  91  92  93  FG  10  9  8  7  6  5  4  3  2  1

# NOTE

Most of the pieces in this book were published first in *The New Yorker*. "The Hotel of the Total Stranger" appeared in *Harper's* as one of the essays in the "One Man's Meat" series. "Death of a Pig" appeared in the *Atlantic Monthly*. "Zoo Revisited" is here published for the first time.

The remarks on humor in Chapter III formed part of an introduction to "A Subtreasury of American Humor," published by Coward-McCann. The remarks on Don Marquis in the same chapter are taken from an introduction to "the lives and times of archy and mehitabel," published by Doubleday. "The Hen (An Appreciation)" is the preface to "A Basic Chicken Guide for the Small Flock Owner," published by Morrow. "Farewell, My Lovely!", a collaboration with Richard L. Strout, appeared first in *The New Yorker* under that title, later as a small book called "Farewell to Model T" published by G. P. Putnam's Sons.

# CONTENTS

### III. THE WONDERFUL WORLD OF LETTERS

# INTRODUCTION

THIRTY YEARS AGO, I sat down one day and wrote the foreword for a book of mine to be called *The Second Tree from the Corner*—a collection of odd (some of them *very* odd) pieces. The book came out, and I gather it is about to come out again. In that 1954 foreword, which will be retained in the new edition, I noted that the book seemed to carry an undertone of indiscriminate farewell. It was to be my swan song, in which I bade goodbye to everybody and every thing. I had grown old—I was fifty-four—and was bathed in the "sweet sorrow of parting." By putting the book together, I was neatening up my affairs, preparatory to the death that I assumed was imminent.

Now, thirty years later, I am again at work writing some introductory remarks for the same book, a man who publicly took his departure three decades ago and who, being still alive, is so hopelessly off schedule as to appear ridiculous in the eyes of the reader. "Goodbye, goodbye!" I sobbed in 1954 and then failed to disappear. It is unnerving, and the whole business puts a heavy strain on a man of my advanced age, to find that he never seems to get done with anything in a clean-cut fashion and must write not just one introduction to a book but two.

I have not reread *The Second Tree from the Corner* in preparation for my current ordeal, but I have prowled around in its pages to see what is still afloat after so long a period of time and have been pleased to discover some old friends. I was glad to encounter Mrs. Wienckus again, the woman who was arrested in Newark, New Jersey, because she was found sleeping in two empty cartons in a hallway. She was arraigned, as some of you may remember, charged with being "disorderly." In all the years that have gone by since my report, I have never lost my admiration for Mrs. Wienckus. She had apparently eliminated everything she couldn't carry with her and had established her own kind of order. Her spirit, I am glad to report, still lives in our latter-day world. I have just been reading a newspaper account of a woman found living in a pup tent deep in the winter woods of Maine—a blood sister to Mrs. Wienckus although of a different stripe. The game wardens who discovered this "tent woman," as she is now called, brought her out of the tent, took her into custody, and turned her over to a mental health institution, presumably because the tiny tent contained nothing much to suggest a civilized life, not even a Hammacher Schlemmer catalogue in whose pages she could have learned of the many conveniences that are available today to any right-minded woman—a portable dry-ice maker, an ultra-sonic cool-mist humidifier, an English heated towel stand, an electronic wine guide, a digital alarm pillbox, an electric kitty litterbox, an oversized electric heating pad, and a cordless electric peppermill. To the wardens the tent must have seemed bare indeed. The woman kept warm at night by heating stones over a small fire and putting them in her sleeping bag. The woods were cold but not the woman. When found she was in good condition. It is encouraging to know that the spirit of Mrs. Wienckus lives on into these desperate days, even though the two women are unlike in other respects.

Another character in *The Second Tree* whom I was glad to greet again was Don Marquis, whose work I tip my hat to in "The Wonderful World of Letters" section of the book. The literary arbiters of Marquis's day never put much stock in him as a poet, but I thought he was greatly endowed. It would now appear that he had another admirer in John F. Kennedy. It was to Marquis that Kennedy apparently turned when he was writing his inaugural address. The famous passage that begins, "Ask not what your country can do for you . . ." is right out of Marquis's poem about Warty Bliggens, the toad. Warty, at ease beneath his toadstool, considered himself to be the center of the universe. The earth existed to grow toadstools for him to sit under, the sun to give him light by day, and the moon and wheeling constellations to make beautiful the night for the sake of Warty Bliggens. You will remember that when they asked the toad to what act of his he imputed this interest on the part of the creator, Warty replied, "Ask rather what the universe has done to deserve me." Kennedy couldn't pass up a chance like that, and the passage turned out to be the high point in his maiden address to the nation. Looking back to those happier days, I feel a renewed surge of affection for the author of archy.

Well, the years have flown by, the world has not stood still. I sometimes draw the curtain against the twilight, but it would be fatuous of me to apologize for my being alive. A much greater miracle is that the book itself is still alive. One of the characters in the book predicted, thirty years ago, that in fifty years only five percent of the people would be reading. I have no statistics at hand that would either support or contradict this prophecy, but I do know that last year (1983) the average family in America watched seven hours of television a day, and it is reasonable to assume that, whatever else they were doing as they sat before the screen, they weren't reading.

Reading, however, is obviously not dead—a staggering number of books and non-books is published every year. Another character in this book of mine—the poet for January in the Old Farmer's Almanac—felt more optimistic about the future of reading than did the prophet quoted above, who would have us down to five percent by the close of the century. The poet, after taking a good look at the twilight,

> Where all's collapse and chaos, now,
> And dust of these obscures the sun . . .

advises the reader to

> . . . take your stand and stay to see
> The wild and frightened and absurd
> Collapsing chaos turn and flee
> Before the grave compulsive word.

As far back as 1954, I thought that was good advice. After a lapse of thirty years, I still think so. One rarely meets the grave compulsive word on the TV screen. To encounter it, one sits down and opens the pages of a book.

—E. B. W.
February 1984

# FOREWORD

A TENDENCY to revisit, to try old places and other times in the
hope of tasting again the sweet sorrow of parting, is discernible
in these pages. The book, in some of its stretches, is a sentimental
journey to the scenes of my crime. I am a goodbye sayer, too, it
would appear from the evidence. There is an account of my bidding goodbye to a complete stranger in a barbershop merely
because he is leaving; and as I look over this book that I have
assembled from so many spare parts, I can't escape the disturbing
realization that the whole thing carries an undertone of indiscriminate farewell. I even knock off the planet Earth at one point,
in an attempt to tidy up the empyrean before somebody else does
it for me. A man who is over fifty, as am I, is sure that he has only
about twenty minutes to live, and it is natural, I suppose, that he
should feel disposed to put his affairs in order, such as they are,
to harvest what fruit he has not already picked up and stored away
against the winter, and to tie his love for the world into a convenient bundle, accessible to all.

Whoever sets pen to paper writes of himself, whether knowingly
or not, and this is a book of revelations: essays, poems, stories,
opinions, reports, drawn from the past, the present, the future, the
city, and the country. I could have called it "Weird Confessions"
as well as not, but "The Second Tree from the Corner" sounds
more genteel and is, in addition, the title of one of the pieces (the
one where the fellow says goodbye to sanity).

xv

Assembling the book has been a sobering experience, revealing, as it has, a man unable to sit still for more than a few minutes at a time, untouched by the dedication required for sustained literary endeavor, yet unable *not* to write. However, I do not come to this foreword in a spirit of derogation or with any idea of offering alibis. If these collected writings resemble a dog's breakfast, I shall insist that it is because of my unusual understanding of dogs and my sympathy for them in their morning problems.

For the most part I have aimed to select material that is not too dependent on the immediate events or portents that inspired it. In three of the chapters, the reader will encounter a section of notes that were published first in the Notes and Comment page of *The New Yorker*. These are, of course, couched in the first person plural, a device as commonplace in journalism as it is harebrained. I do not know how the editorial "we" originated, but I think it must first have been employed in an effort to express a corporate or institutional opinion and that in no time at all the individual charged with formulating this opinion forgot all about his basic responsibility and got talking about himself and peddling his personal prejudices, retaining the "we" and thus giving the impression that the stuff was written by a set of identical twins or the members of a tumbling act. There is nothing I can do about this, and the reader is advised to dismiss it from his mind.

I have not dated the notes, preferring to depend on the reader's perspicacity and good will. Whenever I came across a note that seemed unintelligible without a date, I simply threw it out, serving it right and teaching myself a lesson. Once in a while the reader will stumble on some antique ghost like Hitler, pottering about as though still alive, and will get a momentary jolt. But I am not one to pamper readers, and don't want them daydreaming their way through this book like drivers on a superhighway. This books twists and turns. Go carefully, and remember: the time you save may be your own.

Incidentally, the publication over my signature of items that formed part of the *New Yorker*'s anonymous editorial page is not to be taken as an indication that I am the fellow responsible for that page. The page is the work of many. I am one of the contributors to it. I feel greatly indebted to the magazine for its willingness to let me use these paragraphs, for when something is published first anonymously and then later an author is unveiled, the public draws wrong conclusions about the workings of a magazine and tends to give credit where credit is not due. Theoretically, it is a mistake to break anonymity, and though I am guilty of it, I commit the sin knowingly and for selfish reasons.

Most of the material in the book is presented in exactly the form in which it originally appeared. In a few places I've made slight revisions. Here and there I change a "which" to a "that," in memory of H. W. Ross, who cared deeply about the matter— so deeply, in fact, that I still wince every time I discover myself violating the rule he loved so well. In a couple of places I have changed proper names, for symmetry, or for variety, or to save real people the possible embarrassment of being associated with me in my off-color enterprises.

Although as an observer I try to keep abreast of events, it is a losing game. Progress, deeds, overtake a man. Somebody (I think it was I) once remarked that today's fantasy is tomorrow's news event. The pages that follow confirm the truth of the remark. The future pales into the present. The space platform is old hat. Calculating machines are suffering nervous breakdowns. I wrote the "Song of the Queen Bee" on the strength of information from the Department of Agriculture that bees had not been inseminated by artificial means; but although I composed the poem during lunch hour, and lost not a moment turning it in, it had hardly been off the press when a *Life* photographer sent me graphic evidence that bees had gone the way of all modern flesh. I think there has never been an age more cruel to writers than this one—rendering their stuff obsolete almost before it escapes from the typewriter. On the other hand, human nature is fairly steady and almost changeless: the first piece in the chapter called "Time Present" was written a number of years ago, during the Second World War, but it belongs to the present, and as I reread it I saw that time had stood still.

A book should be the occasion of rejoicing, but it is seldom that, imparting a feeling of completion but not of satisfaction. I suppose a writer, almost by definition, is a person incapable of satisfaction —which is what keeps him at his post. Let us just say that I have tidied up my desk a bit, and flung out a few noisy and ill-timed farewells, like a drunk at a wedding he is enjoying to the hilt and has no real intention of leaving.

—E. B. W.

# I.

# Time Past, Time Future

# A WEEKEND WITH THE ANGELS

(Interlude in a hospital during World War II)

ONE OF the advantages of surgery, to a man at loose ends in Boston, is that it entitles him to a night at a hospital in advance of the operation. In short, it gets him in off the streets. I was instructed to report for my bed not later than three o'clock on Thursday afternoon, although I wasn't to lose my middle turbinate until eight the next morning. That gave me seventeen hours of utter relaxation in comfortable surroundings, dreaming away through the late afternoon, sweating under the arms, wiping my moist palms on the drapes, and marvelling at the strange succession of events that lead a man unerringly into an unimportant misadventure like a nose operation. I had no particular feeling of regret at the idea of giving up a turbinate (which sounded like something the Navy might be able to use in one of its light cruisers); in fact, in a man's middle years there is scarcely a part of the body he would hesitate to turn over to the proper authorities. At my age one jumps at the chance to get rid of something. Half a lifetime with a middle turbinate is enough to satisfy all but the most avid person.

I think the hospital was in Cambridge, but I'm not sure about that, as I was rather depressed on the ride out and when I'm depressed I never look where I'm going. Anyway, it was a very nice place near a small, orderly river (which might easily have been the Charles) and there was a fine big oak just outside my window. The room was tiny but so am I. The bed was a standard crank-up model, complete with drawsheet, rubber pad, and call switch. I had hoped it would have a swan at one end of it, like the boats in the Public Garden, but even without the swan it was a pleasanter accommodation than one can ordinarily expect to get on short notice in Boston.

There seemed no good reason for getting into the bed right away, so I just sat down on a hassock with a copy of the *Atlantic*. After a while a nurse came in.

"I'm Miss Mulqueenie," she said informatively.

"My name is White," I replied. "My temperature is ninety-eight point six, my pulse is seventy-two, and my blood pressure is one hundred and forty over eighty except when I get interested in what I am doing, when it goes up sharply. I'm here for a turbinectomy." Miss Mulqueenie came and sat down by my side. She hung her sphygmomanometer around her neck and drew a pencil and a blank form on me.

"What's your occupation?"

"Writer," I said, searching my memory.

The nurse smiled the knowing smile of a woman who is not easily fooled by men and their little conceits. She then began a careful listing of my clothes and personal effects. About my clothes she seemed a trifle uncertain. "What have you got on underneath your trousers?" she asked, dipping her pencil thoughtfully into her mouth.

"I can't recall," I replied. "It seems ages since I got dressed. This morning seems like a million years ago."

"Well, you must have *some*thing on. What'll I put down?"

"Paisley shawl?" I suggested. She thought a moment and then wrote "underwear" and gave me the list to sign. Then she took my temperature, my blood pressure, and my pulse. My temperature was ninety-eight point six, my pulse was seventy-two, and my blood pressure was one hundred and forty over eighty. "You better get to bed," she said cryptically. And Miss Mulqueenie was gone.

In bed, I felt relaxed and beautiful, as I imagine I shall feel in death. I had not been there long when another nurse appeared. She was in the uniform of a student and her face had the exalted look of a person who is doing a great deal of work and receiving no pay for it—which was, of course, exactly the case. She regarded me closely.

"It says on your card that you're a writer," she began, "but I've never heard of you."

"Did you come in here to harp on my obscurity?" I asked.

"No, I came in here to rub your back." She closed the door and I generously allowed her to rub my back. Later I was given a sedative and slept the uninterrupted sleep of the little-known.

The operation wasn't bad. I quite enjoyed the trip up from my room to the operating parlors, as a closely confined person does enjoy any sort of outing. The morphine had loosened my tongue, and while we waited in the corridor for the surgeon to arrive, the orderly and I let down our hair and had a good chat about fishing tackle. There were several rather distinguished people doing voluntary work in that hospital, and this orderly's face looked familiar. I wouldn't swear to it, but I think it was Governor Saltonstall. You never know whom you'll meet in bed these days. After a few minutes the surgeon was sighted in another part of the building and somebody gave the Governor the go-ahead. He had me halfway through a door leading into an operating room when a nurse caught sight of us. She clicked her tongue in disgust. "No, no," she said, wearily, "that's gall bladder."

The Governor backed me out and we tried our luck in another room. I cautiously put my hand up to my side, where the gall bladder is presumed to be. Everything seemed undisturbed. Soon the surgeon arrived and went to work. Under my skillful direction he removed everything he was supposed to remove and, as far as I could tell, nothing that he wasn't. It was a perfect occasion. It even turned out, in the course of the operation, that *his* father and *my* wife's people were connected—not by blood but in that happy and satisfactory way in which Boston's mystic thread entwines all its sons and daughters.

Because of the war the situation in hospitals is, of course, serious. A civilian feels embarrassed to be there at all, occupying valuable space and wasting the time and strength of the nurses, the student nurses, the nurses' aides, and the Gray Ladies. But I discovered that there is a new spirit in hospitals which, in its own way, is as merciful and resolute as the old, and every bit as mad. A patient, when he enters, receives a booklet reminding him that hospitals are short-handed and asking him not to bother the nurses unnecessarily. If he is a person of any conscience, he takes this quite literally, resolving not to push his call switch unless he is bleeding to death or the room is on fire. He throws himself so violently into the spirit of the emergency that, in the long run, he probably causes just as much trouble as he would have in more relaxed circumstances. I hadn't been off the operating table two hours and was still heavily drugged with morphine and bleeding at the nose when I found myself out of bed, armed with a window pole, engaged in a hand-to-hand encounter with a sticky transom. I enjoyed the nonsensical sensation of being in contact with the enemy. The effort, because of my condition, was rather too much for me, and I just made it back under the covers in time. There was quite a to-do, up and down the halls, when they found I had been out of bed.

As for routine chores, I did them myself, for the most part. Each morning I arose from bed and went at the room, tidying it up and doing all the dozens of things that need doing in an early-morning sickroom. First I would get down and crawl under the bed to retrieve the night's accumulation of blood-soaked paper handkerchiefs, which formed a dismal ring around the scrap basket where I had missed my aim in the dark. Then I'd fold the night blanket neatly and put it away in the bottom drawer of the bureau. I would crank up the bed, take the creases out of the rubber pad, tighten the drawsheet, pat the pillows back into shape, straighten out the *Atlantic Monthly,* and transfer the chrysanthemums into their day vase. Ashtrays had to be emptied, soiled towels removed, the hot-water bottle exhumed from its cold grave at the foot of the bed. One morning, in one of those passionate fits of neatness which overwhelm me from time to time, I spent an hour or so on my hands and knees clearing the room of bobby pins left by a former occupant. It was interesting work but, like all housework, exhausting.

Although there seemed to be, and undoubtedly was, a shortage of help at the hospital, there was one department which was, to my way of thinking, overstaffed. That was the back-rubbing department. There apparently was no schedule or system about back-rubbing—it was just a service a nurse would throw into her routine if she felt like it and had a few minutes to spare. One morning between ten and twelve my back was rubbed three times by as many different angels of mercy. My back, curiously enough, did not need rubbing that morning. I had been up, as usual, doing the housework, and when I finally got things to rights and crawled back into bed at quarter to ten, the blood was coursing through my back. All my back needed was a little while to itself. I took the three rubs without a murmur, but the violence and frequency of the assault increased my nosebleed, and when lunch was brought I was too tired to eat. Right after lunch a nurse I had never seen before, a large, eager girl, waltzed into the room and began peeling the bedclothes off.

"What's up, nurse?" I asked.

"I'm going to rub your back," she replied.

"Look," I said, plucking weakly at the sheets, "what do you say we leave the old backsy-wacksy alone for a few minutes?"

Mostly, however, the days rolled by, hour after hour, and you would never see another living soul. For patriotic reasons I seldom rang and so was seldom visited. Once I had a bath. This was the second morning after the operation. A nurse came in early. Without a word she flung open the door of the commode and extracted a basin, a washcloth, and a piece of soap.

"Can you take your bath?" she asked briskly.

"I always have, in recent years," I replied.

She placed the bathing equipment on the rude table that arched the bed, and handed me a towel. "Take off your uppers and work down. Then roll up your lowers and work up," she snapped. "And don't get the bed wet!"

I waited till she disappeared, then got noiselessly out of bed, removed the basin, emptied it, went into the bathroom which I shared with another fellow, drew a tub, and had a nice bath. Nurses are such formalists.

Of all the memories of this fabulous and salutary weekend, the most haunting is my recollection of the strange visitations of a certain night nurse. She came on duty, I was told, at midnight, and went off at seven. It was her custom to enter my room at a few minutes before five in the morning, when my sleeping potion still held me in thrall, snap on the light, and take a temperature reading. At her entrance I would rouse myself, at enormous physical cost, blink foolishly at the light, and open my mouth to receive, under the thick curly tongue, the thin straight thermometer. The nurse, whose name began with an "A" and ended in a thornbush, would stand in beautiful serenity, gazing peacefully down upon me for the long three minutes required for the recording. Her lips held the faint suggestion of a smile, compounded of scorn and indulgence. Motionless and cool in the lamplight, faithfully discharging her preposterous duty in the awful hour of a day born prematurely, she seemed a creature tinged with madness and beauty. She seemed, but of course could not have been, without flaw. As my drugged senses struggled vainly to catalogue her features, the thermometer would press upward against my tongue and the mercury would begin its long tedious climb toward the normal mark. I have no idea whether she was tall or short, dark or fair, plain or pretty, but in her calm and unreasoning concern about my body heat, at that unconscionable hour, she personified the beauty and lunacy of which life is so subtly blended. On the last morning of my stay I broke the mystical silence that had always before surrounded our ceremony.

"Cousin," I managed to mumble, allowing the thermometer to clash pitilessly against my incisors, "why dost wake me before the dawn for this mild dumbshow?"

She never changed her expression, but I heard words coming surely from her lips. "There's a war on, Bud," she replied. "I got twenty-six readings to take before I go off duty, so just for the heck of it I start with you."

Smiling a tiny proud smile, I raised my right hand and made a V, the way I had seen Churchill do it in the pictures. Then the drug took hold of me again, and when I awoke she was gone. Next day so was I.

# SPEAKING OF COUNTERWEIGHTS

To the Editor of *The New Yorker*:

I noticed in your February 4th issue a story by Richard Lockridge about his career as a counterweight. If you are opening the pages of your magazine to this dubious type of material, I intend to make the most of it. I, too, have a counterweight in my past, and you will be getting off easy if I remember it in under two thousand words.

Unlike Lockridge, I didn't appear in the rôle of counterweight —my lot was cast on the opposite side of the fulcrum. It happened many years ago in Seattle, a frontier settlement of 300,000 people in the shadow of Mount Rainier. The mountain never cast any shadow during my stay, but stood ready to. All it asked was an even break. I wasn't casting any shadow either in those days, but I had a job on a newspaper, the *Times*. I got the job through a friend, and he must have done a magnificent bit of spadework, because the city editor, Johns, took me on without a murmur and apologized for starting me at forty dollars a week. I had never done any newspaper reporting to amount to anything and didn't believe that the *Times* intended to pay me forty dollars—thought it was a gag my friend and Johns had cooked up between them. But it wasn't a gag, it was the Pacific Northwest in a carnival mood.

I turned out to be useless as a reporter and got laid off after eleven months, but not until I had had my affair with the counterweight.

Johns soon realized that in me he had a special problem. Although punctual and neat, I didn't know the meaning of the word "indictment" and was unable to hear anything over the telephone. I could have heard perfectly well over the telephone if the "leg men," as they were called, had simply talked in a natural manner, but they were all keyed up and insisted on spelling out everything in that "B for Boston," "C for Chicago" style. I can't grasp a word when it is spelled out—I have to hear the word itself, and think I am entitled to. Taking a story over the phone, I would get confused and write down the word "Boston" or the word "Chicago" and gradually lose the thread of the narrative. Anyway, Johns saw that his best bet was to keep me away from telephones and courtrooms and let me write feature stories in which you didn't have to know anything except where the space bar on the typewriter was.

There was no dearth of feature material in Seattle. Furthermore, the *Times* was in the habit of using feature stories about itself whenever it got the chance, which was every day. I never knew a newspaper to ramble on so about itself—it was as full of anecdote as a middle-aged author. During my incumbency, the *Times* developed an airtight system for supplying itself with feature material about itself, a system which struck me as unusually ingenious. The publisher, Colonel C. B. Blethen, simply donated a large steel traffic beacon to the city and erected it in front of the Times Building at the intersection of two streets, where it was in every motorist's way. Every day the beacon would be knocked down by a car or a truck, and a reporter (usually me) would dash down and get a feature story about the accident, mentioning that the beacon had been a gift from the publisher of the *Times*. The motorists rarely got injured, so it was permissible for the reporter to use a light, bantering tone

This isn't getting us to the counterweight, but I have no respect for readers who want to hurry an old, white-haired man. One day Johns called me over to his desk and said he would like me to go up to the roof and do a little piece about the new railroad up there.

"How's that again, Mr. Johns?" I asked courteously.

So he explained that the *Times* had a railroad on its roof, which the janitor rode in.

I laughed a hollow laugh to indicate that I understood I was just being kidded, but it turned out that it was all true. Everything about the Seattle *Times* was true, that was the uncanny thing. The *Times* did have a little railroad on the roof and the janitor did ride in it.

"Take a ride in it yourself," said Johns, "and write a story about it. Make a nice little feature."

Everything scared me in those days, and still does. Being in the West, so close to Mount Rainier but never seeing it, scared me. Working for a newspaper, with its noisy preoccupation with life's seamy side, scared me. The faces I saw around the city room and the ringing of the unanswerable phones and the necessity to make my way up in the world all scared me. Actually the city editor was one of the gentlest, most soft-spoken men I have ever encountered, and he did me a service I have always been grateful for. I got stuck one day on a story and finally, with the desperation of youth, I took my problem to him, although it seemed cheeky to bother him. How was I to express a certain thing? (I've forgotten what it was, but I had undoubtedly got bogged down in attempting to put the intricacies of a second-string felony into deathless prose.) I asked him how I could get around my difficulty.

He thought for a minute. Then he said, "Just say the words."

I always remembered that. It was excellent advice and I am still trying to say the words—and my, how they are mounting up this morning! It's a wonder I let a counterweight go as long as this. Well, about this railroad . . .

Johns had told me that the *Times* was the only newspaper in America that had a railroad on its roof, but that was nothing, because you could mention almost anything about the *Times* and it would be the only case of its kind in America. I am sure, for instance, that no other newspaper employed a photographer who went scorching around in a five-passenger Franklin touring car, shouting encouragement to pregnant women. The *Times* had one. He was a thoroughly fascinating man. He went by the name of Matty—only that wasn't it—and was known in many circles. I often went on stories with Matty in his car (the *Times*'s photographers were a motorized unit and supplied transportation to reporters, as well as moral and pictorial support). Matty's Franklin was the apple of his eye, and he always shouted and yelled and jumped up and down as he drove. He didn't feel he was travelling unless he was making a hell of a fuss personally. He was an exceedingly vital man, with a Bert Lahr snarl in his voice and a cockney accent. He would spur his car into a crowd of pedestrians, scattering them chicken fashion and yelling oaths at them. Then he would turn around and laugh a long, loony laugh.

"H'ya, Whitey, old kid, old kid," he would snarl, and lean over and grab me just above the knee with a murderous squeeze. I would jump till my hat squashed against the top, and Matty would howl with pleasure and bounce up and down.

He loved pregnant women—I mean he really had a sort of fondness for them. "I love 'em!" he would shout. "God, I love 'em!" I think the intimation of new life appealed to his sporting spirit—he was glad, with a wild, eerie joy, that a baby was on the way. He could always spot ladies who were *enceinte* and would warp his Franklin alongside and cry out, "H'ya, Mom, h'ya, sweetheart, that's the ticket, that's the old ticket!" Then he'd step down hard on the accelerator and we'd go swaying away on our full elliptical springs. I often think of the small army of today's Seattle citizens, now in the full flower of maturity, who were hailed in embryo with such glad approval.

No, it was no surprise to me to be assigned to cover a railroad on the roof.

I did get a jolt, however, when, escorted by the janitor, I stepped out on the roof and met my assignment face to face. I hadn't expected a railroad conceived in malice. To be frank, I had expected a *toy* railroad of some sort—a publisher's plaything, a narrow gauge, perhaps, with a tiny steam locomotive and two cute little cars. Instead, I encountered an infernal device apparently constructed secretly by djinns out of stolen materials. Around the perimeter of the roof ran a rusty monorail, badly aligned and lightly fastened. Poised in space beyond the edge of the roof and supported by a listless metal arm, which extended outward and downward like one half of a pair of ice tongs, was a car, or cage. Balancing this at the other end of the teeterboard was a counterarm. The wheel, of course, rested on the rail and served as fulcrum —a mobile fulcrum. At the moment, the car was the high end of the seesaw, the counterarm the low end.

"What the hell goes on here?" I asked sullenly.

The janitor explained that there was a garland of electric lights under the eaves of the Times Building and that the railroad had been built to bring these lights within reach, so that when a bulb burned out a new one could be installed. "You'll see when you get in the car. It swings down and puts you right down alongside the bulbs." Here was the Pacific Northwest in a nutshell: a bulb had burned out and the pioneers had countered by building a railroad.

I knew it was time for me to climb aboard.

"Is there anything that keeps the car from sinking down too far under my weight?" I asked, sparring for time.

"You bet," said the janitor amiably. "This counterweight." He pointed to a little block of concrete attached to the counterarm. I looked at the weight and this time I knew I was being kidded. It was about the size of a lady's hatbox in a year of small hats.

"What, that little thing?" I asked, dispirited.

"Sure," he replied. "That's solid concrete."

"What stunted it," I asked, "too many cigarettes?" I was feebly trying to keep up the newspaper tradition of living dangerously with a smile in the heart and a jest on the lips.

"Well, it looks small, but it's heavy," he said. "Besides, I keep bearing down on this arm when I push you around."

"You mean you have to bear down in addition to the weight of the counterweight?"

"Well, that depends," he said. "How much do you weigh?"

"A hundred and forty-five," I replied, quickly adding a cubit to my stature.

"Oh, it's good for a hundred and forty-five, all right," he said. "Go ahead, get in. I'll give you a buggy ride." He seized the counterarm and braced himself.

Taking a last look at the counterweight, which seemed to have shrunk while I was standing there, I grabbed the outer arm and stepped gingerly off the roof into the car. The janitor bore down. I felt the car sink, then rise slightly, then sink again, until gradually there was established between me and the janitor and the counterweight a sort of rough equilibrium. The thought that in another moment still another motion, a forward motion, was to be added to my miserable condition made me feel sick. But in a sense I was happy: all I really asked in those days was the chance to die for a city editor, and here it was, just an easy five-story drop.

"O.K.?" the janitor asked.

"O.K.," I replied, "let's go."

I felt the car move uncertainly forward and heard the wheel grind against the rail. I could feel the janitor bearing down. Bear down, sweet janitor. I wondered what sort of chap he was, this indispensable stranger.

Electric-light bulbs passed slowly in review, close to my left ear. Below, in the yawning street, the *Times* beacon stoically awaited the next direct hit. (From above, this time, I thought.) I glanced east to the Cascades, the lovely mountains through which I had guided my Model T westward in quest of frontiers. Dipping and rising, the car progressed steadily, reached a corner, rounded it, the wheel grinding its flange. I glanced west to the Olympics, tall and stately, the last range, the last frontier waiting to be conquered.

"What time is it?" I asked casually, trying to show the janitor that I was every inch a reporter. The words had hardly fluttered up over the edge of the roof when I realized that it would be quite like a janitor to let go a counterarm in order to pull out a watch. "Never mind!" I shouted hastily. "Never mind! I just saw a clock."

Our course was a triangular one, for the Times Building was modelled after the Times Building in New York and had only three sides. I conscientiously rode the entire distance. It took about four minutes, I think, and seemed longer, with the car so light and birdlike, now up a trifle, now down a bit—this gossamer railroad, this roadbed of thistledown. I could tell by the feeling in my stomach when the janitor was bearing down in good earnest and when he was just coasting.

"How was it?" he asked when I got back to God's roof.

"Fine," I said glibly. "Great little system. I've got my story, all right."

Neither he nor I knew that it would take all these years to write it, but that's the way life is, eh, Lockridge?

—E. B. W.

# AFTERNOON OF AN AMERICAN BOY

W<small>HEN</small> I was in my teens, I lived in Mount Vernon, in the same block with J. Parnell Thomas, who grew up to become chairman of the House Committee on Un-American Activities. I lived on the corner of Summit and East Sidney, at No. 101 Summit Avenue, and Parnell lived four or five doors north of us on the same side of the avenue, in the house the Diefendorfs used to live in.

Parnell was not a playmate of mine, as he was a few years older, but I used to greet him as he walked by our house on his way to and from the depot. He was a good-looking young man, rather quiet and shy. Seeing him, I would call "Hello, Parnell!" and he would smile and say "Hello, Elwyn!" and walk on. Once I remember dashing out of our yard on roller skates and executing a rink turn in front of Parnell, to show off, and he said, "Well! Quite an artist, aren't you?" I remember the words. I was delighted at praise from an older man and sped away along the flagstone sidewalk, dodging the cracks I knew so well.

The thing that made Parnell a special man in my eyes in those days was not his handsome appearance and friendly manner but his sister. Her name was Eileen. She was my age and she was a quiet, nice-looking girl. She never came over to my yard to play, and I never went over there, and, considering that we lived so near each other, we were remarkably uncommunicative; nevertheless, she was the girl I singled out, at one point, to be of special interest to me. Being of special interest to me involved practically nothing on a girl's part—it simply meant that she was under constant surveillance. On my own part, it meant that I suffered an astonishing disintegration when I walked by her house, from embarrassment, fright, and the knowledge that I was in enchanted territory.

In the matter of girls, I was different from most boys of my age. I admired girls a lot, but they terrified me. I did not feel that I possessed the peculiar gifts or accomplishments that girls liked in their male companions—the ability to dance, to play football, to cut up a bit in public, to smoke, and to make small talk. I couldn't do any of these things successfully, and seldom tried. Instead, I stuck with the accomplishments I was sure of: I rode my bicycle sitting backward on the handle bars, I made up poems, I played selections from "Aïda" on the piano. In winter, I tended goal in the hockey games on the frozen pond in the Dell. None of these tricks counted much with girls. In the four years I was in the Mount Vernon High School, I never went to a school dance and I never took a girl to a drugstore for a soda or to the Westchester Playhouse or to Proctor's. I wanted to do these things but did not have the nerve. What I finally did manage to do, however, and what is the subject of this memoir, was far brassier, far gaudier. As an exhibit of teen-age courage and ineptitude, it never fails to amaze me in retrospect. I am not even sure it wasn't un-American.

My bashfulness and backwardness annoyed my older sister very much, and at about the period of which I am writing she began making strong efforts to stir me up. She was convinced that I was in a rut, socially, and she found me a drag in her own social life, which was brisk. She kept trying to throw me with girls, but I always bounced. And whenever she saw a chance she would start the phonograph and grab me, and we would go charging around the parlor in the toils of the one-step, she gripping me as in a death struggle, and I hurling her finally away from me through greater strength. I was a skinny kid but my muscles were hard, and it would have taken an unusually powerful woman to have held me long in the attitude of the dance.

One day, through a set of circumstances I have forgotten, my sister managed to work me into an afternoon engagement she had with some others in New York. To me, at that time, New York was a wonderland largely unexplored. I had been to the Hippodrome a couple of times with my father, and to the Hudson-Fulton Celebration, and to a few matinées; but New York, except as a setting for extravaganzas, was unknown. My sister had heard tales of tea-dancing at the Plaza Hotel. She and a girl friend of hers and another fellow and myself went there to give it a try. The expedition struck me as a slick piece of arrangement on her part. I was the junior member of the group and had been roped in, I imagine, to give symmetry to the occasion. Or perhaps Mother had forbidden my sister to go at all unless another member of the family was along. Whether I was there for symmetry or for decency I can't really remember, but I was there.

The spectacle was a revelation to me. However repulsive the idea of dancing was, I was filled with amazement at the setup. Here were tables where a fellow could sit so close to the dance floor that he was practically on it. And you could order cinnamon toast and from the safety of your chair observe girls and men in close embrace, swinging along, the music playing while you ate the toast, and the dancers so near to you that they almost brushed the things off your table as they jogged by. I was impressed. Dancing or no dancing, this was certainly high life, and I knew I was witnessing a scene miles and miles ahead of anything that took place in Mount Vernon. I had never seen anything like it, and a ferment must have begun working in me that afternoon.

Incredible as it seems to me now, I formed the idea of asking

Parnell's sister Eileen to accompany me to a tea dance at the Plaza. The plan shaped up in my mind as an expedition of unparalleled worldliness, calculated to stun even the most blasé girl. The fact that I didn't know how to dance must have been a powerful deterrent, but not powerful enough to stop me. As I look back on the affair, it's hard to credit my own memory, and I sometimes wonder if, in fact, the whole business isn't some dream that has gradually gained the status of actuality. A boy with any sense, wishing to become better acquainted with a girl who was "of special interest," would have cut out for himself a more modest assignment to start with—a soda date or a movie date—something within reasonable limits. Not me. I apparently became obsessed with the notion of taking Eileen to the Plaza and not to any darned old drugstore. I had learned the location of the Plaza, and just knowing how to get to it gave me a feeling of confidence. I had learned about cinnamon toast, so I felt able to cope with the waiter when he came along. And I banked heavily on the general splendor of the surroundings and the extreme sophistication of the function to carry the day, I guess.

I was three days getting up nerve to make the phone call. Meantime, I worked out everything in the greatest detail. I heeled myself with a safe amount of money. I looked up trains. I overhauled my clothes and assembled an outfit I believed would meet the test. Then, one night at six o'clock, when Mother and Father went downstairs to dinner, I lingered upstairs and entered the big closet off my bedroom where the wall phone was. There I stood for several minutes, trembling, my hand on the receiver, which hung upside down on the hook. (In our family, the receiver always hung upside down, with the big end up.)

I had rehearsed my first line and my second line. I planned to say, "Hello, can I please speak to Eileen?" Then, when she came to the phone, I planned to say, "Hello, Eileen, this is Elwyn White." From there on, I figured I could ad-lib it.

At last, I picked up the receiver and gave the number. As I had suspected, Eileen's mother answered.

"Can I please speak to Eileen?" I asked, in a low, troubled voice.

"Just a minute," said her mother. Then, on second thought, she asked, "Who is it, please?"

"It's Elwyn," I said.

She left the phone, and after quite a while Eileen's voice said, "Hello, Elwyn." This threw my second line out of whack, but I stuck to it doggedly.

"Hello, Eileen, this is Elwyn White," I said.

In no time at all I laid the proposition before her. She seemed dazed and asked me to wait a minute. I assume she went into a huddle with her mother. Finally, she said yes, she would like to go tea-dancing with me at the Plaza, and I said fine, I would call for her at quarter past three on Thursday afternoon, or whatever afternoon it was—I've forgotten.

I do not know now, and of course did not know then, just how great was the mental and physical torture Eileen went through that day, but the incident stacks up as a sort of unintentional un-American activity, for which I was solely responsible. It all went off as scheduled: the stately walk to the depot; the solemn train ride, during which we sat staring shyly into the seat in front of us; the difficult walk from Grand Central across Forty-second to Fifth, with pedestrians clipping us and cutting in between us; the bus ride to Fifty-ninth Street; then the Plaza itself, and the cinnamon toast, and the music, and the excitement. The thundering quality of the occasion must have delivered a mental shock to me, deadening my recollection, for I have only the dimmest memory of leading Eileen onto the dance floor to execute two or three unspeakable rounds, in which I vainly tried to adapt my violent sister-and-brother wrestling act into something graceful and appropriate. It must have been awful. And at six o'clock, emerging, I gave no thought to any further entertainment, such as dinner in town. I simply herded Eileen back all the long, dreary way to Mount Vernon and deposited her, a few minutes after seven, on an empty stomach, at her home. Even if I had attempted to dine her, I don't believe it would have been possible; the emotional strain of the afternoon had caused me to perspire uninterruptedly, and any restaurant would have been justified in rejecting me solely on the ground that I was too moist.

Over the intervening years (all thirty-five of them), I've often felt guilty about my afternoon at the Plaza, and a few years ago, during Parnell's investigation of writers, my feeling sometimes took the form of a guilt sequence in which I imagined myself on the stand, in the committee room, being questioned. It went something like this:

PARNELL: Have you ever written for the screen, Mr. White?

ME: No, sir.

PARNELL: Have you ever been, or are you now, a member of the Screen Writers' Guild?

ME: No, sir.

PARNELL: Have you ever been, or are you now, a member of the Communist Party?

ME: No, sir.

Then, in this imaginary guilt sequence of mine, Parnell digs deep and comes up with the big question, calculated to throw me.

PARNELL: Do you recall an afternoon, along about the middle of the second decade of this century, when you took my sister to the Plaza Hotel for tea under the grossly misleading and false pretext that you knew how to dance?

And as my reply comes weakly, "Yes, sir," I hear the murmur run through the committee room and see reporters bending over their notebooks, scribbling hard. In my dream, I am again seated with Eileen at the edge of the dance floor, frightened, stunned, and happy—in my ears the intoxicating drumbeat of the dance, in my throat the dry, bittersweet taste of cinnamon.

I don't know about the guilt, really. I guess a good many girls might say that an excursion such as the one I conducted Eileen on belongs in the un-American category. But there must be millions of aging males, now slipping into their anecdotage, who recall their Willie Baxter period with affection, and who remember some similar journey into ineptitude, in that precious, brief moment in life before love's pages, through constant reference, had become dog-eared, and before its narrative, through sheer competence, had lost the first, wild sense of derring-do.

# ZOO REVISITED

*Or the Life and Death of Olie Hackstaff*

## I. THE BUFFALO RANGE

Pause here, my soul, and pause then here my son, which art my
    soul,
Here stands the finished bison by the last water hole.
Here sleeps entombed forever in the brown sensate robe
The seminal imperative in the suspended globe.
Low droops the bearded head and low the small and hateful eye;
The plains where burned the fires of dung are dust and the trails
    are dry.
Here stands incarcerate the bull, with his expended fire,
*Bos americanus* in the twilight of desire.
Here stands the bull Myself, alone, with his torrential need,
At home with living death, at rest with reservoirs of seed;
Pause here my self, my soul, my son, by this encrusted rail. . . .

*Don't put your mouth on that dirty old rail!*

## II. END OF MORNING AT BEGINNING OF LIFE, HOME FROM SCHOOL

It's quarter of twelve.
It's fourteen of.
It's thirteen of.
It's twelve of.

The bell will ring in just a sec.
"Dismissed," she'll say. "Dismissed.
Boys, when you go to the cloakroom,
  please
        don't
            shove!"

It's twelve of, it's twelve of,
And still she clings to the short division
(Where the chalk squeaked, the pointer motioned)
  Divider
  Dividend
  And quotient.
    (*The product of the divider and the
    quotient should equal the dividend.*)

There it goes!

The peak of the cap is the visor, unsnap it then snap it,
The peak of the cap . . . unsnap it then snap it.

(Step by step and flag by flag avoiding crack and
block by block the small boy Olie makes his way in
young September's quiet street by hedge and yard
and stoop and drive where blue hydrangeas sadly sway
and grapes are purpling in the arbor:

home is a haven
home for lunch
home is a harbor.)

      (*Kenny Whipple says turtles lay eggs.*)

By hedge and yard and stoop and drive.
I can't wait.
I have to go.

Do they lay eggs or don't they?
And if they do, how do they?

> (*because where would?*
> *even if . . .*)

Why does an older boy like Kenny
Laugh when he tells the rabbit's story?
Why does he hang around the hutch
Where something happens that you have to know—
Something the buck does with the doe,
Something that's sad and terrible to know?
> (*Everybody has to know.*)

I can't wait.
I have to go.

By hedge and yard and stoop and drive:

The Belknaps.
The Gants.
The Immelmans.

Do they lay eggs or don't they?
And if they do, how do they?

Five more houses five more hedges five more . . .
They couldn't possibly.

because where would?
even if.

Home is a harbor,
Home for lunch.

### III. BY THE SEA

This is my get, proprietor, and this the doe.
Have you a room for us who fear the sea?
I am the small boy redivivus, this is me.
Give us a room with bureau space to grow.

"Take Mr. Hackstaff to three nineteen!"

Knock at the door, my bucko, swing her in!
Observe the bed, the chair, the chair, the bed!
Come smell the bureau drawers!
I tarried here a while when I was thee.

Open the drawers take off your things take off
    your coat put on your sneaks throw up the
    sash unpack your bag hang up your coat!
Run a little water in the basin,
I want you to get your hands clean!

        (For what? Were my hands clean in those days?)

Sit down here and put your sneaks on!

(How well I know this sultry scene
where dreaming summer takes her toll
her cruel toll
this sadly overwritten scene
when summer takes complete command
belly to sun and back to sand
how well I know these mourning streets
the lawns the privet and the rose
the bay and the way the wind blows
the tide ebbs and the tide flows

the salted skin the burning air
the combed scalp the sand in hair
oh windblown scene oh dune and mallow . . .)

*The spacious ballroom is ideal for dancing*

His name was redivivus
And they called him Red for short.
    "I'm checking out of three nineteen.
    Will you send a boy for the bags?"


## IV. THE SWORD

"Make me a sword!"

(Man lives alone and by the sword.)
"What for? [You mean for the wars, the debatable
  wars?] You get the stick from the cellar."

"For the scabbard?"

"No, for the sword."

"You have to saw a piece off, to nail across, and
    smooth a place where my hand goes around."

"The grip?"

"Smoothened for the hand, the edges rounded."

"This stick is dusty. Get a cloth. Don't dust
    it here it'll dirty the room take it out
    and dust it not with that new cloth it'll
    ruin it."

"Where is the saw?"

"Hold it, hold the end."
    (The first stroke, sawblade against thumbside. On
this point, my hearty, impale the world. "Hold
the end while I saw a piece off." On this point,
which isn't even sharpened yet, impale the enemy
only don't get hurt. "Hold it steady and don't fool.")

    (Man lives alone and by the sword,
youth dreams alone and girds for right
and dulls his blade against the stone;
the dream fails in the short night.
Man is disarmed and still alone.)

keep your feet dry
don't take cold
be polite shake hands with Mr. Hecatomb
marry a nice girl
pay your bills
look at those hands
don't put your mouth on that dirty old rail


V. Liebestraum


It is at night, when the old woods are still,
The weedy pond first feels the winter's chill.
    (Now night be still and let the cold
    Seal fast the wintry pond!)

    *Still pond, no more moving!*

It is in youth there comes, and one time only,
This dream of love, this flowerform of light,
Perfect in deed and wanting no completion

(Now youth be still and let the dream
Seal fast the faithful heart!)

*Still pond, no more moving!*


VI. THE HOSPITAL

When the grass is long is the time for dying.
Did you know that, nurse?
Death is a wind that rustles our estate,
Turning up fourteen pairs of ecru curtains,
Number forty-eight in the catalogue.
(Bend down, librarian, and taste the page!)
Here is the printed list—the end of Ivy Hall.
Contents of Bedroom Number One, leaving behind
    to the hammer's fall
Five pairs summer blankets, three single blankets—
    Oh sandtoy summer in the mind
    The star (of tin)
    The fish (of tin)
    The crescent moon (of the best quality tin)—
Bend down, librarian, and taste the page,
I'm checking out of three nineteen.
Death is a wind that rustles the estate.
And welcome to the zoo, my dear,
The reptile house, the serpents tonguing
With all their hateful coils of longing,
The lidless eyes the darkness holds
In its own long and scaley folds.
Don't put your mouth on that dirty old rail, nurse!
    When the grass is long is the time for dying,

The grass was a cradle when I was child,
The grass was the bed I had as lover.
My first instruction was from the clover
In the wise field.
The grass was my portion when I was lean,
The warmth in the grass is a gift to the lonely;
The ranks of the leaves were broken only
For me and trouble to pass between.
The grass is my need in this last embrace
   (When the grass is long is the time for dying)
My blood is drink for the roots that are drying,
The strength of the seed is around my face.

don't run with a knife
keep back from a scythe keep back from a saw
when you lean out of the window keep your
    weight low, on the inside.

Low and on the inside, eh, announcer?
Bend down, librarian,
The page is me, and gently hold the place.
   (Notice: These seats are for the
   exclusive use . . .)
And for the Belknaps, the Gants. Do they lay
   eggs or don't they?
Bos, his name is. In the bullpen.
Bend down.
Keep your weight low, nurse, and on the inside.

   "Dr. Ternidad!   Dr. Breese!
    Dr. Ternidad!   Dr. Breese!"

# FAREWELL, MY LOVELY!

*(An aging male kisses an old flame goodbye, circa 1936)* *

I SEE by the new Sears Roebuck catalogue that it is still possible
to buy an axle for a 1909 Model T Ford, but I am not deceived.
The great days have faded, the end is in sight. Only one page in
the current catalogue is devoted to parts and accessories for the
Model T; yet everyone remembers springtimes when the Ford
gadget section was larger than men's clothing, almost as large as
household furnishings. The last Model T was built in 1927, and
the car is fading from what scholars call the American scene—
which is an understatement, because to a few million people who
grew up with it, the old Ford practically *was* the American scene.

It was the miracle God had wrought. And it was patently the
sort of thing that could only happen once. Mechanically uncanny,
it was like nothing that had ever come to the world before. Flourishing industries rose and fell with it. As a vehicle, it was hard-
working, commonplace, heroic; and it often seemed to transmit
those qualities to the persons who rode in it. My own generation
identifies it with Youth, with its gaudy, irretrievable excitements;
before it fades into the mist, I would like to pay it the tribute of
the sigh that is not a sob, and set down random entries in a shape
somewhat less cumbersome than a Sears Roebuck catalogue.

* This piece originally appeared in the *New Yorker* over the pseudonym
Lee Strout White. It was suggested by a manuscript submitted by Richard
L. Strout, of the *Christian Science Monitor*, and Mr. Strout, an amiable
collaborator, has kindly allowed me to include it in this collection. The piece
was published as a little book in 1936 by G. P. Putnam's Sons under the title
"Farewell to Model T."

The Model T was distinguished from all other makes of cars by the fact that its transmission was of a type known as planetary —which was half metaphysics, half sheer fiction. Engineers accepted the word "planetary" in its epicyclic sense, but I was always conscious that it also meant "wandering," "erratic." Because of the peculiar nature of this planetary element, there was always, in Model T, a certain dull rapport between engine and wheels, and even when the car was in a state known as neutral, it trembled with a deep imperative and tended to inch forward. There was never a moment when the bands were not faintly egging the machine on. In this respect it was like a horse, rolling the bit on its tongue, and country people brought to it the same technique they used with draft animals.

Its most remarkable quality was its rate of acceleration. In its palmy days the Model T could take off faster than anything on the road. The reason was simple. To get under way, you simply hooked the third finger of the right hand around a lever on the steering column, pulled down hard, and shoved your left foot forcibly against the low-speed pedal. These were simple, positive motions; the car responded by lunging forward with a roar. After a few seconds of this turmoil, you took your toe off the pedal, eased up a mite on the throttle, and the car, possessed of only two forward speeds, catapulted directly into high with a series of ugly jerks and was off on its glorious errand. The abruptness of this departure was never equalled in other cars of the period. The human leg was (and still is) incapable of letting in a clutch with anything like the forthright abandon that used to send Model T on its way. Letting in a clutch is a negative, hesitant motion, depending on delicate nervous control; pushing down the Ford pedal was a simple, country motion—an expansive act, which came as natural as kicking an old door to make it budge.

The driver of the old Model T was a man enthroned. The car,

with top up, stood seven feet high. The driver sat on top of the
gas tank, brooding it with his own body. When he wanted gasoline,
he alighted, along with everything else in the front seat; the seat
was pulled off, the metal cap unscrewed, and a wooden stick thrust
down to sound the liquid in the well. There were always a couple
of these sounding sticks kicking around in the ratty sub-cushion
regions of a flivver. Refuelling was more of a social function then,
because the driver had to unbend, whether he wanted to or not.
Directly in front of the driver was the windshield—high, uncom-
promisingly erect. Nobody talked about air resistance, and the
four cylinders pushed the car through the atmosphere with a
simple disregard of physical law.

There was this about a Model T: the purchaser never regarded
his purchase as a complete, finished product. When you bought a
Ford, you figured you had a start—a vibrant, spirited framework
to which could be screwed an almost limitless assortment of decorative and functional hardware. Driving away from the agency,
hugging the new wheel between your knees, you were already
full of creative worry. A Ford was born naked as a baby, and a
flourishing industry grew up out of correcting its rare deficiencies
and combatting its fascinating diseases. Those were the great days
of lily-painting. I have been looking at some old Sears Roebuck
catalogues, and they bring everything back so clear.

First you bought a Ruby Safety Reflector for the rear, so that
your posterior would glow in another's car's brilliance. Then you
invested thirty-nine cents in some radiator Moto Wings, a popular
ornament which gave the Pegasus touch to the machine and did
something godlike to the owner. For nine cents you bought a fan-
belt guide to keep the belt from slipping off the pulley.

You bought a radiator compound to stop leaks. This was as
much a part of everybody's equipment as aspirin tablets are of a

medicine cabinet. You bought special oil to prevent chattering, a clamp-on dash light, a patching outfit, a tool box which you bolted to the running board, a sun visor, a steering-column brace to keep the column rigid, and a set of emergency containers for gas, oil, and water—three thin, disc-like cans which reposed in a case on the running board during long, important journeys—red for gas, gray for water, green for oil. It was only a beginning. After the car was about a year old, steps were taken to check the alarming disintegration. (Model T was full of tumors, but they were benign.) A set of anti-rattlers (ninety-eight cents) was a popular panacea. You hooked them on to the gas and spark rods, to the brake pull rod, and to the steering-rod connections. Hood silencers, of black rubber, were applied to the fluttering hood. Shock-absorbers and snubbers gave "complete relaxation." Some people bought rubber pedal pads, to fit over the standard metal pedals. (I didn't like these, I remember.) Persons of a suspicious or pugnacious turn of mind bought a rear-view mirror; but most Model T owners weren't worried by what was coming from behind because they would soon enough see it out in front. They rode in a state of cheerful catalepsy. Quite a large mutinous clique among Ford owners went over to a foot accelerator (you could buy one and screw it to the floor board), but there was a certain madness in these people, because the Model T, just as she stood, had a choice of three foot pedals to push, and there were plenty of moments when both feet were occupied in the routine performance of duty and when the only way to speed up the engine was with the hand throttle.

Gadget bred gadget. Owners not only bought ready-made gadgets, they invented gadgets to meet special needs. I myself drove my car directly from the agency to the blacksmith's, and had the smith affix two enormous iron brackets to the port running board to support an army trunk

People who owned closed models builded along different lines: they bought ball grip handles for opening doors, window anti-rattlers, and de-luxe flower vases of the cut-glass anti-splash type. People with delicate sensibilities garnished their car with a device called the Donna Lee Automobile Disseminator—a porous vase guaranteed, according to Sears, to fill the car with a "faint clean odor of lavender." The gap between open cars and closed cars was not as great then as it is now: for $11.95, Sears Roebuck converted your touring car into a sedan and you went forth renewed. One agreeable quality of the old Fords was that they had no bumpers, and their fenders softened and wilted with the years and permitted the driver to squeeze in and out of tight places.

Tires were 30 x 3½, cost about twelve dollars, and punctured readily. Everybody carried a Jiffy patching set, with a nutmeg grater to roughen the tube before the goo was spread on. Everybody was capable of putting on a patch, expected to have to, and did have to.

During my association with Model T's, self-starters were not a prevalent accessory. They were expensive and under suspicion. Your car came equipped with a serviceable crank, and the first thing you learned was how to Get Results. It was a special trick, and until you learned it (usually from another Ford owner, but sometimes by a period of appalling experimentation) you might as well have been winding up an awning. The trick was to leave the ignition switch off, proceed to the animal's head, pull the choke (which was a little wire protruding through the radiator) and give the crank two or three nonchalant upward lifts. Then, whistling as though thinking about something else, you would saunter back to the driver's cabin, turn the ignition on, return to the crank, and this time, catching it on the down stroke, give it a quick spin with plenty of That. If this procedure was followed, the engine almost always responded—first with a few scattered explosions, then with a tumultuous gunfire, which you checked by racing around to the driver's seat and retarding the throttle. Often, if the emergency brake hadn't been pulled all the way back, the car advanced on you the instant the first explosion occurred and you would hold it back by leaning your weight against it. I can still feel my old Ford nuzzling me at the curb, as though looking for an apple in my pocket.

In zero weather, ordinary cranking became an impossibility, except for giants. The oil thickened, and it became necessary to jack up the rear wheels, which, for some planetary reason, eased the throw.

The lore and legend that governed the Ford were boundless. Owners had their own theories about everything; they discussed mutual problems in that wise, infinitely resourceful way old women discuss rheumatism. Exact knowledge was pretty scarce, and often proved less effective than superstition. Dropping a camphor ball into the gas tank was a popular expedient; it seemed to have a tonic effect on both man and machine. There wasn't much to base exact knowledge on. The Ford driver flew blind. He didn't know the temperature of his engine, the speed of his car, the amount of his fuel, or the pressure of his oil (the old Ford lubricated itself by what was amiably described as the "splash system"). A speedometer cost money and was an extra, like a windshield-wiper. The dashboard of the early models was bare save for an ignition key; later models, grown effete, boasted an ammeter which pulsated alarmingly with the throbbing of the car. Under the dash was a box of coils, with vibrators which you adjusted, or thought you adjusted. Whatever the driver learned of his motor, he learned not through instruments but through sudden developments. I remember that the timer was one of the vital organs about which there was ample doctrine. When everything else had been checked, you "had a look" at the timer. It was an extravagantly odd little device, simple in construction, mysterious in function. It contained a roller, held by a spring, and there were four contact points on the inside of the case against which, many people believed, the roller rolled. I have had a timer apart on a sick Ford many times. But I never really knew what I was up to—I was just showing off before God. There were almost as many schools of thought as there were timers. Some people, when things went wrong, just clenched their teeth and gave the timer a smart crack with a wrench. Other people opened it up and blew on it. There was a school that held that the timer needed large amounts of oil; they fixed it by frequent baptism. And there was a school that was positive it was meant to run dry as a bone; these people were continually taking it off and wiping it. I remember once spitting into a timer; not in anger, but in a spirit of research. You see, the Model T driver moved in the realm of metaphysics. He believed his car could be hexed.

One reason the Ford anatomy was never reduced to an exact science was that, having "fixed" it, the owner couldn't honestly claim that the treatment had brought about the cure. There were too many authenticated cases of Fords fixing themselves—restored naturally to health after a short rest. Farmers soon discovered this, and it fitted nicely with their draft-horse philosophy: "Let 'er cool off and she'll snap into it again."

A Ford owner had Number One Bearing constantly in mind. This bearing, being at the front end of the motor, was the one that always burned out, because the oil didn't reach it when the car was climbing hills. (That's what I was always told, anyway.) The oil used to recede and leave Number One dry as a clam flat; you had to watch that bearing like a hawk. It was like a weak heart—you could hear it start knocking, and that was when you stopped to let her cool off. Try as you would to keep the oil supply right, in the end Number One always went out. "Number One Bearing burned out on me and I had to have her replaced," you would say, wisely; and your companions always had a lot to tell about how to protect and pamper Number One to keep her alive.

Sprinkled not too liberally among the millions of amateur witch doctors who drove Fords and applied their own abominable cures were the heaven-sent mechanics who could really make the car talk. These professionals turned up in undreamed-of spots. One time, on the banks of the Columbia River in Washington, I heard the rear end go out of my Model T when I was trying to whip it up a steep incline onto the deck of a ferry. Something snapped; the car slid backward into the mud. It seemed to me like the end of the trail. But the captain of the ferry, observing the withered remnant, spoke up.

"What's got her?" he asked.

"I guess it's the rear end," I replied, listlessly. The captain leaned over the rail and stared. Then I saw that there was a hunger in his eyes that set him off from other men.

"Tell you what," he said, carelessly, trying to cover up his eagerness, "let's pull the son of a bitch up onto the boat, and I'll help you fix her while we're going back and forth on the river."

We did just this. All that day I plied between the towns of Pasco and Kennewick, while the skipper (who had once worked in a Ford garage) directed the amazing work of resetting the bones of my car.

Springtime in the heyday of the Model T was a delirious season. Owning a car was still a major excitement, roads were still wonderful and bad. The Fords were obviously conceived in madness: any car which was capable of going from forward into reverse without any perceptible mechanical hiatus was bound to be a mighty challenging thing to the human imagination. Boys used to veer them off the highway into a level pasture and run wild with them, as though they were cutting up with a girl. Most everybody used the reverse pedal quite as much as the regular foot brake—it distributed the wear over the bands and wore them all down evenly. That was the big trick, to wear all the bands down evenly, so that the final chattering would be total and the whole unit scream for renewal.

The days were golden, the nights were dim and strange. I still recall with trembling those loud, nocturnal crises when you drew up to a signpost and raced the engine so the lights would be bright enough to read destinations by. I have never been really planetary since. I suppose it's time to say goodbye. Farewell, my lovely!

# THE DECLINE OF SPORT

## (A Preposterous Parable)

In the third decade of the supersonic age, sport gripped the nation in an ever-tightening grip. The horse tracks, the ballparks, the fight rings, the gridirons, all drew crowds in steadily increasing numbers. Every time a game was played, an attendance record was broken. Usually some other sort of record was broken, too—such as the record for the number of consecutive doubles hit by left-handed batters in a Series game, or some such thing as that. Records fell like ripe apples on a windy day. Customs and manners changed, and the five-day business week was reduced to four days, then to three, to give everyone a better chance to memorize the scores.

Not only did sport proliferate but the demands it made on the spectator became greater. Nobody was content to take in one event at a time, and thanks to the magic of radio and television nobody had to. A Yale alumnus, class of 1962, returning to the Bowl with 197,000 others to see the Yale-Cornell football game would take along his pocket radio and pick up the Yankee Stadium, so that while his eye might be following a fumble on the Cornell twenty-two-yard line, his ear would be following a man going down to second in the top of the fifth, seventy miles away. High in the blue sky above the Bowl, skywriters would be at work writing the scores of other major and minor sporting contests, weaving an interminable record of victory and defeat, and using the new high-visibility pink news-smoke perfected by Pepsi-Cola engineers. And in the frames of the giant video sets, just behind the goalposts, this same alumnus could watch Dejected win the Futurity before a record-breaking crowd of 349,872 at Belmont, each of whom was tuned to the Yale Bowl and following the World Series game in the video and searching the sky for further news of events either under way or just completed. The effect of this vast cyclorama of sport was to divide the spectator's attention, over-subtilize his appreciation, and deaden his passion. As the fourth supersonic decade was ushered in, the picture changed and sport began to wane.

A good many factors contributed to the decline of sport. Substitutions in football had increased to such an extent that there were very few fans in the United States capable of holding the players in mind during play. Each play that was called saw two entirely new elevens lined up, and the players whose names and faces you had familiarized yourself with in the first period were seldom seen or heard of again. The spectacle became as diffuse as the main concourse in Grand Central at the commuting hour.

Express motor highways leading to the parks and stadia had become so wide, so unobstructed, so devoid of all life except automobiles and trees that sport fans had got into the habit of travelling enormous distances to attend events. The normal driving speed had been stepped up to ninety-five miles an hour, and the distance between cars had been decreased to fifteen feet. This put an extraordinary strain on the sport lover's nervous system, and he arrived home from a Saturday game, after a road trip of three hundred and fifty miles, glassy-eyed, dazed, and spent. He hadn't really had any relaxation and he had failed to see Czlika (who had gone in for Trusky) take the pass from Bkeeo (who had gone in for Bjallo) in the third period, because at that moment a youngster named Lavagetto had been put in to pinch-hit for Art Gurlack in the bottom of the ninth with the tying run on second, and the skywriter who was attempting to write "Princeton 0–Lafayette 43" had banked the wrong way, muffed the "3," and distracted everyone's attention from the fact that Lavagetto had been whiffed.

Cheering, of course, lost its stimulating effect on players, because cheers were no longer associated necessarily with the immediate scene but might as easily apply to something that was happening somewhere else. This was enough to infuriate even the steadiest performer. A football star, hearing the stands break into a roar before the ball was snapped, would realize that their minds were not on him, and would become dispirited and grumpy. Two or three of the big coaches worried so about this that they considered equipping all players with tiny ear sets, so that they, too, could keep abreast of other sporting events while playing, but the idea was abandoned as impractical, and the coaches put it aside in tickler files, to bring up again later.

I think the event that marked the turning point in sport and started it downhill was the Midwest's classic Dust Bowl game of 1975, when Eastern Reserve's great right end, Ed Pistachio, was shot by a spectator. This man, the one who did the shooting, was seated well down in the stands near the forty-yard line on a bleak October afternoon and was so saturated with sport and with the disappointments of sport that he had clearly become deranged. With a minute and fifteen seconds to play and the score tied, the Eastern Reserve quarterback had whipped a long pass over Army's heads into Pistachio's waiting arms. There was no other player anywhere near him, and all Pistachio had to do was catch the ball and run it across the line. He dropped it. At exactly this moment, the spectator—a man named Homer T. Parkinson, of 35 Edgemere Drive, Toledo, O.—suffered at least three other major disappointments in the realm of sport. His horse, Hiccough, on which he had a five-hundred-dollar bet, fell while getting away from the starting gate at Pimlico and broke its leg (clearly visible in the video); his favorite shortstop, Lucky Frimstitch, struck out and let three men die on base in the final game of the Series (to which Parkinson was tuned); and the Governor Dummer soccer team, on which Parkinson's youngest son played goalie, lost to Kent, 4-3, as recorded in the sky overhead. Before anyone could stop him, he drew a gun and drilled Pistachio, before 954,000 persons, the largest crowd that had ever attended a football game and the *second*-largest crowd that had ever assembled for any sporting event in any month except July.

This tragedy, by itself, wouldn't have caused sport to decline, I suppose, but it set in motion a chain of other tragedies, the cumulative effect of which was terrific. Almost as soon as the shot was fired, the news flash was picked up by one of the skywriters directly above the field. He glanced down to see whether he could spot the trouble below, and in doing so failed to see another skywriter approaching. The two planes collided and fell, wings locked, leaving a confusing trail of smoke, which some observers tried to interpret as a late sports score. The planes struck in the middle of the nearby eastbound coast-to-coast Sunlight Parkway, and a motorist driving a convertible coupé stopped so short, to avoid hitting them, that he was bumped from behind. The pileup of cars that ensued involved 1,482 vehicles, a record for eastbound parkways. A total of more than three thousand persons lost their lives in the highway accident, including the two pilots, and when panic broke out in the stadium, it cost another 872 in dead and injured. News of the disaster spread quickly to other sports arenas, and started other panics among the crowds trying to get to the exits, where they could buy a paper and study a list of the dead. All in all, the afternoon of sport cost 20,003 lives, a record. And nobody had much to show for it except one small Midwestern boy who hung around the smoking wrecks of the planes, captured some aero news-smoke in a milk bottle, and took it home as a souvenir.

From that day on, sport waned. Through long, noncompetitive Saturday afternoons, the stadia slumbered. Even the parkways fell into disuse as motorists rediscovered the charms of old, twisty roads that led through main streets and past barnyards, with their mild congestions and pleasant smells.

# THE HOUR OF LETDOWN

W<small>HEN</small> the man came in, carrying the machine, most of us looked up from our drinks, because we had never seen anything like it before. The man set the thing down on top of the bar near the beerpulls. It took up an ungodly amount of room and you could see the bartender didn't like it any too well, having this big, ugly-looking gadget parked right there.

"Two rye-and-water," the man said.

The bartender went on puddling an Old-Fashioned that he was working on, but he was obviously turning over the request in his mind.

"You want a double?" he asked, after a bit.

"No," said the man. "Two rye-and-water, please." He stared straight at the bartender, not exactly unfriendly but on the other hand not affirmatively friendly.

Many years of catering to the kind of people that come into saloons had provided the bartender with an adjustable mind. Nevertheless, he did not adjust readily to this fellow, and he did not like the machine—that was sure. He picked up a live cigarette that was idling on the edge of the cash register, took a drag out of it, and returned it thoughtfully. Then he poured two shots of rye whiskey, drew two glasses of water, and shoved the drinks in front of the man. People were watching. When something a little out of the ordinary takes place at a bar, the sense of it spreads quickly all along the line and pulls the customers together.

46

The man gave no sign of being the center of attention. He laid a five-dollar bill down on the bar. Then he drank one of the ryes and chased it with water. He picked up the other rye, opened a small vent in the machine (it was like an oil cup) and poured the whiskey in, and then poured the water in.

The bartender watched grimly. "Not funny," he said in an even voice. "And furthermore, your companion takes up too much room. Why'n you put it over on that bench by the door, make more room here."

"There's plenty of room for everyone here," replied the man.

"I ain't amused," said the bartender. "Put the goddam thing over near the door like I say. Nobody will touch it."

The man smiled. "You should have seen it this afternoon," he said. "It was magnificent. Today was the third day of the tournament. Imagine it—three days of continuous brainwork! And against the top players in the country, too. Early in the game it gained an advantage; then for two hours it exploited the advantage brilliantly, ending with the opponent's king backed in a corner. The sudden capture of a knight, the neutralization of a bishop, and it was all over. You know how much money it won, all told, in three days of playing chess?"

"How much?" asked the bartender.

"Five thousand dollars," said the man. "Now it wants to let down, wants to get a little drunk."

The bartender ran his towel vaguely over some wet spots. "Take it somewheres else and get it drunk there!" he said firmly. "I got enough troubles."

The man shook his head and smiled. "No, we like it here." He pointed at the empty glasses. "Do this again, will you, please?"

The bartender slowly shook his head. He seemed dazed but dogged. "You stow the thing away," he ordered. "I'm not ladling out whiskey for jokestersmiths."

" 'Jokesmiths,' " said the machine. "The word is 'jokesmiths.' "

A few feet down the bar, a customer who was on his third high-ball seemed ready to participate in this conversation to which we had all been listening so attentively. He was a middle-aged man. His necktie was pulled down away from his collar, and he had eased the collar by unbuttoning it. He had pretty nearly finished his third drink, and the alcohol tended to make him throw his support in with the underprivileged and the thirsty.

"If the machine wants another drink, give it another drink," he said to the bartender. "Let's not have haggling."

The fellow with the machine turned to his new-found friend and gravely raised his hand to his temple, giving him a salute of gratitude and fellowship. He addressed his next remark to him, as though deliberately snubbing the bartender.

"You know how it is when you're all fagged out mentally, how you want a drink?"

"Certainly do," replied the friend. "Most natural thing in the world."

There was a stir all along the bar, some seeming to side with the bartender, others with the machine group. A tall, gloomy man standing next to me spoke up.

"Another whiskey sour, Bill," he said. "And go easy on the lemon juice."

"Picric acid," said the machine, sullenly. "They don't use lemon juice in these places."

"That does it!" said the bartender, smacking his hand on the bar. "Will you put that thing away or else beat it out of here. I ain't in the mood, I tell you. I got this saloon to run and I don't want lip from a mechanical brain or whatever the hell you've got there."

The man ignored this ultimatum. He addressed his friend, whose glass was now empty.

"It's not just that it's all tuckered out after three days of chess," he said amiably. "You know another reason it wants a drink?"

"No," said the friend. "Why?"

"It cheated," said the man.

At this remark, the machine chuckled. One of its arms dipped slightly, and a light glowed in a dial.

The friend frowned. He looked as though his dignity had been hurt, as though his trust had been misplaced. "Nobody can cheat at chess," he said. "Simpossible. In chess, everything is open and above the board. The nature of the game of chess is such that cheating is impossible."

"That's what I used to think, too," said the man. "But there *is* a way."

"Well, it doesn't surprise me any," put in the bartender. "The first time I laid my eyes on that crummy thing I spotted it for a crook."

"Two rye-and-water," said the man.

"You can't have the whiskey," said the bartender. He glared at the mechanical brain. "How do I know it ain't drunk already?"

"That's simple. Ask it something," said the man.

The customers shifted and stared into the mirror. We were all in this thing now, up to our necks. We waited. It was the bartender's move.

"Ask it what? Such as?" said the bartender.

"Makes no difference. Pick a couple big figures, ask it to multiply them together. You couldn't multiply big figures together if you were drunk, could you?"

The machine shook slightly, as though making internal preparations.

"Ten thousand eight hundred and sixty-two, multiply it by ninety-nine," said the bartender, viciously. We could tell that he was throwing in the two nines to make it hard.

The machine flickered. One of its tubes spat, and a hand changed position, jerkily.

"One million seventy-five thousand three hundred and thirty-eight," said the machine.

Not a glass was raised all along the bar. People just stared gloomily into the mirror; some of us studied our own faces, others took carom shots at the man and the machine.

Finally, a youngish, mathematically minded customer got out a piece of paper and a pencil and went into retirement. "It works out," he reported, after some minutes of calculating. "You can't say the machine is drunk!"

Everyone now glared at the bartender. Reluctantly he poured two shots of rye, drew two glasses of water. The man drank his drink. Then he fed the machine its drink. The machine's light grew fainter. One of its cranky little arms wilted.

For a while the saloon simmered along like a ship at sea in calm weather. Every one of us seemed to be trying to digest the situation, with the help of liquor. Quite a few glasses were refilled. Most of us sought help in the mirror—the court of last appeal.

The fellow with the unbuttoned collar settled his score. He walked stiffly over and stood between the man and the machine. He put one arm around the man, the other arm around the machine. "Let's get out of here and go to a good place," he said.

The machine glowed slightly. It seemed to be a little drunk now.

"All right," said the man. "That suits me fine. I've got my car outside."

He settled for the drinks and put down a tip. Quietly and a trifle uncertainly he tucked the machine under his arm, and he and his companion of the night walked to the door and out into the street.

The bartender stared fixedly, then resumed his light housekeeping. "So he's got his car outside," he said, with heavy sarcasm. "Now isn't that nice!"

A customer at the end of the bar near the door left his drink, stepped to the window, parted the curtains, and looked out. He watched for a moment, then returned to his place and addressed the bartender. "It's even nicer than you think," he said. "It's a Cadillac. And which one of the three of them d'ya think is doing the driving?"

# THE MORNING
## OF THE DAY THEY DID IT

My purpose is to tell how it happened and to set down a few impressions of that morning while it is fresh in memory. I was in a plane that was in radio communication with the men on the platform. To put the matter briefly, what was intended as a military expedient turned suddenly into a holocaust. The explanation was plain enough to me, for, like millions of others, I was listening to the conversation between the two men and was instantly aware of the quick shift it took. That part is clear. What is not so clear is how I myself survived, but I am beginning to understand that, too. I shall not burden the reader with an explanation, however, as the facts are tedious and implausible. I am now in good health and fair spirits, among friendly people on an inferior planet, at a very great distance from the sun. Even the move from one planet to another has not relieved me of the nagging curse that besets writing men—the feeling that they must produce some sort of record of their times.

The thing happened shortly before twelve noon. I came out of my house on East Harding Boulevard at quarter of eight that morning, swinging my newspaper and feeling pretty good. The March day was mild and springlike, the warmth and the smells doubly welcome after the rotten weather we'd been having. A gentle wind met me on the Boulevard, frisked me, and went on.

A man in a leather cap was loading bedsprings into a van in front of No. 220. I remember that as I walked along I worked my tongue around the roof of my mouth, trying to dislodge a prune skin. (These details have no significance; why write them down?)

A few blocks from home there was a Contakt plane station and I hurried in, caught the 8:10 plane, and was soon aloft. I always hated a jet-assist takeoff right after breakfast, but it was one of the discomforts that went with my job. At ten thousand feet our small plane made contact with the big one, we passengers were transferred, and the big ship went on up to fifty thousand, which was the height television planes flew at. I was a script writer for one of the programs. My tour of duty was supposed to be eight hours.

I should probably explain here that at the period of which I am writing, the last days of the planet earth, telecasting was done from planes circling the stratosphere. This eliminated the coaxial cable, a form of relay that had given endless trouble. Coaxials worked well enough for a while, but eventually they were abandoned, largely because of the extraordinary depredations of earwigs. These insects had developed an alarming resistance to bugspray and were out of control most of the time. Earwigs increased in size and in numbers, and the forceps at the end of their abdomen developed so that they could cut through a steel shell. They seemed to go unerringly for coaxials. Whether the signals carried by the cables had anything to do with it I don't know, but the bugs fed on these things and were enormously stimulated. Not only did they feast on the cables, causing the cables to disintegrate, but they laid eggs in them in unimaginable quantities, and as the eggs hatched the television images suffered greatly, there was more and more flickering on the screen, more and more eyestrain and nervous tension among audiences, and of course a further debasement of taste and intellectual life in general. Finally the coaxials were given up, and after much experimenting by Westinghouse and the Glenn Martin people a satisfactory substitute was found in the high-flying planes. A few of these planes, spotted around the country, handled the whole television load nicely. Known as Stratovideo planes, they were equipped with studios; many programs originated in the air and were transmitted directly, others were beamed to the aircraft from ground stations and then relayed. The planes flew continuously, twenty-four hours a day, were refuelled in air, and dropped down to ten thousand feet every eight hours to meet the Contakt planes and take on new shifts of workers.

I remember that as I walked to my desk in the Stratoship that morning, the nine-o'clock news had just ended and a program called "Author, Please!" was going on, featuring Melonie Babson, a woman who had written a best-seller on the theme of euthanasia, called "Peace of Body." The program was sponsored by a dress-shield company.

I remember, too, that a young doctor had come aboard the plane with the rest of us. He was a newcomer, a fellow named Cathcart, slated to be the physician attached to the ship. He had introduced himself to me in the Contakt plane, had asked the date of my Tri-D shot, and had noted it down in his book. (I shall explain about these shots presently.) This doctor certainly had a brief life in our midst. He had hardly been introduced around and shown his office when our control room got a radio call asking if there was a doctor in the stratosphere above Earthpoint F-plus-6, and requesting medical assistance at the scene of an accident.

F-plus-6 was almost directly below us, so Dr. Cathcart felt he ought to respond, and our control man gave the word and asked for particulars and instructions. It seems there had been a low-altitude collision above F-plus-6 involving two small planes and killing three people. One plane was a Diaheliper, belonging to an aerial diaper service that flew diapers to rural homes by helicopter. The other was one of the familiar government-owned sprayplanes that worked at low altitudes over croplands, truck gardens, and commercial orchards, delivering a heavy mist of the deadly Tri-D solution, the pesticide that had revolutionized agriculture, eliminated the bee from nature, and given us fruits and vegetables of undreamed-of perfection but very high toxicity.

The two planes had tangled and fallen onto the observation tower of a whooping-crane sanctuary, scattering diapers over an area of half a mile and releasing a stream of Tri-D. Cathcart got his medical kit, put on his parachute, and paused a moment to adjust his pressurizer, preparatory to bailing out. Knowing that he wouldn't be back for a while, he asked if anybody around the shop was due for a Tri-D shot that morning, and it turned out that Bill Foley was. So the Doctor told Foley to come along, and explained that he would give him his injection on the way down. Bill threw me a quick look of mock anguish, and started climbing into his gear. This must have been six or seven minutes past nine.

It seems strange that I should feel obliged to explain Tri-D shots. They were a commonplace at this time—as much a part of a person's life as his toothbrush. The correct name for them was Anti-Tri-D, but people soon shortened the name. They were simply injections that everyone had to receive at regular twenty-one-day intervals, to counteract the lethal effect of food, and the notable thing about them was the great importance of the twenty-one-day period. To miss one's Tri-D shot by as much as a couple of hours might mean serious consequences, even death. Almost every day there were deaths reported in the papers from failure to get the injection at the proper time. The whole business was something like insulin control in diabetes. You can easily imagine the work it entailed for doctors in the United States, keeping the entire population protected against death by poisoning.

As Dr. Cathcart and Bill eased themselves out of the plane through the chute exit, I paused briefly and listened to Miss Babson, our author of the day.

"It is a grand privilege," she was saying, "to appear before the television audience this morning and face this distinguished battery of critics, including my old sparring partner, Ralph Armstrong, of the *Herald Tribune*. I suppose after Mr. Armstrong finishes with me I will be a pretty good candidate for euthanasia myself. Ha. But seriously, ladies and gentlemen, I feel that a good book is its own defense."

The authoress had achieved a state of exaltation already. I knew that her book, which she truly believed to be great, had been suggested to her by an agent over a luncheon table and had been written largely by somebody else, whom the publisher had had to bring in to salvage the thing. The final result was a run-of-the-can piece of rubbish easily outselling its nearest competitor.

Miss Babson continued, her exaltation stained with cuteness:

"I have heard my novel criticized on the ground that the theme of euthanasia is too daring, and even that it is anti-Catholic. Well, I can remember, way back in the dark ages, when a lot of things that are accepted as commonplace today were considered daring or absurd. My own father can recall the days when dairy cows were actually bred by natural methods. The farmers of those times felt that the artificial-breeding program developed by our marvellous experiment stations was highfalutin nonsense. Well, we all know what has happened to the dairy industry, with many of our best milch cows giving milk continuously right around the clock, in a steady stream. True, the cows do have to be propped up and held in position in special stanchions and fed intravenously, but I always say it isn't the hubbub that counts, it's the butterfat.

And I doubt if even Mr. Armstrong here would want to return to the days when a cow just gave a bucket of milk and then stopped to rest."

Tiring of the literary life, I walked away and looked out a window. Below, near the layer of cumulus, the two chutes were visible. With the help of binoculars I could see Bill manfully trying to slip his chute over next to the Doc, and could see Cathcart fumbling for his needle. Our telecandid man was at another window, filming the thing for the next newscast, as it was a new wrinkle in the Tri-D world to have somebody getting his shot while parachuting.

I had a few chores to do before our program came on, at eleven-five. "Town Meeting of the Upper Air" was the name of it. "Town Meeting" was an unrehearsed show, but I was supposed to brief the guests, distribute copies of whatever prepared scripts there were, explain the cuing, and make everybody happy generally. The program we were readying that morning had had heavy advance billing, and there was tremendous interest in it everywhere, not so much because of the topic ("Will the fear of retaliation stop aggression?") or even the cast of characters, which included Major General Artemus T. Recoil, but because of an incidental stunt we were planning to pull off. We had arranged a radio hookup with the space platform, a gadget the Army had succeeded in establishing six hundred miles up, in the regions of the sky beyond the pull of gravity. The Army, after many years of experimenting with rockets, had not only got the platform established but had sent two fellows there in a Spaceship, and also a liberal supply of the New Weapon.

The whole civilized world had read about this achievement, which swung the balance of power so heavily in our favor, and everyone was aware that the damned platform was wandering around in its own orbit at a dizzy distance from the earth and not subject to gravitational pull. Every kid in America had become an astrophysicist overnight and talked knowingly of exhaust velocities, synergy curves, and Keplerian ellipses. Every subway rider knew that the two men on the platform were breathing oxygen thrown off from big squash vines that they had taken along. The *Reader's Digest* had added to the fun by translating and condensing several German treatises on rockets and space travel, including the great *Wege zur Raumschiffahrt*. But to date, because of security regulations and technical difficulties, there had been no radio-television hookup. Finally we got clearance from Washington, and General Recoil agreed to interview the officers on the platform as part of the "Town Meeting" program. This was big stuff—to hear directly from the Space Platform for Checking Aggression, known pretty generally as the SPCA.

I was keyed up about it myself, but I remember that all that morning in the plane I felt disaffected, and wished I were not a stratovideo man. There were often days like that in the air. The plane, with its queer cargo and its cheap goings on, would suddenly seem unaccountably remote from the world of things I admired. In a physical sense we were never very remote: the plane circled steadily in a fixed circle of about ten miles diameter, and I was never far from my own home on East Harding Boulevard. I could talk to Ann and the children, if I wished, by radiophone.

In many respects mine was a good job. It paid two hundred and twenty-five dollars a week, of which two hundred and ten was withheld. I should have felt well satisfied. Almost everything in the way of social benefits was provided by the government—medical care, hospitalization, education for the children, accident insurance, fire and theft, old-age retirement, Tri-D shots, vacation expense, amusement and recreation, welfare and well-being, Christmas and good will, rainy-day resource, staples and supplies, beverages and special occasions, babysitzfund—it had all been worked out. Any man who kept careful account of his pin money could get along all right, and I guess I should have been happy. Ann never complained much, except about one thing. She found that no matter how we saved and planned, we never could afford to buy flowers. One day, when she was a bit lathered up over household problems, she screamed, "God damn it, I'd rather live dangerously and have one dozen yellow freesias!" It seemed to prey on her mind.

Anyway, this was one of those oppressive days in the air for me. Something about the plane's undeviating course irritated me; the circle we flew seemed a monstrous excursion to nowhere. The engine noise (we flew at subsonic speed) was an unrelieved whine. Usually I didn't notice the engines, but today the ship sounded in my ears every minute, reminding me of a radiotherapy chamber, and there was always the palpable impact of vulgar miracles—the very nature of television—that made me itchy and fretful.

Appearing with General Recoil on "Town Meeting of the Upper Air" were to be Mrs. Florence Gill, president of the Women's Auxiliary of the Sons of Original Matrons; Amory Buxton, head of the Economics and Withholding Council of the United Nations; and a young man named Tollip, representing one of the small, ineffectual groups that advocated world federation. I rounded up this stable of intellects in the reception room, went over the procedure with them, gave the General a drink (which seemed to be what was on his mind), and then ducked out to catch the ten-o'clock news and to have a smoke.

I found Pete Everhardt in the control room. He looked bushed. "Quite a morning, Nuncle," he said. Pete not only had to keep his signal clean on the nine-o'clock show (Melonie Babson was a speaker who liked to range all over the place when she talked) but he had to keep kicking the ball around with the two Army officers on the space platform, for fear he would lose them just as they were due to go on. And on top of that he felt obliged to stay in touch with Dr. Cathcart down below, as a matter of courtesy, and also to pick up incidental stuff for subsequent newscasts.

I sat down and lit a cigarette. In a few moments the day's authoress wound up her remarks and the news started, with the big, tense face of Ed Peterson on the screen dishing it out. Ed was well equipped by nature for newscasting; he had the accents of destiny. When he spread the news, it penetrated in depth. Each event not only seemed fraught with meaning, it seemed fraught with Ed. When he said "I predict . . ." you felt the full flow of his pipeline to God.

To the best of my recollection the ten-o'clock newscast on this awful morning went as follows:

(Announcer) "Good morning. Tepky's Hormone-Enriched Dental Floss brings you Ed Peterson and the news."

(Ed) "Flash! Three persons were killed and two others seriously injured a few minutes ago at Earthpoint F-plus-6 when a government sprayplane collided with a helicopter of the Diaheliper Company. Both pilots were thrown clear. They are at this moment being treated by a doctor released by parachute from Stratovideo Ship 3, from which I am now speaking. The sprayplane crashed into the observation tower of a whooping-crane sanctuary, releasing a deadly mist of Tri-D and instantly killing three wardens who were lounging there watching the love dance of the cranes. Diapers were scattered widely over the area, and these sterile garments proved invaluable to Dr. Herbert L. Cathcart in bandaging the wounds of the injured pilots, Roy T. Bliss and Homer Schenck. [Here followed a newsreel shot showing Cathcart winding a diaper around the head of one of the victims.] You are now at the scene of the disaster," droned Ed. "This is the first time in the history of television that an infant's napkin has appeared in the role of emergency bandage. Another first for American Tel. & Vid.!

"Washington! A Senate committee, with new facts at its disposal, will reopen the investigation to establish the blame for Pearl Harbor.

"Chicago! Two members of the Department of Sanitation were removed from the payroll today for refusal to take the loyalty oath. Both are members of New Brooms, one of the four hundred thousand organizations on the Attorney General's subversive list.

"Hollywood! It's a boy at the Roscoe Pews. Stay tuned to this channel for a closeup of the Caesarean section during the eleven-o'clock roundup!

"New York! Flash! The Pulitzer Prize in editorial writing has been awarded to Frederick A. Mildly, of the New York *Times*, for his nostalgic editorial 'The Old Pumphandle.'

"Flash! Donations to the Atlantic Community Chest now stand at a little over seven hundred billion dollars. Thanks for a wonderful job of giving—I mean that from my heart.

"New York! The vexing question of whether Greek athletes will be allowed to take part in next year's Olympic Games still deadlocks the Security Council. In a stormy session yesterday the Russian delegate argued that the presence of Greek athletes at the games would be a threat to world peace. Most of the session was devoted to a discussion of whether the question was a procedural matter or a matter of substance.

"Flash! Radio contact with the two United States Army officers on the Space Platform for Checking Aggression, known to millions of listeners as the SPCA, has definitely been established, despite rumors to the contrary. The television audience will hear their voices in a little more than one hour from this very moment. You will *not* see their faces. Stay tuned! This is history, ladies and gentlemen—the first time a human voice freed from the pull of gravity has been heard on earth. The spacemen will be interviewed by Major General Artemus T. Recoil on the well-loved program 'Town Meeting of the Upper Air.'

"I predict: that because of SPCA and the Army's Operation Space, the whole course of human destiny will be abruptly changed, and that the age-old vision of peace is now on the way to becoming a reality."

Ed finished and went into his commercial, which consisted of digging a piece of beef gristle out of his teeth with dental floss

I rubbed out my cigarette and walked back toward my cell. In the studio next ours, "The Bee" was on the air, and I paused for a while to watch. "The Bee" was a program sponsored by the Larry Cross Pollination Company, aimed principally at big orchardists and growers—or rather at their wives. It was an interminable mystery-thriller sort of thing, with a character called the Bee, who always wore a green hood with two long black feelers. Standing there in the aisle of the plane, looking into the glass-enclosed studio, I could see the Bee about to strangle a red-haired girl in slinky pajamas. This was America's pollination hour, an old standby, answer to the housewife's dream. The Larry Cross outfit was immensely rich. I think they probably handled better than eighty per cent of all fertilization in the country. Bees, as I have said, had become extinct, thanks to the massive doses of chemicals, and of course this had at first posed a serious agricultural problem, as vast areas were without natural pollination. The answer came when the Larry Cross firm was organized, with the slogan "We Carry the Torch for Nature." The business mushroomed, and branch offices sprang up all over the nation. During blossom time, field crews of highly trained men fanned out and pollinized everything by hand—a huge job and an arduous one. The only honey in the United States was synthetic—a blend of mineral oil and papaya juice. Ann hated it with a morbid passion.

When I reached my studio I found everybody getting ready for the warmup. The Town Crier, in his fusty costume, stood holding his bell by the clapper, while the makeup man touched up his face for him. Mrs. Gill, the S.O.M. representative, sat gazing contemptuously at young Tollip. I had riffled through her script earlier, curious to find out what kind of punch she was going to throw. It was about what I expected. Her last paragraph contained the suggestion that all persons who advocated a revision of the Charter of the United Nations be automatically deprived of their citizenship. "If these well-meaning but misguided persons," ran the script, "with their utopian plans for selling this nation down the river are so anxious to acquire world citizenship, I say let's make it easy for them—let's take away the citizenship they've already got and see how they like it. As a lineal descendant of one of the Sons of Original Matrons, I am sick and tired of these cuckoo notions of one world, which come dangerously close to simple treachery. We've enough to do right here at home without . . ."

And so on. In my mind's ear I could already hear the moderator's salutary and impartial voice saying, "Thank you, Mrs. Florence Gill."

At five past eleven, the Crier rang his bell. "Hear ye! See ye! Town Meetin' today! Listen to both sides and make up your own minds!" Then George Cahill, the moderator, started the ball rolling.

I glanced at Tollip. He looked as though his stomach were filling up with gas. As the program got under way, my own stomach began to inflate, too, the way it often did a few hours after breakfast. I remember very little of the early minutes of that morning's Town Meeting. I recall that the U.N. man spoke first, then Mrs. Gill, then Tollip (who looked perfectly awful). Finally the moderator introduced General Recoil, whose stomach enjoyed the steadying effects of whiskey and who spoke in a loud, slow, confident voice, turning frequently to smile down on the three other guests.

"We in the Army," began the General, "don't pretend that we know all the answers to these brave and wonderful questions. It is not the Army's business to know whether aggression is going to occur or not. Our business is to put on a good show if it *does* occur. The Army is content to leave to the United Nations and to idealists like Mr. Tollip the troublesome details of political progress. I certainly don't know, ladies and gentlemen, whether the fear of retaliation is going to prevent aggression, but I *do* know that there is no moss growing on we of Operation Space. As for myself, I guess I am what you might call a retaliatin' fool. [Laughter in the upper air.] Our enemy is well aware that we are now in a most unusual position to retaliate. That knowledge on the part of our enemy is, in my humble opinion, a deterrent to aggression. If I didn't believe that, I'd shed this uniform and get into a really well-paid line of work, like professional baseball."

*Will this plane never quit circling? (I thought). Will the words never quit going round and round? Is there no end to this noisy carrousel of indigestible ideas? Will no one ever catch the brass ring?*

"But essentially," continued the General, "our job is not to deal with the theoretical world of Mr. Tollip, who suggests that we merge in some vast superstate with every Tom, Dick, and Harry, no matter what their color or race or how underprivileged they are, thus pulling down our standard of living to the level of the lowest common denominator. Our job is not to deal with the diplomatic world of Mr. Buxton, who hopes to find a peaceful solution around a conference table. No, the Army must face the world as it is. We know the enemy is strong. In our dumb way, we think it is just horse sense for us to be stronger. And I'm proud, believe me, ladies and gentlemen, proud to be at one end of the interplanetary conversation that is about to take place on this very, *very* historic morning. The achievement of the United States Army in establishing the space platform—which is literally a man-made planet—is unparalleled in military history. We have led the way into space. We have given Old Lady Gravity the slip. We have got there, and we have got there fustest with the mostest. [Applause.]

"I can state without qualification that the New Weapon, in the capable hands of the men stationed on our platform, brings the entire globe under our dominion. We can pinpoint any spot, anywhere, and sprinkle it with our particular brand of thunder. Mr. Moderator, I'm ready for this interview if the boys out there in space are ready."

Everyone suspected that there might be a slipup in the proceedings at this point, that the mechanical difficulties might prove insuperable. I glanced at the studio clock. The red sweep hand was within a few jumps of eleven-thirty—the General had managed his timing all right. Cahill's face was tenser than I had ever seen it before. Because of the advance buildup, a collapse at this moment would put him in a nasty hole, even for an old experienced m.c. But at exactly eleven-thirty the interview started, smooth as silk. Cahill picked it up from the General.

"And now, watchers of television everywhere, you will hear a conversation between Major General Artemus T. Recoil, who pioneered Operation Space, and two United States Army officers on the platform—Major James Obblington, formerly of Brooklyn, New York, now of Space, and Lieutenant Noble Trett, formerly of Sioux City, Iowa, now of Space. Go ahead, General Recoil!"

"Come in, Space!" said the General, his tonsils struggling in whiskey's undertow, his eyes bearing down hard on the script. "Can you hear me, Major Obblington and Lieutenant Trett?"

"I hear you," said a voice. "This is Trett." The voice, as I remember it, astonished me because of a certain laconic quality that I had not expected. I believe it astonished everyone. Trett's voice was cool, and he sounded as though he were right in the studio.

"Lieutenant Trett," continued the General, "tell the listeners here on earth, tell us, in your position far out there in free space, do you feel the pull of gravity?"

"No, sir, I don't," answered Trett. In spite of the "sir," Trett sounded curiously listless, almost insubordinate.

"Yet you are perfectly comfortable, sitting there on the platform, with the whole of earth spread out before you like a vast target?"

"Sure I'm comfortable."

The General waited a second, as though expecting amplification, but it failed to come. "Well, ah, how's the weather up there?" he asked heartily.

"There isn't any," said Trett.

"No weather? No weather in space? That's very interesting."

"The hell it is," said Trett. "It's God-damn dull. This place is a dump. Worse than some of the islands in the Pacific."

"Well, I suppose it must get on your nerves a bit. That's all part of the game. Tell us, Lieutenant, what's it like to be actually a part of the solar system, with your own private orbit?"

"It's all right, except I'd a damn sight rather get drunk," said Trett.

I looked at Cahill. He was swallowing his spit. General Recoil took a new hold on his script.

"And you say you don't feel the pull of gravity, not even a little?"

"I just told you I didn't feel any pull," said Trett. His voice now had a surly quality.

"Well, ah," continued the General, who was beginning to tremble, "can you describe, briefly, for the television audience—" But it was at this point that Trett, on the platform, seemed to lose interest in talking with General Recoil and started chinning with Major Obblington, his sidekick in space. At first the three voices clashed and blurred, but the General, on a signal from the moderator, quit talking, and the conversation that ensued between Trett and Obblington was audible and clear. Millions of listeners must have heard the dialogue.

"Hey, Obie," said Trett, "you want to know something else I don't feel the pull of, besides gravity?"

"What?" asked his companion.

"Conscience," said Trett cheerfully. "I don't feel my conscience pulling me around."

"Neither do I," said Obblington. "I ought to feel some pulls but I don't."

"I also don't feel the pull of duty."

"Check," said Obblington.

"And what is even more fantastic, I don't feel the pull of dames."

Cahill made a sign to the General. Stunned and confused by the turn things had taken, Recoil tried to pick up the interview and get it back on the track. "Lieutenant Trett," he commanded, "you will limit your remarks to the—"

Cahill waved him quiet. The next voice was the Major's.

"Jesus, now that you mention it, I don't feel the pull of dames, either! Hey, Lieutenant—you suppose gravity has anything to do with sex?"

"God damn if I know," replied Trett. "I know I don't *weigh* anything, and when you don't weigh anything, you don't seem to *want* anything."

The studio by this time was paralyzed with attention. The General's face was swollen, his mouth was half open, and he struggled for speech that wouldn't come.

Then Trett's cool, even voice again: "See that continent down there, Obie? That's where old Fatso Recoil lives. You feel drawn toward that continent in any special way?"

"Naa," said Obblington.

"You feel like doing a little shooting, Obie?"

"You're rootin' tootin' I feel like shootin'."

"Then what are we waiting for?"

I am, of course, reconstructing this conversation from memory. I am trying to report it faithfully. When Trett said the words "Then what are we waiting for?" I quit listening and dashed for the phones in the corridor. As I was leaving the studio, I turned for a split second and looked back. The General had partially recovered his power of speech. He was mumbling something to Cahill. I caught the words "phone" and "Defense Department."

The corridor was already jammed. I had only one idea in my head—to speak to Ann. Pete Everhardt pushed past me. He said crisply, "This is it." I nodded. Then I glanced out of a window. High in the east a crazy ribbon of light was spreading upward. Lower down, in a terrible parabola, another streak began burning through. The first blast was felt only slightly in the plane. It must have been at a great distance. It was followed immediately by two more. I saw a piece of wing break up, saw one of the starboard engines shake itself loose from its fastenings and fall. Near the phone booths, the Bee, still in costume, fumbled awkwardly for a parachute. In the crush one of his feelers brushed my face. I never managed to reach a phone. All sorts of things flashed through my mind. I saw Ann and the children, their heads in diapers. I saw again the man in the leather cap, loading bedsprings. I heard again Pete's words, "This is it," only I seemed to hear them in translation: "Until the whole wide world to nothingness do sink." (How durable the poets are!) As I say, I never managed the phone call. My last memory of the morning is of myriads of bright points of destruction where the Weapon was arriving, each pyre in the characteristic shape of an artichoke. Then a great gash, and the plane tumbling. Then I lost consciousness.

I cannot say how many minutes or hours after that the earth finally broke up. I do not know. There is, of course, a mild irony in the fact that it was the United States that was responsible. Insofar as it can be said of any country that it had human attributes, the United States was well-meaning. Of that I am convinced. Even I, at this date and at this distance, cannot forget my country's great heart and matchless ingenuity. I can't in honesty say that I believe we were wrong to send the men to the platform—it's just that in any matter involving love, or high explosives, one can never foresee all the factors. Certainly I can't say with any assurance that Tollip's theory was right; it seems hardly likely that anyone who suffered so from stomach gas could have been on the right track. I did feel sympathetic toward some of his ideas, perhaps because I suffered from flatulence myself. Anyway, it was inevitable that it should have been the United States that developed the space platform and the new weapon that made the H-bomb obsolete. It was inevitable that what happened, at last, was conceived in good will.

Those times—those last days of earth! I think about them a lot. A sort of creeping ineptitude had set in. Almost everything in life seemed wrong to me, somehow, as though we were all hustling down a blind alley. Many of my friends seemed mentally confused, emotionally unstable, and I have an idea I seemed the same to them. In the big cities, horns blew before the light changed, and it was clear that motorists no longer had the capacity to endure the restrictions they had placed on their own behavior. When the birds became extinct (all but the whooping crane), I was reasonably sure that human beings were on the way out, too. The cranes survived only because of their dance—which showmen were quick to exploit. (Every sanctuary had its television transmitter, and the love dance became a more popular spectacle than heavyweight prizefighting.) Birds had always been the symbol of freedom. As soon as I realized that they were gone, I felt that the significance had gone from my own affairs. (I was a cranky man, though—I must remember that, too—and am not trying here to suggest anything beyond a rather strong personal sadness at all this.)

Those last days! There were so many religions in conflict, each ready to save the world with its own dogma, each perfectly intolerant of the other. Every day seemed a mere skirmish in the long holy war. It was a time of debauch and conversion. Every week the national picture magazines, as though atoning for past excesses, hid their cheesecake carefully away among four-color reproductions of the saints. Television was the universal peepshow—in homes, schools, churches, bars, stores, everywhere. Children early formed the habit of gaining all their images at second hand, by looking at a screen; they grew up believing that anything perceived directly was vaguely fraudulent. Only what had been touched with electronics was valid and real. I think the decline in the importance of direct images dated from the year television managed to catch an eclipse of the moon. After that, nobody ever looked at the sky, and it was as though the moon had joined the shabby company of buskers. There was really never a moment when a child, or even a man, felt free to look away from the television screen—for fear he might miss the one clue that would explain everything.

In many respects I like the planet I'm on. The people here have no urgencies, no capacity for sustained endeavor, but merely tackle things by fits and starts, leaving undone whatever fails to hold their interest, and so, by witlessness and improvidence, escape many of the errors of accomplishment. I like the apples here better than those on earth. They are often wormy, but with a most wonderful flavor. There is a saying here: "Even a very lazy man can eat around a worm.

But I would be lying if I said I didn't miss that other life, I loved it so.

# II.

# Time Present

# ABOUT MYSELF

I AM A man of medium height. I keep my records in a Weis Folder Re-order Number 8003. The unpaid balance of my estimated tax for the year 1945 is item 3 less the sum of items 4 and 5. My eyes are gray. My Selective Service order number is 10789. The serial number is T1654. I am in Class IV-A, and have been variously in Class 3-A, Class I-A(H), and Class 4-H. My social security number is 067-01-9841. I am married to U.S. Woman Number 067-01-9807. Her eyes are gray. This is not a joint declaration, nor is it made by an agent; therefore it need be signed only by me—and, as I said, I am a man of medium height.

I am the holder of a quit-claim deed recorded in Book 682, Page 501, in the county where I live. I hold Fire Insurance Policy Number 424747, continuing until the 23 day of October in the year nineteen hundred forty-five, at noon, and it is important that the written portions of all policies covering the same property read exactly alike. My cervical spine shows relatively good alignment with evidence of proliferative changes about the bodies consistent with early arthritis. (Essential clinical data: pain in neck radiating to mastoids and occipito-temporal region, not constant, moderately severe; patient in good general health and working.) My operator's licence is Number 16200. It expired December 31, 1943, more than a year ago, but I am still carrying it and it appears to be serving the purpose. I shall renew it when I get time. I have made, published, and declared my last will and testament, and it thereby revokes all other wills and codicils at any time heretofore made by me. I hold Basic A Mileage Ration 108950, O.P.A. Form R-525-C. The number of my car is 18-388. Tickets A-14 are valid through March 21st.

I was born in District Number 5903, New York State. My birth is registered in Volume 3/58 of the Department of Health. My father was a man of medium height. His telephone number was 484. My mother was a housewife. Her eyes were blue. Neither parent had a social security number and neither was secure socially. They drove to the depot behind an unnumbered horse.

I hold Individual Certificate Number 4320-209 with the Equitable Life Assurance Society, in which a corporation hereinafter called the employer has contracted to insure my life for the sum of two thousand dollars. My left front tire is Number 48KE8846, my right front tire is Number 63T6895. My rear tires are, from left to right, Number 6N4M5384 and Number A26E5806D. I brush my hair with Whiting-Adams Brush Number 010 and comb my hair with Pro-Phy-Lac-Tic Comb Number 1201. My shaving brush is sterilized. I take Pill Number 43934 after each meal and I can get more of them by calling ELdorado 5-6770. I spray my nose with De Vilbiss Atomizer Number 14. Sometimes I stop the pain with Squibb Pill, Control Number 3K49979 (aspirin). My wife (Number 067-01-9807) takes Pill Number 49345.

I hold War Ration Book 40289EW, from which have been torn Airplane Stamps Numbers 1, 2, and 3. I also hold Book 159378CD, from which have been torn Spare Number 2, Spare Number 37, and certain other coupons. My wife holds Book 40288EW and Book 159374CD. In accepting them, she recognized that they remained the property of the United States Government.

I have a black dog with cheeks of tan. Her number is 11032. It is an old number. I shall renew it when I get time. The analysis of her prepared food is guaranteed and is Case Number 1312. The ingredients are: Cereal Flaked feeds (from Corn, Rice, Bran, and Wheat), Meat Meal, Fish Liver and Glandular Meal, Soybean Oil Meal, Wheat Bran, Corn Germ Meal, 5% Kel-Centrate [containing Dried Skim Milk, Dehydrated Cheese, Vitamin $B_1$ (Thiamin), Flavin Concentrate, Carotene, Yeast, Vitamin A and D Feeding Oil (containing 3,000 U.S.P. units Vitamin A and 400 U.S.P. units Vitamin D per gram), Diastase (Enzyme), Wheat Germ Meal, Rice Polish Extract], 1 1/2% Calcium Carbonate, .00037% Potassium Iodide, and 1/4% Salt. She prefers offal.

When I finish what I am now writing it will be late in the day. It will be about half past five. I will then take up Purchase Order Number 245-9077-B-Final, which I received this morning from the Office of War Information and which covers the use of certain material they want to translate into a foreign language. Attached to the order are Standard Form Number 1034 (white) and three copies of Standard Form Number 1034a (yellow), also "Instructions for Preparation of Voucher by Vendor and Example of Prepared Voucher." The Appropriation Symbol of the Purchase Order is 1153700.001-501. The requisition number is B-827. The allotment is X5-207.1-R2-11. Voucher shall be prepared in ink, indelible pencil, or typewriter. For a while I will be vendor preparing voucher. Later on, when my head gets bad and the pain radiates, I will be voucher preparing vendor. I see that there is a list of twenty-one instructions which I will be following. Number One on the list is: "Name of payor agency as shown in the block 'appropriation symbol and title' in the upper left-hand corner of the Purchase Order." Number Five on the list is: "Vendor's personal account or invoice number," but whether that means Order Number 245-9077-B-Final, or Requisition B-827, or Allotment X5-207.1-R2-11, or Appropriation Symbol 1153700.001-501, I do not know, nor will I know later on in the evening after several hours of meditation, nor will I be able to find out by consulting Woman 067-01-9807, who is no better at filling out forms than I am, nor after taking Pill Number 43934, which tends merely to make me drowsy.

I owe a letter to Corporal 32413654, Hq and Hq Sq., VII AAF S.C., APO 953, c/o PM San Francisco, Calif., thanking him for the necktie he sent me at Christmas. In 1918 I was a private in the Army. My number was 4,345,016. I was a boy of medium height. I had light hair. I had no absences from duty under G.O. 31, 1912, or G.O. 45, 1914. The number of that war was Number One.

# THE DOOR

Everything (he kept saying) is something it isn't. And everybody is always somewhere else. Maybe it was the city, being in the city, that made him feel how queer everything was and that it something else. Maybe (he kept thinking) it was the names of the things. The names were tex and frequently koid. Or they were flex and oid or they were duroid (sani) or flexsan (duro), but everything was glass (but not quite glass) and the thing that you touched (the surface, washable, crease-resistant) was rubber, only it wasn't quite rubber and you didn't quite touch it but almost. The wall, which was glass but thrutex, turned out on being approached not to be a wall, it was something else, it was an opening or doorway—and the doorway (through which he saw himself approaching) turned out to be something else, it was a wall. And what he had eaten not having agreed with him.

He was in a washable house, but he wasn't sure. Now about those rats, he kept saying to himself. He meant the rats that the Professor had driven crazy by forcing them to deal with problems which were beyond the scope of rats, the insoluble problems. He meant the rats that had been trained to jump at the square card with the circle in the middle, and the card (because it was something it wasn't) would give way and let the rat into a place where the food was, but then one day it would be a trick played on the rat, and the card would be changed, and the rat would jump but the card wouldn't give way, and it was an impossible situation (for a rat) and the rat would go insane and into its eyes would come the unspeakably bright imploring look of the frustrated, and after the convulsions were over and the frantic racing around, then the passive stage would set in and the willingness to let anything be done to it, even if it was something else.

He didn't know which door (or wall) or opening in the house to jump at, to get through, because one was an opening that wasn't a door (it was a void, or koid) and the other was a wall that wasn't an opening, it was a sanitary cupboard of the same color. He caught a glimpse of his eyes staring into his eyes, in the thrutex, and in them was the expression he had seen in the picture of the rats—weary after convulsions and the frantic racing around, when they were willing and did not mind having anything done to them. More and more (he kept saying) I am confronted by a problem which is incapable of solution (for this time even if he chose the right door, there would be no food behind it) and that is what madness is, and things seeming different from what they are. He heard, in the house where he was, in the city to which he had gone (as toward a door which might, or might not, give way), a noise—not a loud noise but more of a low prefabricated humming. It came from a place in the base of the wall (or stat) where the flue carrying the filterable air was, and not far from the Minipiano, which was made of the same material nailbrushes are made of, and which was under the stairs. "This, too, has been tested," she said, pointing, but not at it, "and found viable." It wasn't a loud noise, he kept thinking, sorry that he had seen his eyes, even though it was through his own eyes that he had seen them.

First will come the convulsions (he said), then the exhaustion, then the willingness to let anything be done. "And you better believe it *will* be."

All his life he had been confronted by situations which were incapable of being solved, and there was a deliberateness behind all this, behind this changing of the card (or door), because they would always wait till you had learned to jump at the certain card (or door)—the one with the circle—and then they would change it on you. There have been so many doors changed on me, he said, in the last twenty years, but it is now becoming clear that it is an impossible situation, and the question is whether to jump again, even though they ruffle you in the rump with a blast of air—to make you jump. He wished he wasn't standing by the Minipiano. First they would teach you the prayers and the Psalms, and that would be the right door (the one with the circle), and the long sweet words with the holy sound, and that would be the one to jump at to get where the food was. Then one day you jumped and it didn't give way, so that all you got was the bump on the nose, and the first bewilderment, the first young bewilderment.

I don't know whether to tell her about the door they substituted or not, he said, the one with the equation on it and the picture of the amoeba reproducing itself by division. Or the one with the photostatic copy of the check for thirty-two dollars and fifty cents. But the jumping was so long ago, although the bump is . . . how those old wounds hurt! Being crazy this way wouldn't be so bad if only, if only. If only when you put your foot forward to take a step, the ground wouldn't come up to meet your foot the way it does. And the same way in the street (only I may never get back to the street unless I jump at the right door), the curb coming up to meet your foot, anticipating ever so delicately the weight of the body, which is somewhere else. "We could take your name," she said, "and send it to you." And it wouldn't be so bad if only you could read a sentence all the way through without jumping (your eye) to something else on the same page; and then (he kept thinking) there was that man out in Jersey, the one who started to chop his trees down, one by one, the man who

began talking about how he would take his house to pieces, brick
by brick, because he faced a problem incapable of solution, probably, so he began to hack at the trees in the yard, began to pluck
with trembling fingers at the bricks in the house. Even if a house
is not washable, it is worth taking down. It is not till later that
the exhaustion sets in.

But it is inevitable that they will keep changing the doors on
you, he said, because that is what they are for; and the thing is
to get used to it and not let it unsettle the mind. But that would
mean not jumping, and you can't. Nobody can not jump. There
will be no not-jumping. Among rats, perhaps, but among people
never. Everybody has to keep jumping at a door (the one with
the circle on it) because that is the way everybody is, specially
some people. You wouldn't want me, standing here, to tell you,
would you, about my friend the poet (deceased) who said, "My
heart has followed all my days something I cannot name"? (It
had the circle on it.) And like many poets, although few so beloved, he is gone. It killed him, the jumping. First, of course,
there were the preliminary bouts, the convulsions, and the calm
and the willingness.

I remember the door with the picture of the girl on it (only
it was spring), her arms outstretched in loveliness, her dress (it
was the one with the circle on it) uncaught, beginning the slow,
clear, blinding cascade—and I guess we would all like to try that
door again, for it seemed like the way and for a while it was the
way, the door would open and you would go through winged
and exalted (like any rat) and the food would be there, the way
the Professor had it arranged, everything O.K., and you had chosen
the right door for the world was young. The time they changed
that door on me, my nose bled for a hundred hours—how do you
like that, Madam? Or would you prefer to show me further
through this so strange house, or you could take my name and

send it to me, for although my heart has followed all my days
something I cannot name, I am tired of the jumping and I do
not know which way to go, Madam, and I am not even sure that
I am not tried beyond the endurance of man (rat, if you will)
and have taken leave of sanity. What are you following these
days, old friend, after your recovery from the last bump? What
is the name, or is it something you cannot name? The rats have
a name for it by this time, perhaps, but I don't know what they
call it. I call it plexikoid and it comes in sheets, something like
insulating board, unattainable and ugli-proof.

And there was the man out in Jersey, because I keep thinking
about his terrible necessity and the passion and trouble he had
gone to all those years in the indescribable abundance of a house-
holder's detail, building the estate and the planting of the trees
and in spring the lawn-dressing and in fall the bulbs for the
spring burgeoning, and the watering of the grass on the long light
evenings in summer and the gravel for the driveway (all had tc
be thought out, planned) and the decorative borders, probably,
the perennials and the bug spray, and the building of the house
from plans of the architect, first the sills, then the studs, then the
full corn in the ear, the floors laid on the floor timbers, smoothed,
and then the carpets upon the smooth floors and the curtains
and the rods therefor. And then, almost without warning, he
would be jumping at the same old door and it wouldn't give:
they had changed it on him, making life no longer supportable
under the elms in the elm shade, under the maples in the maple
shade.

"Here you have the maximum of openness in a small room."

It was impossible to say (maybe it was the city) what made
him feel the way he did, and I am not the only one either, he kept
thinking—ask any doctor if I am. The doctors, they know how
many there are, they even know where the trouble is only they

don't like to tell you about the prefrontal lobe because that means making a hole in your skull and removing the work of centuries. It took so long coming, this lobe, so many, many years. (Is it something you read in the paper, perhaps?) And now, the strain being so great, the door having been changed by the Professor once too often . . . but it only means a whiff of ether, a few deft strokes, and the higher animal becomes a little easier in his mind and more like the lower one. From now on, you see, that's the way it will be, the ones with the small prefrontal lobes will win because the other ones are hurt too much by this incessant bumping. They can stand just so much, eh, Doctor? (And what is that, pray, that you have in your hand?) Still, you never can tell, eh, Madam?

He crossed (carefully) the room, the thick carpet under him softly, and went toward the door carefully, which was glass and he could see himself in it, and which, at his approach, opened to allow him to pass through; and beyond he half expected to find one of the old doors that he had known, perhaps the one with the circle, the one with the girl her arms outstretched in loveliness and beauty before him. But he saw instead a moving stairway, and descended in light (he kept thinking) to the street below and to the other people. As he stepped off, the ground came up slightly, to meet his foot.

# TWO LETTERS, BOTH OPEN

New York, N. Y.
12 April 1951

The American Society for the Prevention of Cruelty to Animals
York Avenue and East 92nd Street
New York 28, N. Y.

Dear Sirs:

I have your letter, undated, saying that I am harboring an unlicensed dog in violation of the law. If by "harboring" you mean getting up two or three times every night to pull Minnie's blanket up over her, I am harboring a dog all right. The blanket keeps slipping off. I suppose you are wondering by now why I don't get her a sweater instead. That's a joke on you. She has a knitted sweater, but she doesn't like to wear it for sleeping; her legs are so short they work out of a sweater and her toenails get caught in the mesh, and this disturbs her rest. If Minnie doesn't get her rest, she feels it right away. I do myself, and of course with this night duty of mine, the way the blanket slips and all, I haven't had any real rest in years. Minnie is twelve.

In spite of what your inspector reported, she has a license. She is licensed in the State of Maine as an unspayed bitch, or what is more commonly called an "unspaded" bitch. She wears her metal license tag but I must say I don't particularly care for it, as it is in the shape of a hydrant, which seems to me a feeble gag, besides being pointless in the case of a female. It is hard to believe that any state in the Union would circulate a gag like that and make people pay money for it, but Maine is always thinking of something. Maine puts up roadside crosses along the highways to mark the spots where people have lost their lives in motor accidents, so the highways are beginning to take on the appearance of a cemetery, and motoring in Maine has become a solemn experience, when one thinks mostly about death. I was driving along a road near Kittery the other day thinking about death and all of a sudden I heard the spring peepers. That changed me right away and I suddenly thought about life. It was the nicest feeling.

You asked about Minnie's name, sex, breed, and phone number. She doesn't answer the phone. She is a dachshund and can't reach it, but she wouldn't answer it even if she could, as she has no interest in outside calls. I did have a dachshund once, a male, who was interested in the telephone, and who got a great many calls, but Fred was an exceptional dog (his name was Fred) and I can't think of anything offhand that he *wasn't* interested in. The telephone was only one of a thousand things. He loved life—that is, he loved life if by "life" you mean "trouble," and of course the phone is almost synonymous with trouble. Minnie loves life, too, but her idea of life is a warm bed, preferably with an electric pad, and a friend in bed with her, and plenty of shut-eye, night and day. She's almost twelve. I guess I've already mentioned that. I got her from Dr. Clarence Little in 1939. He was using dachshunds in his cancer-research experiments (that was before Winchell was running the thing) and he had a couple of extra puppies, so I wheedled Minnie out of him. She later had puppies by her own father, at Dr. Little's request. What do you think about *that* for a scandal? I know what Fred thought about it. He was some put out.

Sincerely yours,

E. B. White

New York, N. Y.

12 April 1951

Collector of Internal Revenue
Divisional Office
Bangor, Maine
Dear Sir:

I have your notice about a payment of two hundred and some-odd dollars that you say is owing on my 1948 income tax. You say a warrant has been issued for the seizure and sale of my place in Maine, but I don't know as you realize how awkward that would be right at this time, because in the same mail I also received a notice from the Society for the Prevention of Cruelty to Animals here in New York taking me to task for harboring an unlicensed dog in my apartment, and I have written them saying that Minnie is licensed in Maine, but if you seize and sell my place, it is going to make me look pretty silly with the Society, isn't it? Why would I license a dog in Maine, they will say, if I don't live there? I think it is a fair question. I have written the Society, but purposely did not mention the warrant of seizure and sale. I didn't want to mix them up, and it might have sounded like just some sort of cock and bull story. I have always paid my taxes promptly, and the Society would think I was kidding, or something.

Anyway, the way the situation shapes up is this: I am being accused in New York State of dodging my dog tax, and accused in Maine of being behind in my federal tax, and I believe I'm going to have to rearrange my life somehow or other so that everything can be brought together, all in one state, maybe Delaware or some state like that, as it is too confusing for everybody this way. Minnie, who is very sensitive to my moods, knows there is something wrong and that I feel terrible. And now *she* feels terrible. The other day it was the funniest thing, I was packing a suitcase for a trip home to Maine, and the suitcase was lying open on the floor and when

I wasn't looking she went and got in and lay down. Don't you think that was cute?

If you seize the place, there are a couple of things I ought to explain. At the head of the kitchen stairs you will find an awfully queer boxlike thing. I don't want you to get a false idea about it, as it looks like a coffin, only it has a partition inside, and two small doors on one side. I don't suppose there is another box like it in the entire world. I built it myself. I made it many years ago as a dormitory for two snug-haired dachshunds, both of whom suffered from night chill. Night chill is the most prevalent dachshund disorder, if you have never had one. Both these dogs, as a matter of fact, had rheumatoid tendencies, as well as a great many other tendencies, specially Fred. He's dead, damn it. I would feel a lot better this morning if I could just see Fred's face, as he would know instantly that I was in trouble with the authorities and would be all over the place, hamming it up. He was something.

About the tax money, it was an oversight, or mixup. Your notice says that the "first notice" was sent last summer. I think that is correct, but when it arrived I didn't know what it meant as I am no mind reader. It was cryptic. So I sent it to a lawyer, fool-fashion, and asked him if *he* knew what it meant. I asked him if it was a tax bill and shouldn't I pay it, and he wrote back and said, No, no, no, no, it isn't a tax bill. He advised me to wait till I got a bill, and then pay it. Well, that was all right, but I was building a small henhouse at the time, and when I get building something with my own hands I lose all sense of time and place. I don't even show up for meals. Give me some tools and some second-handed lumber and I get completely absorbed in what I am doing. The first thing I knew, the summer was gone, and the fall was gone, and it was winter. The lawyer must have been building something, too, because I never heard another word from him.

To make a long story short, I am sorry about this non-payment, but you've got to see the whole picture to understand it, got to see my side of it. Of course I will forward the money if you haven't seized and sold the place in the meantime. If you have, there are a couple of other things on my mind. In the barn, at the far end of the tieups, there is a goose sitting on eggs. She is a young goose and I hope you can manage everything so as not to disturb her until she has brought off her goslings. I'll give you one, if you want. Or would they belong to the federal government anyway, even though the eggs were laid before the notice was mailed? The cold frames are ready, and pretty soon you ought to transplant the young broccoli and tomato plants and my wife's petunias from the flats in the kitchen into the frames, to harden them. Fred's grave is down in the alder thicket beyond the dump. You have to go down there every once in a while and straighten the headstone, which is nothing but a couple of old bricks that came out of a chimney. Fred was restless, and his headstone is the same way—doesn't stay quiet. You have to keep at it.

I am sore about your note, which didn't seem friendly. I am a friendly taxpayer and do not think the government should take a threatening tone, at least until we have exchanged a couple of letters kicking the thing around. Then it might be all right to talk about selling the place, if I proved stubborn. I showed the lawyer your notice about the warrant of seizure and sale, and do you know what he said? He said, "Oh, that doesn't mean anything, it's just a form." What a crazy way to look at a piece of plain English. I honestly worry about lawyers. They never write plain English themselves, and when you give them a bit of plain English to read, they say, "Don't worry, it doesn't mean anything." They're hopeless, don't you think they are? To me a word is a word, and I wouldn't dream of writing anything like "I am going to get out a warrant to seize and sell your place" unless I meant it, and I can't believe that my government would either.

The best way to get into the house is through the woodshed, as there is an old crocus sack nailed on the bottom step and you can wipe the mud off on it. Also, when you go in through the woodshed, you land in the back kitchen right next to the cooky jar with Mrs. Freethy's cookies. Help yourself, they're wonderful.

Sincerely yours,

E. B. White

# ANSWERS TO HARD QUESTIONS

Dear Mrs. Post—When we have two women guests and they sit at the right and left of my husband and our two half-grown children at the right and left of me, how should the maid serving proceed around the table? When the guest of honor at the right of my husband is served first, if the maid has to walk around him to serve the lady on his left next, the extra time consumed makes service even slower. And yet, if she starts with the lady at the right of my husband and goes around the table to the right, serving my husband last, she also serves the second lady to everything after the choicest pieces are gone. What would you suggest?
—*From Emily Post's column in the Boston Globe.*

The key to this situation is the two half-grown children. No matter what sort of erratic course a maid may pursue around a dinner table, the eyes of a half-grown child will follow her, as though by magnetic influence. This grim gaze contributes to the general feeling of the passage of time. Conversation drags, finally dies. Only the steady tramp-tramp-tramp of the maid and the harsh click of serving spoon against dish relieve the silence. Sometimes an unusually quick half-grown child will reach out a hand as the dish is going by and take something off it. This lessens the actual time consumed in serving the meal, but on the whole there is no satisfactory way of routing a waitress at such a gathering. Guests and hostess alike must simply resign themselves to the fact that the household is understaffed and the party ill-conceived. All dinners end at last, and this one will, too.

❦

Dear Sisters—Can any of you tell me how to keep my dog from making his bed on the dining room table. As soon as we go out or go to bed he gets on it.—*Letter in the Boston Globe.*

With a dog like that you should never go out, and you should never go to bed. Stay in, and stay up.

❦

L. D. writes: Is there any likelihood that the temporary physical condition a man is in would have an effect on his offspring? In other words, should a man hesitate about becoming a father during the time he is suffering from hay fever?—*Health column in the Chicago Tribune.*

This is a question many a man has had to face, alone with his God. Sensitivity to pollen, the male element of flowers, is at once an exalted and a pitiable condition and inevitably suggests to a prospective progenitor the disquieting potentialities inherent in all propagation. Like father like son is the familiar saying: big sneeze, little sneeze. There is little doubt that allergy to hay, so deep-seated, so shattering, is inheritable; and it is just as certain that a sensitive man, during the season of his great distress, is as eager for life and love as in the periods when his mucosae are relaxed. We cannot conscientiously advise any man to abstain from fatherhood on a seasonal, or foliage, basis. The time not to become a father is eighteen years before a world war.

❦

Miss F.: How does one announce a secret marriage, when the bride does not live at home?—*Vogue.*

There is only one correct way to announce a secret marriage, no matter where the bride lives. Use invisible ink.

Q. When a man does not believe in tipping and is eating in a place where tipping is customary, what should he do?—*Letter to the Charleroi (Pa.) Mail.*

Tip.

Q. I took out a marriage license in Camden and we lived together for 15 years. Then he left me. Another man wants to marry me. I remember now that some way we forgot to get married. Do I need a divorce? M. F.—*Philadelphia Record.*

No, honey. Some way you just won't need a divorce.

What is the correct response when someone calls you on the telephone and asks for you by name?—*From "Mind Your Manners" in the World-Telegram.*

Not only is there no "correct" response when this disagreeable thing happens, but there is no real response possible—in the true sense of the word. Anything you say is a makeshift. Hundreds of "responses" have been tried by millions of phone users; every one has proved either evasive or ridiculous or rude.

Let us say your name is Brinckerhoff. The phone rings and you answer it and a voice says, "I would like to speak to Mr. Brincker-hoff, please." You are in an impossible situation. You can say, "This is I," and be put down for a purist or a poseur. Or you can say, "This is me," and be taken for a tough. Or, rather desperately, you can reply, "This is he," or "This is Brinckerhoff," or "This is Mr. Brinckerhoff," referring to yourself grandiloquently in the third person, in the manner of dictators and kings. Believe us, when a man starts referring to himself in the third person, the end of the good life is not far off. To the listener you sound either down-right silly or deliberately vainglorious. Your "response" has a slightly moldy, undemocratic sound, as when, in the presence of a servant, you refer to your wife as "Mrs. Brinckerhoff" instead of as "Esther."

Now, suppose you go off on an entirely different tack when the phone rings and someone asks for you by name. Suppose you say, with forced cheeriness, "Speaking!" What a pitiful attempt! The word has hardly rolled off your tongue when it becomes meaning-less, for you are no longer speaking but are listening—listening, and hoping against hope that it isn't somebody you can't stand. Or let's take a few other conventional "responses" and see how miserably they fail:

Voice: "I would like to speak to Mr. Brinckerhoff, please."
Response: "You are." This is too rude, too familiar.
Voice: "I would like to speak to Mr. Brinckerhoff, please."
Response: "Why?" This is evasive, prying.
Voice: "I would like to speak to Mr. Brinckerhoff, please."
Response: "Go ahead!" Peremptory, unfriendly.

No, there is no "correct" response in this situation. There is no response that is anything but discouraging. It is the most difficult and disturbing phase of one's telephonic life. Unques-tionably it was not foreseen by Mr. Bell when he was so blithely tinkering with his little magnets and diaphragms. If only a voice could have whispered, "I would like to speak to Mr. Alexander Graham Bell, please," how much that might have saved the world! Bell would have laid down his tools with a tired sigh, a man who knew when he was licked.

# THE RETORT TRANSCENDENTAL

In May of the year 1927 I bought a World's Classics edition of "Walden" for, I think, ninety cents and slipped it in my pocket for convenient reading. Since then I have carried it about with me on the cars and in buses and boats, as it is the most amusing detective story I possess. There is, however, a danger in rereading a book, or rather in dipping frequently into the same book: the trouble is you begin to learn some of the lines. In my case, with "Walden," I have recently found that when someone asks me a simple question I reply with a direct quote.

I go into a restaurant, we'll say, at the lunch hour, and the headwaiter approaches me, accusingly.

"All alone?" he asks.

"I feel it wholesome to be alone the greater part of the time," I reply. "To be in company, even with the best, is soon wearisome and dissipating. I love to be alone." Then I glare triumphantly at the waiter and snatch the napkin from the plate.

Or I am walking along the street and meet an acquaintance—someone I haven't seen in a long time and don't care if I never see again.

"Where y'been all this time?" he demands.

"If a man does not keep pace with his companions," I retort, "perhaps it is because he hears a different drummer."

Actually, I suppose, I don't say that at all; yet it often seems to me as though I were saying it. More and more I find it difficult to distinguish clearly between what I am saying and what I might easily be saying. Maybe it's the times. At any rate, Thoreau answers a surprisingly large number of the commonest questions that get thrown at me these days. He is a Johnny-on-the-spot for all ordinary occasions and situations.

I enter a room.

"Won't you sit down?" asks my hostess, indicating a vacancy.

"I would rather sit on a pumpkin and have it all to myself," I reply, accepting the velvet cushion with weary resignation.

"What would you like to drink?" she continues.

"Let me have a draught of undiluted morning air," I snarl. "If men will not drink of this at the fountainhead of the day, why, then, we must even bottle up some and sell it in the shops, for the benefit of those who have lost their subscription ticket to morning time in the world." Then I slump into my cushion and wait for the clear amber liquor and the residual olive.

"Know any good books?" my partner asks at dinner. Slowly I swing my head around, bruising my chin on the hard, rough wing of my collar, my eyes glazed with the strain of evening. I place my lips to her ear.

"Much is published," I whisper, cryptically, "but little printed. We are in danger of forgetting the language which all things and events speak without metaphor, which alone is copious and standard."

Or I am at home, getting ready, perhaps, to escort my wife to a soirée.

"What's it like out tonight?" she asks, glancing anxiously at her rubbers in the corner of the closet.

"This is a delicious evening," I hear my voice saying, "when the whole body is one sense, and imbibes delight through every pore."

Next morning, seeing my suit lying rumpled and mussed on the chair beside the bed, she will inquire, "You got anything to go to the presser's?"

"No, my dear," I reply. "Every day our garments become more assimilated to ourselves, receiving the impress of the wearer's character. If you have any enterprise before you, try it in your old clothes." (I am glad to say my wife doesn't mind Thoreau any more and simply calls the presser.)

The situations are endless, the answers inexhaustible. I recall that one of my angriest and boldest retorts was made on a day when a couple of silly, giggling girls arrived at our house and began effervescing.

"Isn't this an attractive place?" they squealed.

"On the contrary," I snapped, "I sometimes dream of a larger and more populous house, standing in a golden age, of enduring materials, and without gingerbread work, which shall consist of only one room, a vast, rude, substantial primitive hall, without ceiling or plastering, with bare rafters and purlins supporting a sort of lower heaven over one's head—useful to keep off rain and snow; where the king and queen posts stand out to receive your homage, when you have done reverence to the prostrate Saturn of an older dynasty on stepping over the sill; a cavernous house, wherein you must reach up a torch upon a pole to see the roof . . . a house whose inside is as open and manifest as a bird's nest."

The girls sobered up instantly and were quiet and tractable the rest of their visit. But I don't know—I'm afraid I shall have to put "Walden" away and buy another book to travel with. Or possibly a link puzzle. One doesn't remember anything much from long association with a link puzzle.

# THE SECOND TREE
# FROM THE CORNER

"Ever have any bizarre thoughts?" asked the doctor.

Mr. Trexler failed to catch the word. "What kind?" he said.

"Bizarre," repeated the doctor, his voice steady. He watched his patient for any slight change of expression, any wince. It seemed to Trexler that the doctor was not only watching him closely but was creeping slowly toward him, like a lizard toward a bug. Trexler shoved his chair back an inch and gathered himself for a reply. He was about to say "Yes" when he realized that if he said yes the next question would be unanswerable. Bizarre thoughts, bizarre thoughts? Ever have any bizarre thoughts? What kind of thoughts *except* bizarre had he had since the age of two?

Trexler felt the time passing, the necessity for an answer. These psychiatrists were busy men, overloaded, not to be kept waiting. The next patient was probably already perched out there in the waiting room, lonely, worried, shifting around on the sofa, his mind stuffed with bizarre thoughts and amorphous fears. Poor bastard, thought Trexler. Out there all alone in that misshapen antechamber, staring at the filing cabinet and wondering whether to tell the doctor about that day on the Madison Avenue bus.

Let's see, bizarre thoughts. Trexler dodged back along the dreadful corridor of the years to see what he could find. He felt the doctor's eyes upon him and knew that time was running out. Don't be so conscientious, he said to himself. If a bizarre thought is indicated here, just reach into the bag and pick anything at all. A man as well supplied with bizarre thoughts as you are should have no difficulty producing one for the record. Trexler darted into the bag, hung for a moment before one of his thoughts, as a hummingbird pauses in the delphinium. No, he said, not that one. He darted to another (the one about the rhesus monkey), paused, considered. No, he said, not that.

Trexler knew he must hurry. He had already used up pretty nearly four seconds since the question had been put. But it was an impossible situation—just one more lousy, impossible situation such as he was always getting himself into. When, he asked himself, are you going to quit maneuvering yourself into a pocket? He made one more effort. This time he stopped at the asylum, only the bars were lucite—fluted, retractable. Not here, he said. Not this one.

He looked straight at the doctor. "No," he said quietly. "I never have any bizarre thoughts."

The doctor sucked in on his pipe, blew a plume of smoke toward the rows of medical books. Trexler's gaze followed the smoke. He managed to make out one of the titles, "The Genito-Urinary System." A bright wave of fear swept cleanly over him, and he winced under the first pain of kidney stones. He remembered when he was a child, the first time he ever entered a doctor's office, sneaking a look at the titles of the books—and the flush of fear, the shirt wet under the arms, the book on t.b., the sudden knowledge that he was in the advanced stages of consumption, the quick vision of the hemorrhage. Trexler sighed wearily. Forty years, he thought, and I still get thrown by the title of a medical book. Forty years and I still can't stay on life's little bucky horse. No wonder I'm sitting here in this dreary joint at the end of this woebegone afternoon, lying about my bizarre thoughts to a doctor who looks, come to think of it, rather tired.

The session dragged on. After about twenty minutes, the doctor rose and knocked his pipe out. Trexler got up, knocked the ashes out of his brain, and waited. The doctor smiled warmly and stuck out his hand. "There's nothing the matter with you—you're just scared. Want to know how I know you're scared?"

"How?" asked Trexler.

"Look at the chair you've been sitting in! See how it has moved back away from my desk? You kept inching away from me while I asked you questions. That means you're scared."

"Does it?" said Trexler, faking a grin. "Yeah, I suppose it does."

They finished shaking hands. Trexler turned and walked out uncertainly along the passage, then into the waiting room and out past the next patient, a ruddy pin-striped man who was seated on the sofa twirling his hat nervously and staring straight ahead at the files. Poor, frightened guy, thought Trexler, he's probably read in the *Times* that one American male out of every two is going to die of heart disease by twelve o'clock next Thursday. It says that in the paper almost every morning. And he's also probably thinking about that day on the Madison Avenue bus.

A week later, Trexler was back in the patient's chair. And for several weeks thereafter he continued to visit the doctor, always toward the end of the afternoon, when the vapors hung thick above the pool of the mind and darkened the whole region of the East Seventies. He felt no better as time went on, and he found it impossible to work. He discovered that the visits were becoming routine and that although the routine was one to which he certainly did not look forward, at least he could accept it with cool resignation, as once, years ago, he had accepted a long spell with a dentist who had settled down to a steady fooling with a couple of dead teeth. The visits, moreover, were now assuming a pattern recognizable to the patient.

Each session would begin with a résumé of symptoms—the dizziness in the streets, the constricting pain in the back of the neck, the apprehensions, the tightness of the scalp, the inability to concentrate, the despondency and the melancholy times, the feeling of pressure and tension, the anger at not being able to work, the anxiety over work not done, the gas on the stomach. Dullest set of neurotic symptoms in the world, Trexler would think, as he obediently trudged back over them for the doctor's benefit. And then, having listened attentively to the recital, the doctor would spring his question: "Have you ever found anything that gives you relief?" And Trexler would answer, "Yes. A drink." And the doctor would nod his head knowingly.

As he became familiar with the pattern Trexler found that he increasingly tended to identify himself with the doctor, transferring himself into the doctor's seat—probably (he thought) some rather slick form of escapism. At any rate, it was nothing new for Trexler to identify himself with other people. Whenever he got into a cab, he instantly became the driver, saw everything from the hackman's angle (and the reaching over with the right hand, the nudging of the flag, the pushing it down, all the way down along the side of the meter), saw everything—traffic, fare, everything— through the eyes of Anthony Rocco, or Isidore Freedman, or Matthew Scott. In a barbershop, Trexler was the barber, his fingers curled around the comb, his hand on the tonic. Perfectly natural, then, that Trexler should soon be occupying the doctor's chair, asking the questions, waiting for the answers. He got quite interested in the doctor, in this way. He liked him, and he found him a not too difficult patient.

It was on the fifth visit, about halfway through, that the doctor turned to Trexler and said, suddenly, "What do you want?" He gave the word "want" special emphasis.

"I d'know," replied Trexler uneasily. "I guess nobody knows the answer to that one."

"Sure they do," replied the doctor.

"Do you know what you want?" asked Trexler narrowly.

"Certainly," said the doctor. Trexler noticed that at this point the doctor's chair slid slightly backward, away from him. Trexler stifled a small, internal smile. Scared as a rabbit, he said to himself. Look at him scoot!

"What do you want?" continued Trexler, pressing his advantage, pressing it hard.

The doctor glided back another inch away from his inquisitor. "I want a wing on the small house I own in Westport. I want more money, and more leisure to do the things I want to do."

Trexler was just about to say, "And what are those things you want to do, Doctor?" when he caught himself. Better not go too far, he mused. Better not lose possession of the ball. And besides, he thought, what the hell goes on here, anyway—me paying fifteen bucks a throw for these séances and then doing the work myself, asking the questions, weighing the answers. So he wants a new wing! There's a fine piece of theatrical gauze for you! A new wing.

Trexler settled down again and resumed the role of patient for the rest of the visit. It ended on a kindly, friendly note. The doctor reassured him that his fears were the cause of his sickness, and that his fears were unsubstantial. They shook hands, smiling.

Trexler walked dizzily through the empty waiting room and the doctor followed along to let him out. It was late; the secretary had shut up shop and gone home. Another day over the dam. "Goodbye," said Trexler. He stepped into the street, turned west toward Madison, and thought of the doctor all alone there, after hours, in that desolate hole—a man who worked longer hours than his secretary. Poor, scared, overworked bastard, thought Trexler. And that new wing!

It was an evening of clearing weather, the Park showing green and desirable in the distance, the last daylight applying a high lacquer to the brick and brownstone walls and giving the street scene a luminous and intoxicating splendor. Trexler meditated, as he walked, on what he wanted. "What do you want?" he heard again. Trexler knew what he wanted, and what, in general, all men wanted; and he was glad, in a way, that it was both inexpressible and unattainable, and that it wasn't a wing. He was satisfied to remember that it was deep, formless, enduring, and impossible of fulfillment, and that it made men sick, and that when you sauntered along Third Avenue and looked through the doorways into the dim saloons, you could sometimes pick out from the unregenerate ranks the ones who had not forgotten, gazing steadily into the bottoms of the glasses on the long chance that they could get another little peek at it. Trexler found himself renewed by the remembrance that what he wanted was at once great and microscopic, and that although it borrowed from the nature of large deeds and of youthful love and of old songs and early intimations, it was not any one of these things, and that it had not been isolated or pinned down, and that a man who attempted to define it in the privacy of a doctor's office would fall flat on his face.

Trexler felt invigorated. Suddenly his sickness seemed health, his dizziness stability. A small tree, rising between him and the light, stood there saturated with the evening, each gilt-edged leaf perfectly drunk with excellence and delicacy. Trexler's spine registered an ever so slight tremor as it picked up this natural disturbance in the lovely scene. "I want the second tree from the corner, just as it stands," he said, answering an imaginary question from an imaginary physician. And he felt a slow pride in realizing that what he wanted none could bestow, and that what he had none could take away. He felt content to be sick, unembarrassed at being afraid; and in the jungle of his fear he glimpsed (as he had so often glimpsed them before) the flashy tail feathers of the bird courage.

Then he thought once again of the doctor, and of his being left there all alone, tired, frightened. (The poor, scared guy, thought Trexler.) Trexler began humming "Moonshine Lullaby," his spirit reacting instantly to the hypodermic of Merman's healthy voice. He crossed Madison, boarded a downtown bus, and rode all the way to Fifty-second Street before he had a thought that could rightly have been called bizarre.

# NOTES ON OUR TIMES

### Mrs. Wienckus

THE Newark police arrested a very interesting woman the other day—a Mrs. Sophie Wienckus—and she is now on probation after being arraigned as disorderly. Mrs. Wienckus interests us because her "disorderliness" was simply her capacity to live a far more self-contained life than most of us can manage. The police complained that she was asleep in two empty cartons in a hallway. This was her preferred method of bedding down. All the clothes she possessed she had on—several layers of coats and sweaters. On her person were bankbooks showing that she was ahead of the game to the amount of $19,799.09. She was a working woman—a domestic—and, on the evidence, a thrifty one. Her fault, the Court held, was that she lacked a habitation.

"Why didn't you rent a room?" asked the magistrate. But he should have added parenthetically "(and the coat hangers in the closet and the cord that pulls the light and the dish that holds the soap and the mirror that conceals the cabinet where lives the aspirin that kills the pain)." Why didn't you rent a room "(with the rug that collects the dirt and the vacuum that sucks the dirt and the man that fixes the vacuum and the fringe that adorns the shade that dims the lamp and the desk that holds the bill for the installment on the television set that tells of the wars)?" We feel that the magistrate oversimplified his question.

Mrs. Wienckus may be disorderly, but one pauses to wonder where the essential disorder really lies. All of us are instructed to

seek hallways these days (except school children, who crawl under
the desks), and it was in a hallway that they found Mrs. Wienckus,
all compact. We read recently that the only hope of avoiding in-
flation is through ever increasing production of goods. This to us is
always a terrifying conception of the social order—a theory of the
good life through accumulation of objects. We lean toward the
order of Mrs. Wienckus, who has eliminated everything except
what she can conveniently carry, whose financial position is solid,
and who can smile at Rufus Rastus Johnson Brown. We salute a
woman whose affairs are in such excellent order in a world untidy
beyond all belief.

### Rainmakers

When he was told that people were bringing suit against the
makers of rain, Mayor O'Dwyer, the rainmaker, said, "Somebody
doesn't want it to rain, I take it." This remark belongs right up
with the more cocky utterances of self-reliant man, alongside
Hague's famous pronouncement: "I am the law." It was almost
as though the Mayor had said, "I am the rain." By putting in
their place those who took an opposite view of rain, he reduced
precipitation to simple dogma. His was not a demagogic remark,
like Hague's—simply an Olympian remark, innocent and infinitely
remote. Somebody indeed doesn't want it to rain—some almost,
but not quite, forgotten man. How about this fellow? He interests
us. Crotchety, probably. Or maybe an inveterate picnicker. But a
man, nevertheless—two arms, two legs, an umbrella, and a habit
of looking to the limitless sky for his rewards and punishments, not
to a city father.

An arresting quality in modern man is his attitude toward his
natural surroundings, a quality likely to get him in trouble and

even shorten his stay on earth. He commonly thinks of himself as having been here since the beginning—older than the crab— and he also likes to think he's destined to stay to the bitter end. Actually, he is a late comer, and there are moments when he shows every sign of being an early leaver—a patron who bows out after a few gaudy and memorable scenes. It is entirely in keeping with man's feeling about nature that when he suddenly notices his drinking fountain losing pressure, he should ascend to heaven and beat a cloud over the ears. Petulance, coupled with insatiable curiosity, and the will to dominate. "Somebody doesn't want it to rain, I take it," said the Mayor, while the lightning played all around his words.

The city presumably feels it has a pretty good legal loophole. Even if a plane goes up and seeds a cloud, and rain falls, the wet people down below will have to prove that the seed germinated, that the rain was in fact the fruit of the seed. This may be hard to prove. Legally, rainmaking may be in the clear as a device. Philosophically, rainmaking is anything but in the clear —it is in a misty mid-region. There is more to rain than meets the kitchen tap of a city dweller; rain is part of the stuff of melancholia, part of darkness, of husbandry, of sport, and of retailing. Everyone talks about the weather because the weather is every man's chattel. The suicide often holds off until it rains, and the pilot who seeds a cloud may be seeding a man, too, and causing the ultimate and unbearable teardrop. The rain pilot's flight is a long, long flight—into the wild gray yonder.

New York's water shortage is caused less by lack of rain than by lack of foresight, lack of a decent feeling for nature. The remedy, it seems to us, is not the manufacture of rain but the correct use and distribution of whatever rain naturally arrives on earth. If, as the rainmakers would have it, man does invade the sky and nudge clouds, his flight will, we predict, be but the beginning of such practices, and we shall find the makers of lightning also aloft, to satisfy the desires of the manufacturers of lightning rods, who may decide that lightning is in short supply and devise a way of setting more of it loose. This, in turn, will be an affront to insurance companies, who must stand the cost of retopping chimneys that get hit by the bolts. In short, it is conceivable that man may have to set an arbitrary limit to his domain—draw a line where he ends and God begins. The Mayor may think he is the rain, but when he pours he may have a surprise coming.

### The Dream of the American Male

Dorothy Lamour is the girl above all others desired by the men in Army camps. This fact was turned up by *Life* in a routine study of the unlimited national emergency. It is a fact which illuminates the war, the national dream, and our common unfulfillment. If you know what a soldier wants, you know what Man wants, for a soldier is young, sexually vigorous, and is caught in a line of work which leads toward a distant and tragic conclusion. He personifies Man. His dream of a woman can be said to be Everyman's dream of a woman. In desiring Lamour, obviously his longing is for a female creature encountered under primitive conditions and in a setting of great natural beauty and mystery. He does not want this woman to make any sudden or nervous movement. She should be in a glade, a swale, a grove, or a pool below a waterfall. This is the setting in which every American youth first encountered Miss Lamour. They were in a forest; she had walked slowly out of the pool and stood dripping in the ferns.

The dream of the American male is for a female who has an essential languor which is not laziness, who is unaccompanied except by himself, and who does not let him down. He desires a beautiful, but comprehensible, creature who does not destroy a perfect situation by forming a complete sentence. She is compounded of moonlight and shadows, and has a slightly husky voice, which she uses only in song or in an attempt to pick up a word or two that he teaches her. Her body, if concealed at all, is concealed by a water lily, a frond, a fern, a bit of moss, or by a sarong —which is a simple garment carrying the implicit promise that it will not long stay in place. For millions of years men everywhere have longed for Dorothy Lamour. Now, in the final complexity of an age which has reached its highest expression in the instrument panel of a long-range bomber, it is a good idea to remember that Man's most persistent dream is of a forest pool and a girl coming out of it unashamed, walking toward him with a wavy motion, childlike in her wonder, a girl exquisitely untroubled, as quiet and accommodating and beautiful as a young green tree. That's all he really wants. He sometimes wonders how this other stuff got in—the instrument panel, the night sky, the full load, the moment of exultation over the blackened city below. . . .

## Biographee

We have a letter this morning from Wheeler Sammons, publisher of Who's Who in America. It is a long, chatty letter, full of shoptalk. He speaks intimately of his "next scheduled stuffing," of the "currency-of-content provided by the biographee's coöperation," and of "revisionary data." The thing that impresses us particularly about this letter from Mr. Sammons (and we have had many others) is his introductory remark. He starts with an apology: ". . . I appreciate your every moment is under pressure."

Mr. Sammons undoubtedly believes this to be true of his biographees, that their every moment is under pressure. He must think of himself as running a stable of thoroughbreds, in which there is no horse of no account, no horse that isn't terribly busy. But it is a delusion, a dream. A great many of the most consistently indolent characters in the United States are listed in *Who's Who*, and some of them haven't felt an ounce of pressure since 1910, when their first book came out. They are men who have made their mark, have joined a club, and are content to let bygones be bygones. We speak with knowledge about this matter. A biographee of no small inactivity ourself, we can state positively that we are under no pressure at the moment—except the tiny pressure connected with writing this ephemeral paragraph. After it is done, we intend to walk slowly to Central Park in the mild sunshine and visit the baby camel for a routine checkup, then to a saloon, where we shall pass the early afternoon hours in deep torpor over a glass of May wine—a biographee as near inert as a horned toad.

## Country Dwellers

People are retreating to the deep country in these June days, fleeing the heat, searching for roots, a department-store peasantry in slacks and espadrilles, ploughing the fields of summer with their roan station wagons. Of country living, which they know only hurriedly, they make a sort of masque, dressing for a walk-on part in the play Nature. "Dig in the garden," says *Vogue*, "in a Chinese laundryman's jumper of blue or white cotton, pulled over trousers to match or over a cotton skirt. Keep all the scarfs you find in Mexico, Brittany, or Mittel-Europa. Order from Haiti the wooden armchairs with seats and backs of natural matting. And for your country bathroom, have rows of bottles covered in wicker cases and soap-dishes of bleached pearwood from Jean-Michel Frank." There is something almost frenzied in this advice to persons returning to the land—a frenzy which only half cloaks the strange guilt of the dispossessed. A dogwood tree is dragged down a hill behind a caterpillar tractor. A setting of duck eggs is rushed five hundred miles by motorcar to be placed under a hen. Nervous country dwellers, wistfully hoping to keep the world alive by rearranging its bloom and warming its embryos.

### Professor Piccard—Before

Professor Piccard, traveller in the outer spheres, has announced his intention of making another ascent, this time borne aloft by 2,000 small balloons instead of by one big one. If he carries out his plan, the trip should be of profound interest to logicians—for the professor this time will invade not only the stratosphere but that equally vaporous region, the Realm of Probability. Usually, you see, the Professor relies, for his descent, on letting some gas out of his bag; but on this occasion he will rely on the fitful bursting of some of the little balloons in the rarefied air to which they are exposed. He hopes that only "some" of the little balloons, not all of them, will give way, and feels that probability is on his side.

The calculation of probability has long occupied the night thoughts of gambling men, and the coin-flippers of the world will brood endlessly on the idea of 2,000 little supporting balloons, some of which must hold, some of which must let go. What, they will want to know, are the chances of having 2,000 balloons, all subjected to bursting conditions, explode at comfortable intervals? It is not probable, yet it is conceivable, that 2,000 balloons, rising into an unfavorable zone, might explode as one, just as it is conceivable that a coin, tossed fifty times, might show heads in all fifty flips. And there is still another, larger question which comes up, it seems to us: What effect does rarefied air have on the very law itself? Can anyone state, authoritatively, that there exists any such thing as probability so far from the core of earth? We wish Dr. Abraham Wolf and Dr. William Fleetwood Sheppard, who wrote the fascinating chapters on probability in the Britannica, would write us an equation covering the probable interval of explosion of 2,000 little balloons dangling an inquisitive professor in the already improbable blue.

### Professor Piccard—After

Dr. Piccard, of the upper air, brings to scientific fields the highest quality of madness. This sprightly little explorer, the jackanapes of the stratosphere, cunningly soars aloft in a basket borne upward by a galaxy of toy balloons, suddenly whips out a gun and takes pot shots at his own supports. "So I took my pistol and killed about a dozen of them," he explained. It was the sort of plot Harpo Marx might hatch, with his hair straying and his eyes too bright. Dr. Piccard descended in flames, and when he jumped out, according to the papers, he was choked with laughter.

### The Home

Homemaking reared its chintzy little head the other day when the ladies of the American Home Economics Association decided that maybe the Home should rate a Cabinet position, to be called the Department of the American Home. It is a noble idea and would unquestionably attract the wrong people. If we had a Secretary of the Home, like a Secretary of State or a Secretary of Commerce, she would probably be a lady whose emphasis would be upon vitamins and lampshades. She would be against mice. The

American Home, given Cabinet status, would continue to move (as it has moved in the last few years) in the wrong direction. The American Kitchen would become more and more stagy and unlivable; the American Cellar would finally and forever emerge as a rumpus room, above ground; the Home as a whole would tend to become collapsible, transparent, mobile, washable, sterile, and devoid of human life.

Home is too delicate an organism to be federalized. The eviction of even so small a thing as a mouse threatens its balance; the absence of a hummingbird from the delphiniums can destroy its tone. Some of the most vital and dependable homes we have ever been in were ones in which the economics were deplorable; some of the barest of homes were ones which, physically, were the answer to an economist's dream. Home was quite a place when people stayed there, but Home Economics is just another in the long line of activities that take ladies away. Of the home economists we have met in our lifetime, all had one trait in common: not one of them was at home.

## Censorship

We are delighted with the recent censorship ruling in the matter of motion-picture harems. Some scenes in a Paramount picture now in production are set in a harem, and after careful deliberation the censors have decided to allow this type of polyform allure *provided* the boudoir does not contain the sultan. The girls can mill about among the pillows, back and side having gone bare, but no male eye must gaze upon them—save, of course, yours, lucky reader. This harem-but-no-sultan decision belongs in the truly great body of opinion interpreting the American moral law. It takes its place alongside the celebrated 1939 ruling on the exposure of

female breasts in the Flushing World of Tomorrow, which provided that one breast could be presented publicly but not two,
and thereby satisfied the two seemingly irreconcilable groups:
the art-lovers, who demanded breasts but were willing to admit
that if you'd seen one you'd seen them both, and the decency
clique, who held out for concealment but were agreed that the
fact of concealing one breast established the essential reticence
of the owner and thereby covered the whole situation, or chest.
That subtle and far-reaching ruling carried the Fair, as we know,
safely through two difficult seasons, and we imagine that the
aseptic harem will do as much for Hollywood.

### Sound

The sound truck, or Free Speech on Wheels, won its first brush
with the law by a close decision in the Supreme Court. We have
an idea, however, that the theme of amplification is not dead
and will recur in many variations. The Court found itself in a
snarl; free speech became confused with free extension-of-speech,
noise with ideas wrapped in noise. A sound truck, it seems to us,
is not a man on a soapbox—it is Superman on a tower of suds.
The distinction will eventually have to be drawn. Loud speaking
is not the same thing as plain speaking; the loudspeaker piles
decibel on decibel and not only is capable of disturbing the peace
but through excess of volume can cause madness and death,
whereas the human voice is a public nuisance only to the extent
that it aggravates the normal human resentment against the whole
principle of free speech. Amplified sound is already known among
military men as a weapon of untried potency, and we will probably suffer from it if there is another war.

Up till now, modern man has meekly accepted the miracle of

his enlarged vocal cords. He has acquiesced in jumboism. A modern baby is born amplified, for even the nursery is wired for sound and the infant's earliest cries are carried over a private distress system to the ears of its mother in the living room—along with street noises that drift in through the open nursery window. (Note to political candidates: Always park your sound truck under nursery windows and your remarks will be picked up by an interior network and carried to uneasy elders.) One wonders, though, how much longer the human race will string along with its own electrical gifts, and how long the right to speak can remain innocent of wattage. We have a feeling that only if this issue is met will the principle of free speech survive. There are always plenty of people who are eager to stifle opinion they don't admire, and if the opinion happens to be expressed in a volume of sound that is in itself insufferable, the number of people who will want to stifle both the sound *and* the fury will greatly increase. Amplification, therefore, is something like alcohol: it can heighten our meanings, but it can also destroy our reason.

In radio it is understood that whatever else happens, there must never be a silence. This hard condition is most noticeable in the aerial forums, in which the performers are expected to offer an immediate opinion on any subject, and do. Someone must always be speaking, either the ringmaster or one of the experts. The rule seems to be: make sense if you can, but if you can't make sense say something anyway. If you listen to one of these nervous exercises in intellectual rough-and-tumble, it is plain that a large part of the effort goes simply into preventing a lull in the conversation. The Quakers take a more sensible view of silence; they

accord it equal recognition with sound. We doubt that radio will
ever amount to a damn as long as it is haunted by the fear of
nobody speaking.

## The Age of Dust

On a sunny morning last week, we went out and put up a swing
for a little girl, age three, under an apple tree—the tree being
much older than the girl, the sky being blue, the clouds white.
We pushed the little girl for a few minutes, then returned to the
house and settled down to an article on death dust, or radiological
warfare, in the July *Bulletin of the Atomic Scientists*, Volume
VI, No. 7.

The article ended on a note of disappointment. "The area that
can be poisoned with the fission products available to us today
is disappointingly small; it amounts to not more than two or three
major cities per month." At first glance, the sentence sounded
satirical, but a rereading convinced us that the scientist's disappointment was real enough—that it had the purity of detachment.
The world of the child in the swing (the trip to the blue sky and
back again) seemed, as we studied the ABC of death dust, more
and more a dream world with no true relation to things as they
are or to the real world of discouragement over the slow rate of
the disappearance of cities.

Probably the scientist-author of the death-dust article, if he were
revising his literary labors with a critical eye, would change the
wording of that queer sentence. But the fact is, the sentence got
written and published. The terror of the atom age is not the
violence of the new power but the speed of man's adjustment to
it—the speed of his acceptance. Already bombproofing is on ap-
proximately the same level as mothproofing. Two or three major

cities per month isn't much of an area, but it is a start. To the
purity of science (which hopes to enlarge the area) there seems to
be no corresponding purity of political thought, never the same detachment. We sorely need, from a delegate in the Security Council,
a statement as detached in its way as the statement of the scientist
on death dust. This delegate (and it makes no difference what
nation he draws his pay from) must be a man who has not adjusted to the age of dust. He must be a person who still dwells in
the mysterious dream world of swings, and little girls in swings.
He must be more than a good chess player studying the future;
he must be a memoirist remembering the past.

We couldn't seem to separate the little girl from radiological
warfare—she seemed to belong with it, although inhabiting another sphere. The article kept getting back to her. "This is a novel
type of warfare, in that it produces no destruction, except to life."
The weapon, said the author, can be regarded as a horrid one, or,
on the other hand, it "can be regarded as a remarkably humane
one. In a sense, it gives each member of the target population
[including each little girl] a choice of whether he will live or die."
It turns out that the way to live—if that be your choice—is to
leave the city as soon as the dust arrives, holding "a folded, dam-
pened handkerchief" over your nose and mouth. We went out-
doors again to push the swing some more for the little girl, who is
always forgetting her handkerchief. At lunch we watched her try
to fold her napkin. It seemed to take forever.

As we lay in bed that night, thinking of cities and target popu-
lations, we saw the child again. This time she was with the other
little girls in the subway. When the train got to 242nd Street,
which is as far as it goes into unreality, the children got off. They
started to walk slowly north. Each child had a handkerchief, and
every handkerchief was properly moistened and folded neatly—
the way it said in the story.

### Trance

That delicious Sabbath trance induced by the study of the Sunday *Times* reaches its glassiest phase when we get into the changeless ads on the garden page of the Drama-Screen-Radio-Music-Dance-Art-Stamps-Resorts-Travel-Gardens-Women's News-Bridge Section. It is here, among the strange accoutrements of the horticultural life, that we forget, losing ourself completely. The senses float in pale regions of total intellectual stupor. A flexible blade to increase the efficiency of the lawn mower which we know we will never push over lawns measureless to man; a citronella candle to banish the imaginary mosquito from the imaginary porch on the fancied terrible summer night; twenty pachysandras for one dollar —how calm we feel, reading about them, how sweetly safe and indolent behind the walls of this stifling room in town! Here is a device for dehydrating vegetables, here a treatise on the breeding of earthworms for the feeding of hens in confinement, here a lovely silver gazing ball for the informal coppice. As our lids slowly droop, the scene expands and lightens, and we stand in the centre of this unearthly pleasure spot, this garden close, this green maze, with the cutworms and the laying pullets creeping around our feet, the liquid repellent for dogs and beetles gurgling over the mossy stones of the artificial brook, and an incredibly beautiful woman staring steadily into the gazing ball. No matter that this is the century of trouble: it is Sunday in the living room and there is a panacea for every ill.

### Cowboy

We commend to historians the steer wrestler who has been commuting between Chicago and New York by plane, in order to throw steers in the rodeos of both cities. In this pendulous cowboy, if cowboy is the word for him, our century comes to a sort of head: the winged ranch hand, his eye on two steers at once, and the steers a thousand miles apart yet capable of being thrown by the winged, neither steer needing to be thrown, each existing only to be thrown. The cowboy rises from the head of the fallen animal, dusts the seat of his pants, walks stiff-legged to the waiting airliner. The spectators, yearning for the open West and its herds of cattle on the ranges, rise from their mezzanine seats, stiff-legged, dust off their unfulfilled desires, walk to the exits.

### Heavier Than Air

The first time we ever saw a large, heavy airplane drop swiftly out of the sky for a landing, we thought the maneuver had an element of madness in it. We haven't changed our opinion much in thirty years. During that time, to be sure, a great many planes have dropped down and landed successfully, and the feat is now generally considered to be practicable, even natural. Anyone who, like us, professes to find something implausible in it is himself thought to be mad. The other morning, after the Convair dived into the East River, an official of the Civil Aeronautics Board said that the plane was "on course and every circumstance was normal" —a true statement, aeronautically speaking. It was one of those statements, though, that illuminate the new normalcy, and it encouraged us to examine the affair more closely, to see how far the world has drifted toward accepting the miraculous as the commonplace. Put yourself, for a moment, at the Convair's controls and let us take a look at this day's normalcy. The speed of a Convair, approaching an airport, is about a hundred and forty miles an hour, or better than two miles a minute. We don't know the weight of the plane, but let us say that it is heavier than a grand piano. There are passengers aboard. The morning is dark, drizzly. The skies they are ashen and sober. You are in the overcast. Below, visibility is half a mile. (A few minutes ago it was a mile, but things have changed rather suddenly.) If your forward speed is two miles per minute and you can see half a mile after you get out of the overcast, that means you'll be able to see what you're in for in the next fifteen seconds. At the proper moment, you break out of the overcast and, if you have normal curiosity, you look around to see what's cooking. What you see, of course, is Queens—an awful shock at any time, and on this day of rain, smoke, and shifting winds a truly staggering shock. You are close to earth now, doing two miles a minute, every circumstance is normal, and you have a fifteen-second spread between what you *can* see and what you can't. What you hope to see, of course, is Runway 22 rising gently to kiss your wheels, but, as the passenger from Bath so aptly put it, "When I felt water splashing over my feet, I knew it wasn't an airport."

Airplane design has, it seems to us, been fairly static, and designers have docilely accepted the fixed-wing plane as the sensible and natural form. Improvements have been made in it, safety devices have been added, and strict rules govern its flight. But we'd like to see plane designers start playing with ideas less rigid than those that now absorb their fancy. The curse of flight is speed. Or, rather, the curse of flight is that no opportunity exists for dawdling. And so weather is still an enormous factor in air travel. Planes encountering fog are diverted to other airports, and set their passengers down hundreds of miles from where they want to be. In very bad weather, planes are not permitted to leave the ground at all. There are still plenty of people who refuse to fly simply because they don't like to proceed at two miles a minute through thick conditions. Before flight becomes what it ought to be, a new sort of plane will have to be created—perhaps a cross between a helicopter and a fixed-wing machine. Its virtue will be that its power can be used either to propel it rapidly forward or to sustain it vertically. So armed, this airplane will be able to face bad weather with equanimity, and when a pall of melancholy hangs over Queens, this plane will be seen creeping slowly down through the overcast and making a painstaking inspection of Runway 22, instead of coming in like a grand piano.

The above remarks on flying drew a fine letter from a T.W.A. captain. His observations reveal a man so well adjusted to this life that they deserve being published. It isn't every day that you encounter a serene personality, either on land or in the sky. The captain did not take exception to our rather sour view of heavier-than-air flight; he merely testified that the acceptance of aerial hazards made him feel "time-fitted" to his profession and "apt to our second of history." (Stylist as well as pilot.)

To move at a high rate of speed; to feel less secure the closer I come to earth and man; to be able to look ahead with some certainty for 15 seconds;—these factors characterize life in the world today. For most people this constitutes a constant hardship, including a rebellion and fretfulness against life. I suspect that by not merely accepting an unforeseeable future, but by building it into my life I may come closer to living a "normal" 20th century life than those who must still struggle against it.

Well, there you have birdman and philosopher rolled into one —the contemplative pilot, full of semicolons, perfectly sympathetic to modern urgencies, a man with a built-in unforeseeable future who has surrendered himself to his speedy century as proudly and passionately as a bride to her lover. He would be our choice of a pilot if we had to go anywhere by air. Happily, however, our own mind is quiet today, and we shall travel afoot in the Park, time-fitted to the life of a weekly hack, unfretful, grateful for the next fifteen seconds.

The mental poise of this airline pilot in the middle of difficult flight shows man's spirit maintaining a small but significant lead over his instrument panel. Our own earth-bound life, we realize, is schizophrenic. Half the time we feel blissfully wedded to the modern scene, in love with its every mood, amused by its every joke, imperturbable in the face of its threat, bent on enjoying it to the hilt. The other half of the time we are the fusspot moralist, suspicious of all progress, resentful of change, determined to right wrongs, correct injustices, and save the world even if we have to blow it to pieces in the process. These two characters war incessantly in us, and probably in most men. First one is on top, then the other—body and soul always ravaged by the internal slugging match. We envy Captain X, who has come out a whole man instead of a divided one and who is at peace with his environment. We envy all who fly with him through the great sky.

### Railroads

The strong streak of insanity in railroads, which accounts for a child's instinctive feeling for them and for a man's unashamed devotion to them, is congenital; there seems to be no reason to fear that any disturbing improvement in the railroads' condition will set in. Lying at peace but awake in a Pullman berth all one hot night recently, we followed with dreamy satisfaction the familiar symphony of the cars—the diner departing (*furioso*) at midnight, the long, fever-laden silences between runs, the timeless gossip of rail and wheel during the runs, the crescendos and diminuendos, the piffling poop-pooping of the diesel's horn. For the most part, railroading is unchanged from our childhood. The water in which one washes one's face at morn is still without any real wetness, the little ladder leading to the upper is still the symbol of the tremendous adventure of the night, the green clothes hammock still sways with the curves, and there is still no foolproof place to store one's trousers.

Our journey really began several days earlier, at the ticket window of a small station in the country, when the agent showed signs of cracking under the paperwork. "It's hard to believe," he said, "that after all these years I still got to write the word 'Providence' in here every time I make out one of these things. Now, there's no possible conceivable way you could make this journey *without* going through Providence, yet the Company wants the word written in here just the same. O.K., here she goes!" He gravely wrote "Providence" in the proper space, and we experienced anew the reassurance that rail travel is unchanged and unchanging, and that it suits our temperament perfectly—a dash of lunacy, a sense of detachment, not much speed, and no altitude whatsoever.

### Mantis

We found the corpse of a praying mantis on our wife's dressing table the other day and were more than commonly interested in the discovery, since we have been praying lately ourself, and if we were to die suddenly, our remains would probably look as comical in supplication, as dry and light. The mantis (a female) measured three and five-eighths inches from eye to tip of folded wings—a truly formidable bug. Her legs and the leading edge of her wings still held their beautiful grass-green color, and her thorax was the rich, ruddy-brown color of cornstalks. In fact, the mantis, in her desiccated condition, was curiously vegetable-like, a sort of animated twig (animated in retrospect, that is). Her arms were still in the attitude of prayer, her chin resting on one hand in perfect piety. We cannot guess what she prayed for, what she asked: possibly that a dressing table in a city apartment might prove to be a suitable place for depositing eggs. Our own prayers have been of great violence recently; we have implored God to strike down evil persons who are deliberately stirring up a rumpus and creating situations of incalculable mischief for the world. These are idle prayers, or at least badly conceived, and, like the mantis, we may die praying; but many people are muttering such prayers these days, and earnestly. In prayer, we feel more angry than religious.

## Withholding

We have given about a year's thought to the withholding principle of taxation (not to be confused with the pay-as-you-go plan) and are now ready with our conclusion. Our belief is that withholding is a bad way to go about collecting tax money, even though the figures may show that it gets results. It is bad because it implies that the individual is incapable of handling his own affairs. The government as much as says: We know that, if left to your own devices, you will fritter away your worldly goods and tax day will catch you without cash. Or it says: We're not sure you'll come clean in your return, so we will just take the money before it reaches you and you will be saved the trouble and fuss of being honest. This implication is an unhealthy thing to spread around, being contrary to the old American theory that the individual is a very competent little guy indeed. The whole setup of our democratic government assumes that the citizen is bright, honest, and at least as fundamentally sound as a common stock. If you start treating him as something less than that, you are going to get into deep water, in our opinion. The device of withholding tax money, which is clearly confiscatory, since the individual is not allowed to see, taste, or touch a certain percentage of his wages, tacitly brands him as negligent or unthrifty or immature or incompetent or dishonest, or all of those things at once. There is, furthermore, a bad psychological effect in earning money that you never get your paws on. We believe this effect to be much stronger than the government realizes. At any rate, if the American individual is in truth incapable of paying his tax all by himself, then he should certainly be regarded as incapable of voting all by himself, and the Secretary of the Treasury should accompany him into the booth to show him where to put the X.

### Nails

Painted fingernails used to be the mark of the abandoned woman, but they have come a long way in a single generation and a lot of girls now paint their nails who haven't abandoned anything except a couple of bucks for the paint set. The other morning we visited our dental emporium to get our choppers cleaned, and as we reclined in the arms of the female oral hygienist, we were surprised to note that even *her* nails had been painted. Red as a rich man's barn, they insinuated themselves cleverly into our mouth and we felt that if we should close quickly on them we'd get the sudden taste of lobster. And not long ago we had some blood removed from our arm in a hospital and the nurse who tapped us had blood-red nails, as though she had dipped them daintily in our lifestream, as in a fingerbowl. Since there is nothing prettier than a pretty hand, we often wonder why women persist in messing themselves up that way—the same sort of impulse, no doubt, that causes some people to desecrate the lovely shell of a young turtle by painting the Statue of Liberty on it.

### Crab Grass

With lawnmowing just about over for the year, it was a pleasure the other morning to find a letter in the *Tribune* in defense of crab grass. The letter was from Mr. Gilbert G. Brinckerhoff, a retired schoolteacher living in Radburn, New Jersey, and it was the first piece of original thinking we had come across in weeks. Mr. Brinckerhoff, probably alone among homeowners in the United States, has taken the pressure off crab grass and off himself: he has come up with the discovery that you can just leave the stuff alone and survive; you don't have to fight it. Brinckerhoff has developed a lawn that is one hundred per cent crab grass; not a spear of anything else mars its lovely green surface. It makes, he says, a very presentable lawn. What this discovery will do to the Scott Lawn Company, what steps against Brinckerhoff will be taken by an aroused citizenry of Radburn—these are subjects for conjecture. But at least there is one man in America whose energies are not flowing into silly channels and who can stand erect and look something in the face. We admire Brinckerhoff and wish him a long, indolent retirement, much of which can be spent in a rocker on the porch overlooking the weedy plain.

### Remembrance of Things Past

These are the antibiotic days, when even newborn pigs are removed to sanitary surroundings, to be raised on laboratory milk, innocent of any connection with the sow. Pigs are "hatched" nowadays, rather than farrowed. After a few brief swigs of colostrum, they are transferred to the brooder, where an electric heat lamp comforts them, and where they are soon nuzzling the great, many-teated breasts of science and drinking an elixir of terramycin, skim milk, and concentrated vim. (How much of the terramycin finds its way to the consumer in ham and pork, to plague those who have an allergy to that drug and to lower everyone's resistance to Virus X, has not been demonstrated.)

Farmers who have experimented with the artificial method of raising pigs have discovered that it is advisable to retain one link with nature—one remembrance of things past. So the modern pig nursery is equipped with a record-player, and at proper intervals the infants hear the victrola give forth the sounds of suckling— the blissful grunting of sows as they let down their milk. The little pigs respond. A chord is touched. They awake and feed.

Man's separation from his mother, Nature, is quite parallel to the pig's from the sow. The separation, it seems, becomes more complete with every passing year, and may finally reach the point of artifice where, to maintain life at all, we will have to resort to a recording—some recollection of the natural world, some grunting noise that takes us back to reality and stirs us to accept the half-forgotten sources of our original supply.

### Experimentation

The year ends on a note of pure experimentation. Dr. Fritz Zwicky last week tried to hurl some metal slugs out into space, free of the earth's gravitational pull. Dr. Zwicky stood in New Mexico and tossed from there. He was well equipped: he had a rocket that took the slugs for the first forty-mile leg of the journey and then discharged them at high velocity to continue on their own. The desire to toss something in a new way, or to toss it a greater distance, is fairly steady in men and boys. Boys stand on high bridges, chucking chips down wind, or they stand on the shore of a pond, tossing rocks endlessly at a floating bottle, or at a dead cat, observing closely every detail of their experiment, trying to make every stone sail free of the pull of past experience. Then the boys grow older, stand in the desert, still chucking, observing, wondering. They have almost exhausted the earth's possibilities and are going on into the empyrean to throw at the stars, leaving the earth's people frightened and joyless, and leaving some fellow scientists switching over from science to politics and hoping they have made the switch in time.

### Daylight and Darkness

Up early this day, trying to decide whether or not to bequeath our brain to our alma mater, which is making a collection of such stuff. It struck us as odd that the decision will have to be made by the brain itself and that no other part of us—a foot or a gall bladder—can be in on the matter, although all are, in a way, concerned. Our head is small and we fear that our brain may suffer by comparison if arranged on a shelf with others. Spent part of the morning composing an inscription to go with our brain, but all we got was this:

> Observe, quick friend, this quiet noodle,
> This kit removed from its caboodle.
> Here sits a brain at last unhinged,
> On which too many thoughts impinged.

Spent the rest of the morning studying the crisis in the newspapers and watching apple-fall and leaf-fall in our city backyard, where nature is cleverly boxed and has therefore an appearance of special value, as of a jewel so precious that it must always be suitably contained. The day was clear, with a gentle wind, and the small leaves descended singly and serenely, except now and then when a breeze entered and caused a momentary rain of leaves— what one weather prophet on the radio calls "inner mitten" showers. A school of fish paraded slowly counterclockwise in the fountain, and on the wall above us hung seed pods of the polygonum vine. Our complaint about the crisis is not that it is so appalling but that it is so trivial. The consequences of the atomic cataclysm that are being relentlessly published seem mild alongside the burning loveliness of a fall morning, or the flash of a southbound bird, or the wry smell of chrysanthemums in the air. We examined everything said yesterday in the council chambers of the mighty and could find not a single idea that was not trifling, not a noble word of any calibre, not one unhurried observation or natural thought. The newspaper headline prophesying darkness is less moving than the pool of daylight that overflows upon it from the window, illuminating it. The light of day—so hard at times to see, so convincing when seen.

### Air Raid Drill

Five minutes after the all-clear sounded, everyone on our floor of *The New Yorker* offices was back at work. Nobody escaped, in the confusion, to another part of the city or to another planet; nobody tried to prolong the recess period in order to savor his freedom; none seemed desirous of meditating on the heavy implications of an A-bomb drill. To slip back into harness—that was the compelling aim. It was the same story all through the city—eight million well-behaved citizens, docile as lambs, huddled in hallways and tunnels while a hush fell over all. The city fathers were delighted, as indeed they might be. Yet how discouraging, really, such behavior is! It might have been more promising for the future had we all rushed wildly into the streets, punched wardens in the nose, and screamed our defiance of the implausible and crazy design that had led us to this pretty pass. But there was no sign of that. Only one fellow, of all we heard about, questioned the normality of eight million people creeping into the walls like mice. He stepped out on Broadway, gazed up and down, and asked, "What's this—something new?"

We inmates of the nineteenth floor were supposed to proceed, by easy stages, to the tenth floor, and that is exactly what we did. Bubbling with good spirits and bright as birds, we assembled at the elevators and were piped aboard, in lots of a dozen, for the weird descent to the survival chamber, or tenth-floor corridor. This descent from the nineteenth to the tenth is, in our building, the dodge that has been agreed upon as the means of eluding the atom —a queer piece of magic but one that is probably as good as any other. The tenth floor is an important station on the lift, being the first express stop, and in a few minutes the corridor of the tenth was full of people. Cars discharged passengers briskly. There was an overtone of uneasy mirth, rising to a slightly exaggerated pitch, as though each of us had had one cocktail. There was a temptation to clown, reminiscent of grammar-school days, when a fire drill brought sudden relief from classroom tedium. Underneath the mirth and chatter, easily discernible in the faces, was the deep current of loneliness, of fear—the imagination, carefully controlled at the surface level, operating miles down in the dark unfathomable regions.

Our descent from the nineteenth floor to the tenth floor was, we realized, a drop not of nine flights but of eight. This building has no floor called "13"; hence the "fourteenth" floor is a euphemism, and all the other floors above the twelfth are numbered not by a system of mathematics but by witchcraft. In our descent, then, in the cheerful lift, we not only had to evade an atomic explosion by taking a short journey but we had to subtract ten from nineteen and get eight. It occurred to us, gliding by the thirteenth floor and seeing the numeral "14" painted on it, that our atom-splitting scientists had committed the error of impatience and had run on ahead of the rest of the human race. They had dared look into the core of the sun, and had fiddled with it; but it might have been a good idea if they had waited to do that until the rest of us could look the number 13 square in the face. Such is the true nature of our peculiar dilemma.

For a minute or two during our sojourn on the tenth floor, we tried to take stock of our life, tried to understand what had brought us to this ignominious pass. We wondered whether the very qualities that are so generally admired—industry, ingenuity, loyalty, faith—whether they had not played a big part in it. Centuries of good behavior, centuries of brilliant achievement in the arts and sciences, and we take cover in a steel-and-plaster corridor, standing erect and tractable in fantastic assemblage, next to those we love, to await the messy results of some basic mismanagement, some distant fury, some essential cruelty and bestiality.

The papers reported that millions of dollars in manpower were lost by the quiescence of eight million persons. For fifteen minutes, wealth ran down the drain. This, like the missing thirteenth floor, was a mathematical enigma that stopped us cold. What happened, exactly? Who lost what? How can anyone say for sure that millions of dollars were lost? Probably the dollars, like the people, were not lost—just deeply troubled. Like the people, the dollars stood still for a brief while. For a quarter of an hour, no citizen, no dollar, did anything much. Travel, busy-ness, creation, connivance, promotion, shopping—all were at low ebb. It was eerie, but it was not necessarily a loss. The Consolidated Edison Company noted a sharp

dip in the curve of kilowattage, giving stockholders a nasty turn
but relieving consumers of fifteen minutes of expensive electrical
existence. It was one of those intense moments (as at midnight on
December 31st) when it is hard to say what, precisely, is taking
place. People are so addicted to activity that the sudden stoppage
of it gives them a quick sense of something being wrong, when, in
point of fact, it may be the beginning of something being right.

A fellow we stood next to in the corridor, and who survived,
confided to us that the drill was costing *The New Yorker* a pretty
penny, because at that very moment a couple of high-priced lawyers
were in the office and they were being paid by the hour. But what
he failed to say was whether the advice they were peddling was
good or bad. If it should turn out to be bad, then every minute
they were rendered inarticulate was so much gain. We regard the
published estimates of community loss during the test as highly
suspect. Who knows? Maybe if everybody in the world stood still
for a quarter of an hour and looked into the eyes of the next man,
the mischief would come to an end.

## The Distant Music of the Hounds

To perceive Christmas through its wrapping becomes more
difficult with every year. There was a little device we noticed in one
of the sporting-goods stores—a trumpet that hunters hold to their
ears so that they can hear the distant music of the hounds. Something of the sort is needed now to hear the incredibly distant sound
of Christmas in these times, through the dark, material woods that
surround it. "Silent Night," canned and distributed in thundering
repetition in the department stores, has become one of the greatest
of all noisemakers, almost like the rattles and whistles of Election
Night. We rode down on an escalator the other morning through

the silent-nighting of the loudspeakers, and the man just in front of us was singing, "I'm gonna wash this store right outa my hair, I'm gonna wash this store . . ."

The miracle of Christmas is that, like the distant and very musical voice of the hound, it penetrates finally and becomes heard in the heart—over so many years, through so many cheap curtain-raisers. It is not destroyed even by all the arts and craftiness of the destroyers, having an essential simplicity that is everlasting and triumphant, at the end of confusion. We once went out at night with coon-hunters and we were aware that it was not so much the promise of the kill that took the men away from their warm homes and sent them through the cold shadowy woods, it was something more human, more mystical—something even simpler. It was the night, and the excitement of the note of the hound, first heard, then not heard. It was the natural world, seen at its best and most haunting, unlit except by stars, impenetrable except to the knowing and the sympathetic.

Christmas in this year of crisis must compete as never before with the dazzling complexity of man, whose tangential desires and ingenuities have created a world that gives any simple thing the look of obsolescence—as though there were something inherently foolish in what is simple, or natural. The human brain is about to turn certain functions over to an efficient substitute, and we hear of a robot that is now capable of handling the tedious details of psychoanalysis, so that the patient no longer need confide in a living doctor but can take his problems to a machine, which sifts everything and whose "brain" has selective power and the power of imagination. One thing leads to another. The machine that is imaginative will, we don't doubt, be heir to the ills of the imagination; one can already predict that the machine itself may become sick emotionally, from strain and tension, and be compelled at last to consult a medical man, whether of flesh or of steel. We have tended to assume that the machine and the human brain are in conflict. Now the fear is that they are indistinguishable. Man not only is notably busy himself but insists that the other animals follow his example. A new bee has been bred artificially, busier than the old bee.

So this day and this century proceed toward the absolutes of convenience, of complexity, and of speed, only occasionally holding up the little trumpet (as at Christmas time) to be reminded of the simplicities, and to hear the distant music of the hound. Man's inventions, directed always onward and upward, have an odd way of leading back to man himself, as a rabbit track in snow leads eventually to the rabbit. It is one of his more endearing qualities that man should think his tracks lead outward, toward something else, instead of back around the hill to where he has already been; and it is one of his persistent ambitions to leave earth entirely and travel by rocket into space, beyond the pull of gravity, and perhaps try another planet, as a pleasant change. He knows that the atomic age is capable of delivering a new package of energy; what he doesn't know is whether it will prove to be a blessing. This week, many will be reminded that no explosion of atoms generates so hopeful a light as the reflection of a star, seen appreciatively in a pasture pond. It is there we perceive Christmas—and the sheep quiet, and the world waiting.

# III.

# The Wonderful World of Letters

# A CLASSIC WAITS FOR ME

(With apologies to Walt Whitman, plus a trial
membership in the Classics Club)


A classic waits for me, it contains all, nothing is lacking,
Yet all were lacking if taste were lacking, or if the endorsement of
  the right man were lacking.
O clublife, and the pleasures of membership,
O volumes for sheer fascination unrivalled.
Into an armchair endlessly rocking,
Walter J. Black my president,
I, freely invited, cordially welcomed to membership,
My arm around John Kieran, Pearl S. Buck,
My taste in books guarded by the spirits of William Lyon Phelps,
  Hendrik Willem van Loon,
(From your memories, sad brothers, from the fitful risings and
  callings I heard),
I to the classics devoted, brother of rough mechanics, beauty-
  parlor technicians, spot welders, radio-program directors
(It is not necessary to have a higher education to appreciate these
  books),
I, connoisseur of good reading, friend of connoisseurs of good read-
  ing everywhere,
I, not obligated to take any specific number of books, free to
  reject any volume, perfectly free to reject Montaigne, Erasmus,
  Milton,

I, in perfect health except for a slight cold, pressed for time, having
   only a few more years to live,
Now celebrate this opportunity.
Come, I will make the club indissoluble,
I will read the most splendid books the sun ever shone upon,
I will start divine magnetic groups,
    With the love of comrades,
      With the life-long love of distinguished committees.

I strike up for an Old Book.
Long the best-read figure in America, my dues paid, sitter in arm-
   chairs everywhere, wanderer in populous cities, weeping with
   Hecuba and with the late William Lyon Phelps,
Free to cancel my membership whenever I wish,
Turbulent, fleshy, sensible,
Never tiring of clublife,
Always ready to read another masterpiece provided it has the
   approval of my president, Walter J. Black,
Me imperturbe, standing at ease among writers,
Rais'd by a perfect mother and now belonging to a perfect book
   club,
Bearded, sunburnt, gray-neck'd, astigmatic,
Loving the masters and the masters only
(I am mad for them to be in contact with me),
My arm around Pearl S. Buck, only American woman to receive
   the Nobel Prize for Literature,
I celebrate this opportunity.
And I will not read a book nor the least part of a book but has
   the approval of the Committee,
For all is useless without that which you may guess at many times
   and not hit, that which they hinted at,
All is useless without readability.

By God! I will accept nothing which all cannot have their counterpart of on the same terms (89¢ for the Regular Edition or $1.39
for the De Luxe Edition, plus a few cents postage).

I will make inseparable readers with their arms around each other's
necks,
  By the love of classics,
    By the manly love of classics.

# ACROSS THE STREET
# AND INTO THE GRILL

## (With my respects to Ernest Hemingway)

This is my last and best and true and only meal, thought Mr. Perley as he descended at noon and swung east on the beat-up sidewalk of Forty-fifth Street. Just ahead of him was the girl from the reception desk. I am a little fleshed up around the crook of the elbow, thought Perley, but I commute good.

He quickened his step to overtake her and felt the pain again. What a stinking trade it is, he thought. But after what I've done to other assistant treasurers, I can't hate anybody. Sixteen deads, and I don't know how many possibles.

The girl was near enough now so he could smell her fresh receptiveness, and the lint in her hair. Her skin was light blue, like the sides of horses.

"I love you," he said, "and we are going to lunch together for the first and only time, and I love you very much."

"Hello, Mr. Perley," she said, overtaken. "Let's not think of anything."

A pair of fantails flew over from the sad old Guaranty Trust Company, their wings set for a landing. A lovely double, thought Perley, as he pulled. "Shall we go to the Hotel Biltmore, on Vanderbilt Avenue, which is merely a feeder lane for the great streets, or shall we go to Schrafft's, where my old friend Botticelli is captain of girls and where they have the mayonnaise in fiascos?"

"Let's go to Schrafft's," said the girl, low. "But first I must phone Mummy." She stepped into a public booth and dialled true and well, using her finger. Then she telephoned.

As they walked on, she smelled good. She smells good, thought Perley. But that's all right, I add good. And when we get to Schrafft's, I'll order from the menu, which I like very much indeed.

They entered the restaurant. The wind was still west, ruffling the edges of the cookies. In the elevator, Perley took the controls. "I'll run it," he said to the operator. "I checked out long ago." He stopped true at the third floor, and they stepped off into the men's grill.

"Good morning, my Assistant Treasurer," said Botticelli, coming forward with a fiasco in each hand. He nodded at the girl, who he knew was from the West Seventies and whom he desired.

"Can you drink the water here?" asked Perley. He had the fur trapper's eye and took in the room at a glance, noting that there was one empty table and three pretty waitresses.

Botticelli led the way to the table in the corner, where Perley's flanks would be covered.

"Alexanders," said Perley. "Eighty-six to one. The way Chris mixes them. Is this table all right, Daughter?"

Botticelli disappeared and returned soon, carrying the old Indian blanket.

"That's the same blanket, isn't it?" asked Perley.

"Yes. To keep the wind off," said the Captain, smiling from the backs of his eyes. "It's still west. It should bring the ducks in tomorrow, the chef thinks."

Mr. Perley and the girl from the reception desk crawled down under the table and pulled the Indian blanket over them so it was solid and good and covered them right. The girl put her hand on his wallet. It was cracked and old and held his commutation book. "We are having fun, aren't we?" she asked.

"Yes, Sister," he said.

"I have here the soft-shelled crabs, my Assistant Treasurer," said Botticelli. "And another fiasco of the 1926. This one is cold."

"Dee the soft-shelled crabs," said Perley from under the blanket. He put his arm around the receptionist good.

"Do you think we should have a green pokeweed salad?" she asked. "Or shall we not think of anything for a while?"

"We shall not think of anything for a while, and Botticelli would bring the pokeweed if there was any," said Perley. "It isn't the season." Then he spoke to the Captain. "Botticelli, do you remember when we took all the mailing envelopes from the stockroom, spit on the flaps, and then drank rubber cement till the foot soldiers arrived?"

"I remember, my Assistant Treasurer," said the Captain. It was a little joke they had.

"He used to mimeograph pretty good," said Perley to the girl. "But that was another war. Do I bore you, Mother?"

"Please keep telling me about your business experiences, but not the rough parts." She touched his hand where the knuckles were scarred and stained by so many old mimeographings. "Are both your flanks covered, my dearest?" she asked, plucking at the blanket. They felt the Alexanders in their eyeballs. Eighty-six to one.

"Schrafft's is a good place and we're having fun and I love you," Perley said. He took another swallow of the 1926, and it was a good and careful swallow. "The stockroom men were very brave," he said, "but it is a position where it is extremely difficult to stay alive. Just outside that room there is a little bare-assed highboy and it is in the way of the stuff that is being brought up. The hell with it. When you make a breakthrough, Daughter, first you clean out the baskets and the half-wits, and all the time they have the fire escapes taped. They also shell you with old production orders, many of them approved by the general manager in charge of sales. I am boring you and I will not at this time discuss the general manager in charge of sales as we are unquestionably being listened to by that waitress over there who is setting out the decoys."

"I am going to give you my piano," the girl said, "so that when you look at it you can think of me. It will be something between us."

"Call up and have them bring the piano to the restaurant," said Perley. "Another fiasco, Botticelli!"

They drank the sauce. When the piano came, it wouldn't play. The keys were stuck good. "Never mind, we'll leave it here, Cousin," said Perley.

They came out from under the blanket and Perley tipped their waitress exactly fifteen per cent minus withholding. They left the piano in the restaurant, and when they went down the elevator and out and turned in to the old, hard, beat-up pavement of Fifth Avenue and headed south toward Forty-fifth Street, where the pigeons were, the air was as clean as your grandfather's howitzer. The wind was still west.

I commute good, thought Perley, looking at his watch. And he felt the old pain of going back to Scarsdale again.

# BOOK REVIEW

("Malabar Farm," by Louis Bromfield)

Malabar Farm is the farm for me,
It's got what it takes, to a large degree:
Beauty, alfalfa, constant movement,
And a terrible rash of soil improvement.
Far from orthodox in its tillage,
Populous as many a village,
Stuff being planted and stuff being written,
Fields growing lush that were once unfitten,
Bromfield land, whether low or high land,
Has more going on than Coney Island.

When Bromfield went to Pleasant Valley,
The soil was as hard as a bowling alley;
He sprinkled lime and he seeded clover,
And when it came up he turned it over.
From far and wide folks came to view
The things that a writing man will do.
The more he fertilized the fields
The more impressive were his yields,
And every time a field grew fitter
Bromfield would add another critter,
The critter would add manure, despite 'im,
And so it went—ad infinitum.

It proves that a novelist on his toes
Can make a valley bloom like a rose.

Malabar Farm is the farm for me,
A place of unbridled activity.
A farm is always in some kind of tizzy,
But Bromfield's place is *really* busy:
Strangers arriving by every train,
Bromfield terracing against the rain,
Catamounts crying, mowers mowing,
Guest rooms full to overflowing,
Boxers in every room of the house,
Cows being milked to Brahms and Strauss,
Kids arriving by van or pung,
Bromfield up to his eyes in dung,
Sailors, trumpeters, mystics, actors,
All of them wanting to drive the tractors,
All of them eager to husk the corn,
Some of them sipping their drinks till morn;
Bulls in the bull pen, bulls on the loose,
Everyone bottling vegetable juice,
Play producers jousting with bards,
Boxers fighting with St. Bernards,
Boxers fooling with auto brakes,
Runaway cars at the bottom of lakes,
Bromfield diving to save the Boxers,
Moving vans full of bobby-soxers,
People coming and people going,
Everything fertile, everything growing,
Fish in the ponds other fish seducing,
Thrashing around and reproducing,
Whole place teeming with men and pets,

Field mice nesting in radio sets,
Cats in the manger, rats in the nooks,
Publishers scanning the sky for books,
Harvested royalties, harvested grain,
Bromfield scanning the sky for rain,
Bromfield's system proving reliable,
Soil getting rich and deep and friable,
Bromfield phoning, Bromfield haying,
Bromfield watching mulch decaying,
Women folks busy shelling peas,
Guinea fowl up in catalpa trees.
Oh, Bromfield's valley is plenty pleasant—
Quail and rabbit, Boxers, pheasant.
Almost every Malabar day
Sees birth and growth, sees death, decay;
Summer ending, leaves a-falling,
Lecture dates, long distance calling.

Malabar Farm is the farm for me,
It's the proving ground of vivacity.
A soil that's worn out, poor, or lazy
Drives L. Bromfield almost crazy;
Whether it's raining or whether it's pouring,
Bromfield's busy with soil restoring;
From the Hog Lot Field to the Lower Bottom
The things a soil should have, he's got 'em;
Foe of timothy, friend of clover,
Bromfield gives it a going over,
Adds some cobalt, adds some boron.
Not enough? He puts some more on.
Never anything too much trouble,
Almost everything paying double:

Nice fat calves being sold to the sharper,
Nice fat checks coming in from Harper.
Most men cut and cure their hay,
Bromfield cuts it and leaves it lay;
Whenever he gets impatient for rain
He turns his steers in to standing grain;
Whenever he gets in the least depressed
He sees that another field gets dressed;
He never dusts and he never sprays,
His soil holds water for days and days,
And now when a garden piece is hoed
You'll find neither bug nor nematode,
You'll find how the good earth holds the rain.
Up at the house you'll find Joan Fontaine.

Malabar Farm is the farm for me,
It's the greenest place in the whole countree,
It builds its soil with stuff organic,
It's the nearest thing to a planned panic.
Bromfield mows by any old light,
The sun in the morning and the moon at night;
Most tireless of all our writing men,
He sometimes mows until half past ten;
With a solid program of good trash mulch
He stops the gully and he stops the gulch.
I think the world might well have a look
At Louis Bromfield's latest book;
A man doesn't have to be omniscient
To see that he's right—our soil's deficient.
We've robbed and plundered this lovely earth
Of elements of immeasurable worth,
And darned few men have applied their talents

Harder than Louis to restore the balance;
And though his husbandry's far from quiet,
Bromfield had the guts to try it.
A book like his is a very great boon,
And what he's done, I'd like to be doon.

# SHOP TALK

### Poets

THESE are busy days for a poet. Every mail seems to bring some new excitement, some fragrant new project. There is the congress of poets, soon to meet; there is the new anthology of American men poets, nearing completion; and there is the Galleon Press's heroic undertaking—the forthcoming "Who's Who in American Poetry," which, according to a communication we received from them, will be "a complete listing of all major poets." This last project is the one that fires our imagination and awakens our support. The problem of who is a major poet and who is a minor poet is one which has long beset American letters. It has kept poets in a state of nervous tension. It has embarrassed editors and kept them busy apologizing for their distressing errors of judgment. It has kept the whole field of poesy in a peculiarly turbulent and uneasy condition, not conducive to good results. Now, happily, those days will soon be over; America is to have an authoritative listing of major poets. All a person need do, when confronted by a doubtful bard or a poem of uncertain proportions, will be to thumb through "Who's Who in American Poetry" to discover if the writer has attained his majority. The price of the book is $5.

You read, perhaps, about the man who stole four tires from a car in Norfolk, Virginia, and left a purse and a diamond ring untouched on the front seat, with this note: "Roses are red, violets are blue, we like your jewels but your tires are new." The papers said it was a case of a thief who had a flair for poetry. This is palpable nonsense. It was a case of a poet who was willing to attempt any desperate thing, even larceny, in order to place his poem. Clearly, here was a man who had written something and then had gone up and down in the world seeking the precise situation which would activate his poem. It must have meant long nights and days of wandering before he found a car with jewels lying loose in the front seat and four good tires on the wheels. Poets endure much for the sake of their art.

## English Usage

We were interested in what Dr. Henry Seidel Canby had to say about English usage, in the *Saturday Review*. Usage seems to us peculiarly a matter of ear. Everyone has his own prejudices, his own set of rules, his own list of horribles. Dr. Canby speaks of "contact" used as a verb, and points out that careful writers and speakers, persons of taste, studiously avoid it. They do—some of them because the word, so used, makes their gorge rise, others because they have heard that we sensitive lit'ry folk consider it displeasing. The odd thing is that what is true of one noun-verb is not necessarily true of another. To "contact a man" makes us wince; but to "ground a plane because of bad weather" sounds all right. Further, although we are satisfied to "ground a plane," we object to "garaging an automobile." An automobile should not be "garaged"; it should either be "put in a garage" or left out all night.

The contraction "ain't," as Dr. Canby points out, is a great loss to the language. Nice Nellies, schoolteachers, and underdone grammarians have made it the symbol of ignorance and ill-breeding, when in fact it is a handy word, often serving where nothing else will. "Say it ain't so" is a phrase that is right the way it stands, and couldn't be any different. People are afraid of words, afraid of mistakes. One time a newspaper sent us to a morgue to get a story on a woman whose body was being held for identification. A man believed to be her husband was brought in. Somebody pulled the sheet back; the man took one agonizing look, and cried, "My God, it's her!" When we reported this grim incident, the editor diligently changed it to "My God, it's she!"

The English language is always sticking a foot out to trip a man. Every week we get thrown, writing merrily along. Even Dr. Canby, a careful and experienced craftsman, got thrown in his own editorial. He spoke of "the makers of textbooks who are nearly always reactionary, and often unscholarly in denying the right to change to a language that has always been changing . . ." In this case the word "change," quietly sandwiched in between a couple of "to's," unexpectedly exploded the whole sentence. Even inverting the phrases wouldn't have helped. If he had started out "In denying to a language . . . the right to change," it would have come out this way: "In denying to a language that has always been changing the right to change . . ." English usage is sometimes more than mere taste, judgment, and education—sometimes it's sheer luck, like getting across a street.

## The Departure of Eustace Tilley

We looked up Mr. Eustace Tilley this week, on the eve of his departure from the city—his "maiden" departure, as he pointed out. The elegant old gentleman was found in his suite at the Plaza, his portmanteau packed, his mourning doves wrapped in dotted swiss, his head in a sitz bath for a last shampoo. Everywhere, scattered about the place, were grim reminders of his genteel background: a cold bottle of Tavel on the lowboy, a spray of pinks in a cut-glass bowl, an album held with a silver clasp, and his social-security card copied in needlepoint and framed on the wall. We begged the privilege of an interview for The Talk of the Town (or what the French call "Murmures de la Ville"), and he reluctantly granted it.

When we inquired about his destination, Mr. Tilley was evasive. "I should prefer to be grilled on that," he remarked, bitterly.

So we grilled him, naming over all the fashionable watering places, without success.

"Would you say you were going to a spa?" we ventured.

"It has a little of the spa in it, a little of the gulch," replied the renowned fop.

"Oh, the White Mountains," we cried.

"Let it go. Ask me about things of moment, such as the ever-normal granary." Mr. Tilley pulled the plug in the sitz bath, sat down at a dressing table, and began to do his hair.

"Why are you leaving town?" we asked.

"I should say that my departure was in part a matter of temper, in part of expediency."

"You mean you're beating the purge?"

Mr. Tilley let the comb drop into his lap, and turned half around, his magnificent profile etched in light from the window.

"We live in a new world," he said. "St. Bernards are killing little girls. Books, or what pass for books, are being photographed on microfilm. There is a cemetery I want to see," he continued, "a grove where ancient trees shelter the graves and throw their umbrage on the imponderable dead. The branches of these trees, my dear young man, are alive with loudspeakers. I believe Upper Montclair is the place. That is one reason for my departure—I have certain macabre pilgrimages to make, while the lustiness is still in my bones. And besides, the other day I received a letter." He gave us a cryptic glance.

"You mean it contained a threat?" we asked.

"Oh my, no," said Tilley. "It came from the office of a division manager, and began: 'Dear Mr. Tilley, Take two pieces of metal and rub them together for a few seconds.' You see, it is time I took my leave." A waiter carrying a guinea fowl aspic entered the room and buzzed about Mr. Tilley. A fly buzzed about the waiter.

"And then, there are things I want to think about, things on which I can more readily concentrate when I am not in town. I want to think about the Will Rogers memorial."

"Why?" we inquired.

"I don't know why," said Tilley, petulantly. "I simply know what are the things I like to think about, and the Will Rogers memorial is one of them. I want time to examine the new English divorce law, the ever-normal granary (which you forgot to ask me about), the new Knopf book about a man who had a good time, the grasshopper invasion, Hitler's ban on all art that he doesn't understand. I shall perhaps enter a putting tournament, using my old brassie, of course. And I have a strong desire to hear again the wildest sound in all the world."

"You mean timber wolves?" we said.

"I mean cockcrow," snapped Tilley, who by this time was becoming visibly agitated. "I want time to think about many people, alive and dead: Pearl White, Schoolboy Creekmore, Igor Sikorsky —I couldn't begin to name them. I want to think about the custom of skiing in summertime, want to hear a child play thirds on the pianoforte in midafternoon. I shall devote considerable time to studying the faces of motorists drawn up for the red light; in their look of discontent is the answer to the industrial revolution. Did you know that a porcupine has the longest intestine in

Christendom, either because he eats so much wood or in order that he may? It is a fact. There must be something to be learned by thinking about that. Take a person employed by a broadcasting studio to close contracts with mountain people who sing folk songs over the air—what will such a person develop, in the course of time, to correspond to a porcupine's long intestine? Ah, well, it's time to be off."

The elderly eccentric rose, phoned for a bellboy, and gathered his last-minute personal effects into the pocket of his waistcoat. We accompanied him down to the street, where a Victoria was drawn up at the curb, the driver waiting by the head of his old cob. Cameras clicked as Tilley stepped into the carriage and sat down. He held his brassie at his side, stiffly, like a sword. By his side sat a pretty girl, who welcomed him to the carriage and made him comfortable.

"You are wondering, of course, who this young female might be," growled Tilley. We nodded.

"A hostess," said Tilley, coldly. "Provided by the livery stable. Another dubious wonder of the modern world. In the event of emergency, she will be the one to walk to the nearest farmhouse, give the alarm, and be photographed. Well, au revoir!" The coachman whipped up his cob, and the little party rumbled off along Fifty-ninth Street, Tilley brandishing his brassie with great ferocity at a horsefly. As we turned, we discovered to our surprise that the sidewalk, where he had paused a moment, was a pool of tears.

### Critical Dilemma

Some time ago, Mr. James Agee wrote a piece for the *Partisan Review* deflating a number of plays, among them "Oklahoma!," which he said were so bad he had not bothered to see them. We commented briefly at the time on Mr. Agee's critical method, which would seem to spare the critic the irksome experience of becoming acquainted with the material he is criticizing. We thought the matter would end there, but the *Partisan Review* apparently broods a good deal about these questions, and the current issue contains an article passionately defending the no-look-at method of play criticism. It points out that Mr. Agee's estimate of "Oklahoma!," which he arrived at by hearing his friends discuss it, is "scientific in the extreme." He had "seen his object from two separate and known points of view and had placed it accordingly," just as a surveyor, by triangulation, would map "an inaccessible point across a river." We admit that "Oklahoma!" is inaccessible, but we think that any mathematician who tried to determine an unknown triangle by asking his friends how big they thought the known sides and angles were wouldn't even be called partisan; he'd be called dotty.

Actually, we think we understand why a critic shuns "Oklahoma!" if he learns from sources he considers reliable that it is a debasement of art. Having placed it in the category of pseudo-folk art, he stays away because of a deep dread that if he were to attend a performance, at some point in the show he might find himself having fun. No conscientious critic wants to risk the debilitating experience of enjoying something which is clearly on an inferior artistic level. It upsets everything. When the intelligence says "Nuts" and the blood says "Goody," a critic would rather be home writing his review sight unseen, from information supplied by friends.

## A Writer in Arms

William Saroyan, the wingèd, has been talking things over with his draft board. He has given the board its choice of taking his body (and leaving his mind alone) or else deferring both body and mind so that he can go on writing in a civilian capacity. "If they want me as a person, as a body," he said, "the responsibility is theirs. However, I'll insist on one thing and that is that I be a soldier and no more, that I will not be required to write." This dream of divorcing the intellect from soldiering is common to many of us, although few of us manage to use the word "insist" with Mr. Saroyan's charming innocence. The fact is, the Army is the only organization in the world that can compel an independent writer to become a press agent or propagandist. This power which the Army wields is a very grave responsibility—in our opinion just as grave as the power to order a man into a military engagement from which he may not emerge whole. We are, in fact, deeply sympathetic with Mr. Saroyan's feelings in this matter. We would also love to be in his squad when the sergeant hands him a pen and orders him to make like a playwright.

### Estimating the Tax

To a writer, almost everything in life seems a special problem and virtually insoluble. Take a non-wage-earning writer who is trying to estimate his tax; his problem is as special as a wedding cake and twice as intricate. If he estimates that he will earn practically nothing (a tendency that is strong in most writers and that is based on vivid recollections of the past), then he runs the risk of breaking his spirit and throwing himself out of joint. It is dangerous for any writer to predict that he is dying on the vine. On the other hand, if he tries to tone himself up by estimating a huge income, he immediately confronts the disgusting fact that he hasn't money enough to pay the first installment. The whole process, actually, calls for so fine an adjustment of fact and fancy, of hope and memory, that only a truly creative person is capable of tackling it at all.

### Peaks in Journalism

On Labor Day Eve we pawed through the trash on our desk and scrapped everything except one item, which we find indispensable —a clipping from a Lucius Beebe column containing a picture of Dick Maney. We have been saving the clipping through fetid summer weeks, because the publication of the Maney photograph in the *Herald Tribune* sets a mark in journalism which will not be reached again in our time, as the saying goes. Mr. Beebe, whose text the picture illustrates, was telling how he stayed sensibly in town during a hot weekend, and how pleasant this experience was. Nobody even phoned, he wrote. Not even Dick Maney phoned, he continued. And the *Tribune*, suiting the action to the word, gravely produced a picture of Mr. Maney and ran it—a man whose only immediate news value was that he had *not* phoned Lucius Beebe over a hot weekend.

❦

All week we have been thinking about the patient cameraman of Budapest whose triumphant exploit was reported in the *American* recently. This extraordinary person, it appears, spent three days sitting by a bridge over the Danube, lens focussed, shutter cocked, waiting for some unhappy individual to jump off into the water. He was, as the *American* put it, finally "rewarded" with the "above" snapshot. It seems an odd way to spend three days of one's life, an odd reward. Like many news pictures, the suicide snapshot had no intrinsic graphic value (the speck which is the body in mid-air might as well be a tailor's dummy or a sack of sawdust); its value, photographically speaking, is in the explicit authenticity which the caption insists upon. In other words, it is a triumph of virtuosity.

Photography, as a journalistic form, is in the ascendant, with the candid camera challenging the privacy of all, with flashlights exploding in restaurants and theatres in the faces of the unwary, with able-bodied seamen equipped and ready to snap the sinking of their own ship, and with *Life* exposing a fat man in the act of taking off his pants. Today the Leica in steady hands can be as deadly as the revolver, and it enjoys immunity from the Sullivan law. The pictures that result satisfy something in the public, yet there is sometimes a quality in the photographer's art more predatory than reportorial. And we say that knowing that even a despondent man on a bridge is not necessarily an unwilling subject.

❦

Photography is the most self-conscious of the arts. The act of photography has been glorified in the newspicture magazines, and even in the newspapers. Publisher and reader enjoy shoptalk together. The editor continually points to "best shots," or "newspicture of the week," confident that his clientele is following every move of the shutter. Even the staid *Times* published a couple of views of John L. Lewis the other day, and remarked that they were "unretouched." (Imagine retouching a picture of John L. Lewis!) *Life* describes how Margaret Bourke-White leans far out of her plane to snap "such stunning pictures as the one on P. 26." In the writing profession, there is nothing that quite corresponds to this sort of cameraderie. We feel rather left out. Perhaps we make a mistake not to make more fuss about the mechanics of our writing. When we toss off a particularly neat ablative absolute, or kill a hanging participle in the last three seconds of play, maybe our editor should call the matter to the attention of the reader. A writer does a lot of work the reader isn't conscious of, and never gets any credit. This paragraph was exposed for eighteen minutes, in a semi-darkened room. The writer was leaning far out over his typewriter, thinking to beat the band.

Of course, it may be that the art of photography and the art of writing are antithetical. The hope and aim of a word-handler is that he may communicate a thought or an impression to his reader without the reader's realizing that he has been dragged through a series of hazardous or grotesque syntactical situations. In photography, the goal seems to be to prove beyond a doubt that the cameraman, in his great moment of creation, was either hanging by his heels from the rafters or was wedged under the floor with his lens at a knothole.

### Readerhood

We received at *The New Yorker* this morning an exceptionally friendly letter from the publisher of one of the magazines to which we subscribe. It began: "Dear *Time* Subscriber, I hope very much that you will drop in to see us if you are in New York this summer during the World's Fair. As Publisher of *Time* I have always been sorry I could not meet each of our widely-scattered subscribers and talk to you face to face, and I know that all our editors feel the same way."

This expression of mass warmth puts us to shame. We have searched our own heart in vain for its counterpart. The sheer numerical possibilities of the invitation are staggering—six readers in a face-to-face mood would fill our reception room, twelve would tax the utmost divan. But quite apart from the purely dimensional terrors of the situation, we have, in our heart of hearts, not the faintest desire to see a reader—ever. The relationship between reader and magazine is so tenuous, so delicately poised, so chemically active, sometimes so purely spiteful and crotchety, that we feel we should preserve, at all costs, the indispensable boon of complete physical separation. Absence is the very essence of readerhood. Destroy that, and you destroy all. Readers must remain, for editors, a misty though rather laudable group, somewhere out there in the great beyond—like the audience to the actor, a dark, swimming mass of half-people, honored, respected, distant, and inviolate. Once in a coon's age a reader should drop into a magazine office to fight a duel or pay an old account, but such an occasion should be rare and exceptional. By and large, readers will find nothing but grief if they seek out the tangible, routine side of the magazine to which they subscribe. What few *New Yorker* readers have made their unhappy way into these catacombs have departed in sorrow and disillusion. We shall always remember the remark of one of them—a girl—who had come in high hopes of discovering something commensurate with her dream. "My God," she said, gazing around, "but it's dreary!"

### The Future of Reading

In schools and colleges, in these audio-visual days, doubt has been raised as to the future of reading—whether the printed word is on its last legs. One college president has remarked that in fifty years "only five per cent of the people will be reading." For this, of course, one must be prepared. But how prepare? To us it would seem that even if only one person out of a hundred and fifty million should continue as a *reader*, he would be the one worth saving, the nucleus around which to found a university. We think this not impossible person, this Last Reader, might very well stand in the same relation to the community as the queen bee to the colony of bees, and that the others would quite properly dedicate themselves wholly to his welfare, serving special food and building special accommodations. From his nuptial, or intellectual, flight would come the new race of men, linked perfectly with the long past by the unbroken chain of the intellect, to carry on the community. But it is more likely that our modern hive of bees, substituting a coaxial cable for spinal fluid, will try to perpetuate the race through audio-visual devices, which ask no discipline of the mind and which are already giving the room the languor of an opium parlor.

Reading is the work of the alert mind, is demanding, and under ideal conditions produces finally a sort of ecstasy. As in the sexual experience, there are never more than two persons present in the act of reading—the writer, who is the impregnator, and the reader, who is the respondent. This gives the experience of reading a sublimity and power unequalled by any other form of communication. It would be just as well, we think, if educators clung to this great phenomenon and did not get sidetracked, for although books and reading may at times have played too large a part in the educational process, that is not what is happening today. Indeed, there is very little true reading, and not nearly as much writing as one would suppose from the towering piles of pulpwood in the dooryards of our paper mills. Readers and writers are scarce, as are publishers and reporters. The reports we get nowadays are those of men who have not gone to the scene of the accident, which is always farther inside one's own head than it is convenient to penetrate without galoshes.

### Writers At Work

Kenneth Roberts' working methods and ours differ so widely
it is hard to realize we are in the same line of business. We've
just been looking through his book "I Wanted to Write" and
marvelling at his stamina and his discipline. The thought of
writing apparently stimulates Roberts and causes him to sit up-
right at a desk, put in requests to libraries, write friends, examine
sources, and generally raise hell throughout the daylight hours
and far into the night. He works at home (where his privacy is
guarded), writes in longhand, counts the words, keeps a record of
moneys received, and gets a great deal done. Now turn for a
moment to your correspondent. The thought of writing hangs over
our mind like an ugly cloud, making us apprehensive and depressed, as before a summer storm, so that we begin the day by
subsiding after breakfast, or by going away, often to seedy and
inconclusive destinations: the nearest zoo, or a branch post office
to buy a few stamped envelopes. Our professional life has been a
long, shameless exercise in avoidance. Our home is designed for
the maximum of interruption, our office is the place where we
never are. From his remarks, we gather that Roberts is contemptuous of this temperament and setup, regards it as largely a
pose and certainly as a deficiency in blood. It has occurred to us
that perhaps we are not a writer at all but merely a bright clerk
who persists in crowding his destiny. Yet the record is there. Not
even lying down and closing the blinds stops us from writing;
not even our family, and our preoccupation with same, stops us.
We have never counted the words, but we estimated them once
and the estimate was staggering. The only conclusion we can draw
is that there is no such thing as "the writing man," and that after

you have waded through a book like "I Wanted to Write" you still don't know the half of it, and would be a fool to try and find out.

## Death of the Sun

The death of the *Sun*, and the obsequies, reminded us of the death of Freddy the rat. Freddy was a celebrated inhabitant of the *Sun* office, a hated contemporary of Archy's. When Freddy died (following an encounter with a tarantula), they dropped him off the fire escape into an alley, with military honors. That is about what happens when a newspaper dies. Frank Munsey put it into words, and so did the tarantula. The tarantula kept taunting Freddy. "Where I step," he said, "a weed dies." Munsey said it a little more elegantly. "The New York evening-newspaper field," he said in 1924, "is now in good shape through the elimination of an oversupply of evening newspapers. These evening newspapers have been eliminated as individual entities from New York journalism by myself alone." Where I step, a rag dies.

The first duty of a newspaper is to stay alive. And the most important single fact about any newspaper is that it differs from the next newspaper and is owned by a different man, or group of men. This fact (the fact of difference) transcends a newspaper's greatness, a newspaper's honesty, a newspaper's liveliness, or any other quality. The health of the country deteriorates every time a newspaper dies of strangulation or is wiped out in a mercy killing. The solemn fact about the absorption of the *Sun* by Scripps-Howard is not that we lose a conservative paper, or an ancient paper, or an honest paper, or a funny paper, but that we lose a paper—one voice in the choir.

The final statement of the *Sun's* publisher was written in such expensive language as almost to explain the demise of his sheet. Mr. Dewart said, "Mounting costs of production, unaccompanied by commensurate increases in advertising revenue, have made some such course inevitable." That kind of prose takes a heap of newsprint, plenty of typesetting. Archy could have said it quicker, and cheaper.

## 3 D

A friend just back from the Coast tells us that Hollywood is in shock—cameras aimed but not grinding, actors dressed but not performing, writers poised but not creating, and all top-level people studying charts and omens, convinced that TV is the enemy and that a miracle has got to happen to save the day. They have, moreover, pretty much decided that the thing that's wrong with the movies is the photography, and that the miracle that'll save the industry is a new technique, three-dimensional or cycloramic. On the strength of this report, we wangled a couple of seats to Cinerama and went over to see what is going to save the movies. We took our wife along, and she proved the perfect guinea pig. She got seasick on the Grand Canal, slept soundly through the triumphal scene of "Aïda," and left the theatre during the airplane ride through the Rockies, saying that if she was going to fly the mountains she'd go with some pilot who knew *how* to fly.

It is now, apparently, Hollywood's considered opinion that there is too big a separation between screen and audience, and that once this gap is bridged, the industry will be revitalized. (The lion, leaping, must land in your lap; the kiss, delivered, must be delivered where it belongs, on the lips of the person who paid his money at the box office.) This simple-minded notion that art is a matter of tactuality is typical of Hollywood and should surprise no one. As for us, we're sticking to the belief that what the movies need is good pictures. The aim of picturemakers should be to establish the sort of emotional experience that one enjoys when reading a great book or watching a great play—which is a sense of participation by reason of detachment, and is not the experience of getting sent. We're beginning to think that great pictures, although not beyond the skill of Hollywood, are beyond its aspiration. And unless one's aspirations are in good order, one's business chances are dim indeed.

### Calculating Machine

A publisher in Chicago has sent us a pocket calculating machine by which we may test our writing to see whether it is intelligible. The calculator was developed by General Motors, who, not satisfied with giving the world a Cadillac, now dream of bringing perfect understanding to men. The machine (it is simply a celluloid card with a dial) is called the Reading-Ease Calculator and shows four grades of "reading ease"—Very Easy, Easy, Hard, and Very Hard. You count your words and syllables, set the dial, and an indicator lets you know whether anybody is going to understand what you have written. An instruction book came with it, and after mastering the simple rules we lost no time in running a test on the instruction book itself, to see how *that* writer was doing. The poor fellow! His leading essay, the one on the front cover, tested Very Hard.

Our next step was to study the first phrase on the face of the calculator: "How to test Reading-Ease of written matter." There is, of course, no such thing as reading ease of written matter. There is the ease with which matter can be read, but that is a condition of the reader, not of the matter. Thus the inventors and distributors of this calculator get off to a poor start, with a Very Hard instruction book and a slovenly phrase. Already they have one foot caught in the brier patch of English usage.

Not only did the author of the instruction book score badly on the front cover, but inside the book he used the word "personalize" in an essay on how to improve one's writing. A man who likes the word "personalize" is entitled to his choice, but we wonder whether he should be in the business of giving advice to writers. "Whenever possible," he wrote, "personalize your writing by directing it to the reader." As for us, we would as lief Simonize our grandmother as personalize our writing.

In the same envelope with the calculator, we received another training aid for writers—a booklet called "How to Write Better," by Rudolf Flesch. This, too, we studied, and it quickly demonstrated the broncolike ability of the English language to throw whoever leaps cocksurely into the saddle. The language not only can toss a rider but knows a thousand tricks for tossing him, each more gay than the last. Dr. Flesch stayed in the saddle only a moment or two. Under the heading "Think Before You Write," he wrote, "The main thing to consider is your *purpose* in writing. Why are you sitting down to write?" And echo answered: Because, sir, it is more comfortable than standing up.

Communication by the written word is a subtler (and more beautiful) thing than Dr. Flesch and General Motors imagine. They contend that the "average reader" is capable of reading only what tests Easy, and that the writer should write at or below this level. This is a presumptuous and degrading idea. There is no average reader, and to reach down toward this mythical character is to deny that each of us is on the way up, is ascending. ("Ascending," by the way, is a word Dr. Flesch advises writers to stay away from. Too unusual.)

It is our belief that no writer can improve his work until he discards the dulcet notion that the reader is feeble-minded, for writing is an act of faith, not a trick of grammar. Ascent is at the heart of the matter. A country whose writers are following a calculating machine downstairs is not ascending—if you will pardon the expression—and a writer who questions the capacity of the person at the other end of the line is not a writer at all, merely a schemer. The movies long ago decided that a wider communication could be achieved by a deliberate descent to a lower level, and they walked proudly down until they reached the cellar. Now they are groping for the light switch, hoping to find the way out.

We have studied Dr. Flesch's instructions diligently, but we return for guidance in these matters to an earlier American, who wrote with more patience, more confidence. "I fear chiefly," he wrote, "lest my expression may not be *extra-vagant* enough, may not wander far enough beyond the narrow limits of my daily experience, so as to be adequate to the truth of which I have been convinced. . . . Why level downward to our dullest perception always, and praise that as common sense? The commonest sense is the sense of men asleep, which they express by snoring."

Run that through your calculator! It may come out Hard, it may come out Easy. But it will come out whole, and it will last forever.

## Ghostwriting

A course in ghostwriting opens this month at American University, Washington, D. C., and youngsters whose dream is to put words into somebody else's mouth may further their ambition by enrolling. Theirs is a queer dream, but these are queer times. Some university was bound, sooner or later, to make an honest woman out of a ghostwriter, and it's probably no worse than spring football, at that. Dr. Walter P. Bowman, who will teach the course at American, points out that ghostwriters are indispensable today—"indispensable artisans," he calls them. If the course is to face up to realities, Dr. Bowman presumably will not make the mistake of preparing his lectures himself but will locate a behind-the-scenes man on the faculty to get up his stuff for him. The students, for their part, will not waste their own valuable time studying for their exams but will get some bright freshman to come up with the answers. We've been wondering what sort of final examination would be suitable for a course in ghostwriting. Cyrano de Bergerac, an early ghost, is probably the model to go by. If we were running the shop, we'd require every student, as a condition for passing the course, to compose a ballade while fighting a duel.

"Most of the great speeches we hear," said Dr. Bowman, "are written in whole or in part by someone backstage. It is time we recognized the fact." Well, everyone recognizes the fact that public men receive help in writing speeches, but whether the speeches are "great" is something else again. Roosevelt was a great man and an accomplished actor, but his speeches rarely seemed great to us; they seemed exactly what they were—smooth, carefully contrived, and bravely spoken, right up to the studied reference to God in the final sentence. Because of the nature of radio and television, virtually all public utterances nowadays are prefabricated, and while this tends to raise the general level of expression and gets rid of windbags, it also diminishes the chance of greatness. Great speeches are as much a part of a man as his eyeballs or his intestines. If Lincoln had had help on his Gettysburg speech, the thing would almost certainly have started "Eighty-seven years ago . . ."—showing that the ghost was right on the job.

We did a couple of short hitches, years ago, in the ghost world. A fellow who was trying to interest a syndicate in buying a column patterned after O. O. McIntyre turned the job of writing the sample column over to us. He said he was too busy to do it himself. (Imagine being too busy to imitate O. O. McIntyre!) We had plenty of leisure, and we wrote the column, and the other fellow signed it. We felt ghostly but not unhappy, and in no time at all the syndicate itself became too busy to write checks, and the enterprise blew up, as it well deserved to do. Another time, working for an adman who had motor accounts, we were told that the president of one of the motorcar companies was too busy to write a Christmas piece for the house organ, so we wrote it and he signed it. Here, too, nature took its course. The innocent forgery, so out of key with the spirit of Bethlehem, was presumably discovered by the American public—which is extremely sensitive to such things—and people stopped buying that make of car, and it is now out of existence, as it deserves to be, despite our effort to save it with a poem containing the lines:

> Together we sally at top of the morn,
> With frost on the fender and toots on the horn.

American University, if it is bent on adding ghost training to its curriculum, may soon have to decide how far into the shadowy jungles to proceed. An advertisement appeared in the Washington *Post* recently, reading as follows:

Too Busy to Paint? Call on The Ghost Artists. We Paint It— You Sign It. Why Not Give An Exhibition?

It turned out that the man behind this enterprise was Hugh Troy, veteran of many a satirical mission. But let no one be fooled. Mr. Troy's jokes go to the heart of the matter; the sober carry on in earnest what he indicates in fun. Essentially, the thing we find discouraging about the ghost world is not its areas of candid dishonesty but that the whole place smells of the American cult of busyness. Too busy to write. Lincoln probably had as much on his mind as the president of the motorcar company, but when an occasion arose, he got out a pencil and went to work alone. His technique is as good today, despite electronics, as it was then. Few men, however, have that kind of nerve today, or that kind of loneliness. They're all too busy taking their ghost to lunch and filling him in.

### Incubation

A bird sitting on eggs is all eye and tail, a miracle of silent radiation and patience. It is almost impossible to meet, squarely, the accusing gaze of a broody bird, however unjust the accusation may seem. Perhaps this is because the bird's dedication is pure—untainted by expectations of a hatch. (Nobody is more surprised than a hen bird when a shell opens and a chick comes out.) This classic pose of a bird is the despair of creative people: we have never seen a broody artist sitting on an egg except knowingly, in an attitude of sly expectancy.

### In Giving Thanks

The *Old Farmer's Almanac* arrived in time for Thanksgiving, tabulating our blessings and foreshadowing new blessings in the coming year. It is, after all, useful to know the hour of high water on one's next birthday, and the gestation period of the walrus. *Expect clear weather, followed by rain or snow.* This is good advice and we intend to take it.

The *Almanac* is a happy association of astronomy, prophecy, philosophy, and poetry—with random shots of photography thrown in, and a recipe for banana doughnuts. It is a timetable of the verities; in it you can almost hear the heavenly bodies slowing up on their whistle stops. On page 104, the astronomer discusses dawn and dark and the length of twilight. But long before you arrive at page 104, the poet for January has examined twilight:

> Where all's collapse and chaos, now,
> And dust of these obscures the sun . . .

The astronomer, worrying about the length of the twilight, advises that we "subtract from time of sunrise for dawn" and "add to time of sunset for dark." The poet, worrying about the same thing, speaks more resolutely:

> And take your stand and stay to see
> The wild and frightened and absurd
> Collapsing chaos turn and flee
> Before the grave compulsive word.

This is not only good advice, it is tingling. It can be accepted with confidence, and independently of aspects, holidays, heights of high water, and weather.

The thing to take one's stand on is, of course, liberty. Liberty is in a fix everywhere in the world, and men are spoiling to make the earth even less habitable than it now is. The tables of sunrise and sunset for another twelvemonth are almost the only surefire commodity for which to render thanks to God. Each morning, we glance at the political weather map for signs of clearing, but we think it quite likely that we are in for rain or snow. However, we have recently come across some remarks of E. M. Forster's, written in the memorable twilight of 1939. They are sustaining. His is the grave compulsive word. Mr. Forster, a lover of democracy, discerns in the world a sort of aristocracy—an aristocracy of the sensitive, the considerate, and the plucky. This is no Englishman's club; the members are everywhere, he thinks—in all lands, in all ages—"and there is a secret understanding between them when they meet. They represent the true human tradition, the one permanent victory of our queer race over cruelty and chaos." Their pluck, he writes, is not swankiness but the power to endure.

Mr. Forster in 1939 was not optimistic, but he had a nice, steady grip on his pen and found time to write coolly and appreciatively about the sensitive, considerate, and plucky. He felt that "with this type of person knocking about," the experiment of earthly life could by no means be dismissed as a failure. His words of 1939 cause us to give thanks in 1951. We propose to grab a bite of turkey, take our stand, and stay to see.

# SOME REMARKS ON HUMOR*

A NALYSTS have had their go at humor, and I have read some of this interpretative literature, but without being greatly instructed. Humor can be dissected, as a frog can, but the thing dies in the process and the innards are discouraging to any but the pure scientific mind.

In a newsreel theatre the other day I saw a picture of a man who had developed the soap bubble to a higher point than it had ever before reached. He had become the ace soap bubble blower of America, had perfected the business of blowing bubbles, refined it, doubled it, squared it, and had even worked himself up into a convenient lather. The effect was not pretty. Some of the bubbles were too big to be beautiful, and the blower was always jumping into them or out of them, or playing some sort of unattractive trick with them. It was, if anything, a rather repulsive sight. Humor is a little like that: it won't stand much blowing up, and it won't stand much poking. It has a certain fragility, an evasiveness, which one had best respect. Essentially, it is a complete mystery. A human frame convulsed with laughter, and the laughter becoming hysterical and uncontrollable, is as far out of balance as one shaken with the hiccoughs or in the throes of a sneezing fit.

One of the things commonly said about humorists is that they are really very sad people—clowns with a breaking heart. There

* Adapted from the preface to "A Subtreasury of American Humor," Coward-McCann, 1941.

is some truth in it, but it is badly stated. It would be more accurate, I think, to say that there is a deep vein of melancholy running through everyone's life and that the humorist, perhaps more sensible of it than some others, compensates for it actively and positively. Humorists fatten on trouble. They have always made trouble pay. They struggle along with a good will and endure pain cheerfully, knowing how well it will serve them in the sweet by and by. You find them wrestling with foreign languages, fighting folding ironing boards and swollen drainpipes, suffering the terrible discomfort of tight boots (or as Josh Billings wittily called them, "tite" boots). They pour out their sorrows profitably, in a form that is not quite fiction nor quite fact either. Beneath the sparkling surface of these dilemmas flows the strong tide of human woe.

Practically everyone is a manic depressive of sorts, with his up moments and his down moments, and you certainly don't have to be a humorist to taste the sadness of situation and mood. But there is often a rather fine line between laughing and crying, and if a humorous piece of writing brings a person to the point where his emotional responses are untrustworthy and seem likely to break over into the opposite realm, it is because humor, like poetry, has an extra content. It plays close to the big hot fire which is Truth, and sometimes the reader feels the heat.

The world likes humor, but it treats it patronizingly. It decorates its serious artists with laurel, and its wags with Brussels sprouts. It feels that if a thing is funny it can be presumed to be something less than great, because if it were truly great it would be wholly serious. Writers know this, and those who take their literary selves with great seriousness are at considerable pains never to associate their name with anything funny or flippant or nonsensical or "light." They suspect it would hurt their reputation, and they are right. Many a poet writing today signs his real name to his serious verse and a pseudonym to his comical verse, being unwilling to have the public discover him in any but a pensive and heavy moment. It is a wise precaution. (It is often a bad poet, too.)

When I was reading over some of the parody diaries of Franklin P. Adams, I came across this entry for April 28, 1926:

> Read H. Canby's book, *Better Writing*, very excellent. But when he says, "A sense of humour is worth gold to any writer," I disagree with him vehemently. For the writers who amass the greatest gold have, it seems to me, no sense of humour; and I think also that if they had, it would be a terrible thing for them, for it would paralyze them so that they would not write at all. For in writing, emotion is more to be treasured than a sense of humour, and the two are often in conflict.

That is a sound observation. The conflict is fundamental. There constantly exists, for a certain sort of person of high emotional content, at work creatively, the danger of coming to a point where something cracks within himself or within the paragraph under construction—cracks and turns into a snicker. Here, then, is the very nub of the conflict: the careful form of art, and the careless shape of life itself. What a man does with this uninvited snicker (which may closely resemble a sob, at that) decides his destiny. If he resists it, conceals it, destroys it, he may keep his architectural scheme intact and save his building, and the world will never know. If he gives in to it, he becomes a humorist, and the sharp brim of the fool's cap leaves a mark forever on his brow.

I think the stature of humor must vary some with the times. The court fool in Shakespeare's day had no social standing and was no better than a lackey, but he did have some artistic standing and was listened to with considerable attention, there being a well-founded belief that he had the truth hidden somewhere about his person. Artistically he stood probably higher than the humorist of today, who has gained social position but not the ear of the mighty. (Think of the trouble the world would save itself if it would pay some attention to nonsense!) A narrative poet at court, singing of great deeds, enjoyed a higher standing than the fool and was allowed to wear fine clothes; yet I suspect that the ballad singer was more often than not a second-rate stooge, flattering his monarch lyrically, while the fool must often have been a first-rate character, giving his monarch good advice in bad puns.

In the British Empire of our time, satirical humor of the Gilbert and Sullivan sort enjoys a solid position in the realm, and *Punch*, which is as British as vegetable marrow, is socially acceptable everywhere an Englishman is to be found. The *Punch* editors not only write the jokes but they help make the laws of England. Here in America we have an immensely humorous people in a land of milk and honey and wit, who cherish the ideal of the "sense" of humor and at the same time are highly suspicious of anything that is nonserious. Whatever else an American believes or disbelieves about himself, he is absolutely sure he has a sense of humor.

Frank Moore Colby, one of the most intelligent humorists operating in this country in the early years of the century, in an essay called "The Pursuit of Humor" described how the American loves and guards his most precious treasure:

> . . . Now it is the commonest thing in the world to hear people call the absence of a sense of humor the one fatal defect. No matter how owlish a man is, he will tell you that. It is a miserable falsehood, and it does incalculable harm. A life without humor is like a life without legs. You are haunted by a sense of incompleteness, and you cannot go where your friends go. You are also somewhat of a burden. But the only really fatal thing is the shamming of humor when you have it not. There are people whom nature meant to be solemn from their cradle to their grave. They

are under bonds to remain so. In so far as they are true to themselves they are safe company for any one; but outside their proper field they are terrible. Solemnity is relatively a blessing, and the man who was born with it should never be encouraged to wrench himself away.

We have praised humor so much that we have started an insincere cult, and there are many who think they must glorify it when they hate it from the bottom of their hearts. False humorworship is the deadliest of social sins, and one of the commonest. People without a grain of humor in their composition will eulogize it by the hour. Men will confess to treason, murder, arson, false teeth, or a wig. How many of them will own up to a lack of humor? The courage that could draw this confession from a man would atone for everything.

Relatively few American humorists have become really famous, so that their name is known to everyone in the land in the way that many novelists and other solemn literary characters have become famous. Mark Twain made it. He had, of course, an auspicious start, since he was essentially a story teller and his humor was an added attraction. (It was also very, very good.) In the 1920's and 30's, Ring Lardner was the idol of professional humorists and of plenty of other people, too; but I think I am correct in saying that at the height of his career he was not one of the most widely known literary figures in this country, and the name Lardner was not known to the millions but only to the thousands. He never reached Mr. and Mrs. America and all the ships at sea, to the extent that Mark Twain reached them, and I doubt if he ever will. On the whole, humorists who give pleasure to a wide audience are the ones who create characters and tell tales, the ones who are story tellers at heart. Lardner told stories and gave birth to some characters, but I think he was a realist and a parodist and a satirist first of all, not essentially a writer of fiction.

The general public needs something to get a grip on—a Penrod, a Huck Finn, a Br'er Rabbit, or a Father Day. The subtleties of satire and burlesque and nonsense and parody and criticism are not to the general taste; they are for the top (or, if you want, for the bottom) layer of intellect. Clarence Day, for example, was relatively inconspicuous when he was oozing his incomparable "Thoughts without Words," which are his best creations; he became generally known and generally loved only after he had brought Father to life. (Advice to young writers who want to get ahead without any annoying delays: don't write about Man, write about *a* man.)

I was interested, in reading DeVoto's "Mark Twain in Eruption," to come across some caustic remarks of Mr. Clemens's about an anthology of humor which his copyright lawyer had sent him and which Mark described as "a great fat, coarse, offensive volume." He was not amused. "This book is a cemetery," he wrote.

> In this mortuary volume [he went on] I find Nasby, Artemus Ward, Yawcob Strauss, Derby, Burdette, Eli Perkins, the Danbury News Man, Orpheus C. Kerr, Smith O'Brien, Josh Billings, and a score of others, maybe two score, whose writings and sayings were once in everybody's mouth but are now heard of no more and are no longer mentioned. Seventy-eight seems an incredible crop of well-known humorists for one forty-year period to have produced, and yet this book has not harvested the entire crop—far from it. It has no mention of Ike Partington, once so welcome and so well known; it has no mention of Doesticks, nor of the Pfaff crowd, nor of Artemus Ward's numerous and perishable imitators, nor of three very popular Southern humorists whose names I am not able to recall, nor of a dozen other sparkling transients whose light shone for a time but has now, years ago, gone out.
>
> Why have they perished? Because they were merely humorists. Humorists of the "mere" sort cannot survive. Humor is only a

fragrance, a decoration. Often it is merely an odd trick of speech and of spelling, as in the case of Ward and Billings and Nasby and the "Disbanded Volunteer," and presently the fashion passes and the fame along with it.

Not long ago I plunged back fifty to a hundred years into this school of dialect humor that Mark Twain found perishable. Then was the heyday of the crackerbarrel philosopher, sometimes wise, always wise-seeming, and when read today rather dreary. It seemed to me, in reading the dialect boys, that a certain basic confusion often exists in the use of tricky or quaint or illiterate spelling to achieve a humorous effect. I mean, it is not always clear whether the author intends his character to be writing or speaking—and I, for one, feel that unless I know at least this much about what I am reading, I am off to a bad start. For instance, here are some spellings from the works of Petroleum V. Nasby: he spells "would" *wood*, "of" *uv*, "you" *yoo*, "hence" *hentz*, "office" *offis*.

Now, it happens that I pronounce "office" *offis*. And I pronounce "hence" *hentz*, and I even pronounce "of" *uv*. Therefore, I infer that Nasby's character is supposed not to be speaking but to be writing. Yet in either event, justification for this perversion of the language is lacking; for if the character is speaking, the queer spelling is unnecessary, since the pronunciation is almost indistinguishable from the natural or ordinary pronunciation, and if the character is writing, the spelling is most unlikely. Who ever wrote "uv" for "of"? Nobody. Anyone who knows how to write at all knows how to spell a simple word like "of." If you can't spell "of" you wouldn't be able to spell anything and wouldn't be attempting to set words to paper—much less words like "solissitood." A person who can't spell "of" is an illiterate, and the only time such a person attempts to write anything down is in a great crisis. He doesn't write political essays or diaries or letters or satirical paragraphs.

In the case of Dooley, the Irish dialect is difficult but worth the effort, and it smooths out after the first hundred miles. Finley Peter Dunne was a sharp and gifted humorist, who wrote no second-rate stuff, and he had the sympathetic feeling for his character which is indispensable. This same sympathy is discernible in contemporary Jewish humor—in the work of Milt Gross, Arthur Kober, Leonard Q. Ross. It is sympathy, not contempt or derision, that makes their characters live. Lardner's ballplayer was born because the author had a warm feeling for ballplayers, however boyish or goofy. The spelling in all these cases is not a device for gaining a humorous effect but a necessary tool for working the material, which is inherently humorous.

I suspect that the popularity of all dialect stuff derives in part from flattery of the reader—giving him a pleasant sensation of superiority which he gets from working out the intricacies of misspelling, and the satisfaction of detecting boorishness or illiteracy in someone else. This is not the whole story but it has some bearing in the matter. Incidentally, I am told by an authority on juvenile literature that dialect is tops with children. They like to puzzle out the words. When they catch on to the thing, they must feel that first fine glow of maturity—the ability to exercise higher intellectual powers than those of the character they are looking at.

But to get back to Mark Twain and the "great fat, coarse volume" that offended him so:

There are those [he continued], who say that a novel should be a work of art solely, and you must not preach in it, you must not teach in it. That may be true as regards novels but it is not true as regards humor. Humor must not professedly teach, and it must not professedly preach, but it must do both if it would live forever. By forever I mean thirty years. With all its preaching it is not likely to outlive so long a term as that. The very things it preaches about, and which are novelties when it preaches about them, can cease to be novelties and become commonplaces in thirty years. Then that sermon can thenceforth interest no one.

I have always preached. That is the reason that I have lasted thirty years. If the humor came of its own accord and uninvited, I have allowed it a place in my sermon, but I was not writing the sermon for the sake of humor. I should have written the sermon just the same, whether any humor applied for admission or not. I am saying these vain things in this frank way because I am a dead person speaking from the grave. Even I would be too modest to say them in life. I think we never become really and genuinely our entire and honest selves until we are dead— and not then until we have been dead years and years. People ought to start dead, and then they would be honest so much earlier.

I don't think I agree that humor must preach in order to live; it need only speak the truth—and I notice it usually does. But there is no question at all that people ought to start dead.

# DON MARQUIS*

AMONG books of humor by American authors, there are only a handful that rest solidly on the shelf. This book about Archy and Mehitabel, hammered out at such awful cost by the bug hurling himself at the keys, is one of those books. It is funny, it is wise; it goes right on selling, year after year. The sales do not astound me; only the author astounds me, for I know (or think I do) at what cost Don Marquis produced these gaudy and irreverent tales. He was the sort of poet who does not create easily; he was left unsatisfied and gloomy by what he produced; day and night he felt the juices squeezed out of him by the merciless demands of daily newspaper work; he was never quite certified by intellectuals and serious critics of belles lettres. He ended in an exhausted condition—his money gone, his strength gone. Describing the coming of Archy in the Sun Dial column of the New York *Sun* one afternoon in 1916, he wrote: "After about an hour of this frightfully difficult literary labor he fell to the floor exhausted, and we saw him creep feebly into a nest of the poems which are always there in profusion." In that sentence Don Marquis was writing his own obituary notice. After about a lifetime of frightfully difficult literary labor keeping newspapers supplied with copy, he fell exhausted.

* This essay, in a slightly different form, appeared as the introduction to Doubleday's 1950 edition of "the lives and times of archy and mehitabel."

I feel obliged, before going any further, to dispose of one trouble-some matter. The reader will have perhaps noticed that I am capitalizing the name Archy and the name Mehitabel. I mention this because the capitalization of Archy is considered the unfor-givable sin by a whole raft of old Sun Dial fans who have some-how nursed the illogical idea that because Don Marquis's cockroach was incapable of operating the shift key of a typewriter, nobody else could operate it. This is preposterous. Archy himself wished to be capitalized—he was no e. e. cummings. In fact he once flirted with the idea of writing the story of his life all in capital letters, if he could get somebody to lock the shift key for him. Furthermore, I capitalize Archy on the highest authority: wherever in his columns Don Marquis referred to his hero, Archy was capitalized by the boss himself. What higher authority can you ask?

The device of having a cockroach leave messages in his type-writer in the *Sun* office was a lucky accident and a happy solution for an acute problem. Marquis did not have the patience to adjust himself easily and comfortably to the rigors of daily columning, and he did not go about it in the steady, conscientious way that (for example) his contemporary Franklin P. Adams did. Conse-quently Marquis was always hard up for stuff to fill his space. Adams was a great editor, an insatiable proofreader, a good makeup man. Marquis was none of these. Adams, operating his Conning Tower in the *World,* moved in the commodious margins of column-and-a-half width and built up a reliable stable of con-tributors. Marquis, cramped by single-column width, produced his column largely without outside assistance. He never assembled a hard-hitting bunch of contributors and never tried to. He was impatient of hard work and humdrum restrictions, yet expression was the need of his soul. (It is significant that the first words

Archy left in his machine were "expression is the need of my soul.")

The creation of Archy, whose communications were in free verse, was part inspiration, part desperation. It enabled Marquis to use short (sometimes very, very short) lines, which fill space rapidly, and at the same time it allowed his spirit to soar while viewing things from the under side, insect fashion. Even Archy's physical limitations (his inability to operate the shift key) relieved Marquis of the toilsome business of capital letters, apostrophes, and quotation marks, those small irritations that slow up all men who are hoping their spirit will soar in time to catch the edition. Typographically, the *vers libre* did away with the turned or runover line that every single-column practitioner suffers from.

Archy has endeared himself in a special way to thousands of poets and creators and newspaper slaves, and there are reasons for this beyond the sheer merit of his literary output. The details of his creative life make him blood brother to writing men. He cast himself with all his force upon a key, head downward. So do we all. And when he was through his labors, he fell to the floor, spent. He was vain (so are we all), hungry, saw things from the under side, and was continually bringing up the matter of whether he should be paid for his work. He was bold, disrespectful, possessed of the revolutionary spirit (he organized the Worms Turnverein), was never subservient to the boss yet always trying to wheedle food out of him, always getting right to the heart of the matter. And he was contemptuous of those persons who were absorbed in the mere technical details of his writing. "The question is whether the stuff is literature or not." That question dogged his boss, it dogs us all. This book—and the fact that it sells steadily and keeps going into new editions—supplies the answer.

In one sense Archy and his racy pal Mehitabel are timeless. In another sense, they belong rather intimately to an era—an era in American letters when this century was in its teens and its early twenties, an era before the newspaper column had degenerated. In 1916 to hold a job on a daily paper, a columnist was expected to be something of a scholar and a poet—or if not a poet at least to harbor the transmigrated soul of a dead poet. Nowadays, to get a columning job a man need only have the soul of a Peep Tom or a third-rate prophet. There are plenty of loud clowns and bad poets at work on papers today, but there are not many columnists adding to belles lettres, and certainly there is no Don Marquis at work on any big daily, or if there is, I haven't encountered his stuff. This seems to me a serious falling off of the press. Mr. Marquis's cockroach was more than the natural issue of a creative and humorous mind. Archy was the child of compulsion, the stern compulsion of journalism. The compulsion is as great today as it ever was, but it is met in a different spirit. Archy used to come back from the golden companionship of the tavern with a poet's report of life as seen from the under side. Today's columnist returns from the platinum companionship of the night club with a dozen pieces of watered gossip and a few bottomless anecdotes. Archy returned carrying a heavy load of wine and dreams. These later cockroaches come sober from their taverns, carrying a basket of fluff. I think newspaper publishers in this decade ought to ask themselves why. What accounts for so great a falling off?

To interpret humor is as futile as explaining a spider's web in terms of geometry. Marquis was, and is, to me a very funny man, his product rich and satisfying, full of sad beauty, bawdy adventure, political wisdom, and wild surmise; full of pain and jollity, full of exact and inspired writing. The little dedication to this book

. . . to babs
with babs knows what
and babs knows why

is a characteristic bit of Marquis madness. It has the hasty despair, the quick anguish, of an author who has just tossed another book to a publisher. It has the unmistakable whiff of the tavern, and is free of the pretense and the studied affection that so often pollute a dedicatory message.

The days of the Sun Dial were, as one gazes back on them, pleasantly preposterous times and Marquis was made for them, or they for him. *Vers libre* was in vogue, and tons of souped-up prose and other dribble poured from young free-verse artists who were suddenly experiencing a gorgeous release in the disorderly high-sounding tangle of nonmetrical lines. Spiritualism had captured people's fancy also. Sir Arthur Conan Doyle was in close touch with the hereafter, and received frequent communications from the other side. Ectoplasm swirled around all our heads in those days. (It was great stuff, Archy pointed out, to mend broken furniture with.) Souls, at this period, were being transmigrated in Pythagorean fashion. It was the time of "swat the fly," dancing the shimmy, and speakeasies. Marquis imbibed freely of this carnival air, and it all turned up, somehow, in Archy's report. Thanks to Archy, Marquis was able to write rapidly and almost (but not quite) carelessly. In the very act of spoofing free verse, he was enjoying some of its obvious advantages. And he could always let the chips fall where they might, since the burden of responsibility for his sentiments, prejudices, and opinions was neatly shifted to the roach and the cat. It was quite in character for them to write either beautifully or sourly, and Marquis turned it on and off the way an orchestra plays first hot, then sweet.

Archy and Mehitabel, between the two of them, performed the inestimable service of enabling their boss to be profound without sounding self-important, or even self-conscious. Between them, they were capable of taking any theme the boss threw them, and handling it. The piece called "the old trouper" is a good example of how smoothly the combination worked. Marquis, a devoted member of The Players, had undoubtedly had a bellyful of the lamentations of aging actors who mourned the passing of the great days of the theatre. It is not hard to imagine him hastening from his club on Gramercy Park to his desk in the *Sun* office and finding, on examining Archy's report, that Mehitabel was inhabiting an old theatre trunk with a tom who had given his life to the theatre and who felt that actors today don't have it any more— "they don't have it here." (Paw on breast.) The conversation in the trunk is Marquis in full cry, ribbing his nostalgic old actors all in the most wildly fantastic terms, with the tomcat's grandfather (who trooped with Forrest) dropping from the fly gallery to play the beard. This is double-barreled writing, for the scene is funny in itself, with the disreputable cat and her platonic relationship with an old ham, and the implications are funny, with the author successfully winging a familiar type of bore. Double-barreled writing and, on George Herriman's part, double-barreled illustration. It seems to me Herriman deserves much credit for giving the right form and mien to these willful animals. They possess (as he drew them) the great soul. It would be hard to take Mehitabel if she were either more catlike or less. She is cat, yet not cat; and Archy's lineaments are unmistakably those of poet and pest.

Marquis was by temperament a city dweller, and both his little friends were of the city: the cockroach, most common of city bugs; the cat, most indigenous of city mammals. Both, too, were tavern habitués, as was their boss. Here were perfect transmigrations of an American soul, this dissolute feline who was a dancer and always the lady, *toujours gai*, and this troubled insect who was a poet—both seeking expression, both vainly trying to reconcile art and life, both finding always that one gets in the way of the other.

Marquis moved easily from one literary form to another. He was parodist, historian, poet, clown, fable writer, satirist, reporter, and teller of tales. He had everything it takes and more. In this book you will find prose in the guise of bad *vers libre*, you will find poetry that is truly free verse, and you will find rhymed verse. Whatever fiddle he plucked, he always produced a song. I think he was at his best in a piece like "warty bliggens," which has the jewel-like perfection of poetry and contains cosmic reverberations along with high comedy. Beautiful to read, beautiful to think about.

At bottom Don Marquis was a poet, and his life followed the precarious pattern of a poet's existence. He danced on bitter nights with Boreas, he ground out copy on drowsy afternoons when he felt no urge to write and in newspaper offices where he didn't want to be. After he had exhausted himself columning, he tried playwriting and made a pot of money (on "The Old Soak") and then lost it all on another play (about the Crucifixion). He tried Hollywood and was utterly miserable and angry, and came away with a violent, unprintable poem in his pocket describing the place. In his domestic life he suffered one tragedy after another —the death of a young son, the death of his first wife, the death of his daughter, finally the death of his second wife. Then sickness and poverty. All these things happened in the space of a few years. He was never a robust man—usually had a puffy, overweight look and a gray complexion. He loved to drink, and was told by doctors that he mustn't. Some of the old tomcats at The Players remember the day when he came downstairs after a month on the wagon, ambled over to the bar, and announced: "I've conquered that god-damn will power of mine. Gimme a double scotch."

I think the new generation of newspaper readers is missing a lot that we used to have, and I am deeply sensible of what it meant to be a young man when Archy was at the top of his form and when Marquis was discussing the Almost Perfect State in the daily paper. Buying a paper then was quietly exciting, in a way that it has ceased to be.

# IV.

## Nine Songs

# THE RED COW IS DEAD

ISLE OF WIGHT (AP)—Sir Hanson Rowbotham's favorite Red Polled cow is dead. Grazing in the lush pastures of the Wellow Farm, she was bitten on the udder by an adder.—*The Herald Tribune*.

Toll the bell, fellow,
This is a sad day at Wellow:
Sir Hanson's cow is dead,
His red cow,
Bitten on the udder by an adder.

Spread the bad news! What is more sudden,
What sadder than udder stung by adder?
He's never been madder, Sir Hanson Rowbotham.

The Red Polled cow is dead.
The grass was lush at very last,
And the snake (a low sneak)
Passed, hissed,
Struck.

Now a shadow goes across the meadow,
Wellow lies fallow.
The red cow is dead, and the stories go round.
"Bit in the teat by a dog in a fit."
"A serpent took Sir Hanson's cow—
A terrible loss, a king's ransom."

A blight has hit Wight:
The lush grass, the forked lash, the quick gash
Of adder, torn bleeding udder,
The cow laid low,
The polled cow dead, the bell not yet tolled
(A sad day at Wellow),
Sir Hanson's cow,
Never again to freshen, never again
Bellow with passion—
A ruminant in death's covenant,
Smitten, bitten, gone.
Toll the bell, young fellow!

# CONCH

Hold a baby to your ear
  As you would a shell:
Sounds of centuries you hear
  New centuries foretell.

Who can break a baby's code?
  And which is the older—
The listener or his small load?
  The held or the holder?

# VILLAGE REVISITED

(A cheerful lament in which truth, pain, and beauty are
prominently mentioned, and in that order)

In the days of my youth, in the days of my youth,
I lay in West Twelfth Street, writhing with Truth.
I died in Jones Street, dallying with pain,
And flashed up Sixth Avenue, risen again.

In the terrible beautiful age of my prime,
I lacked for sweet linen but never for time.
The tree in the alley was potted in gold,
The girls on the buses would never grow old.

Last night with my love I returned to these haunts
To visit Pain's diggings and try for Truth's glance;
I was eager and ardent and waited as always
The answering click to my ring in the hallways,
But Truth hardly knew me, and Pain wasn't in
(It scarcely seemed possible Pain wasn't in).

Beauty recalled me. We bowed in the Square,
In the wonderful westerly Waverly air.
She had a new do, I observed, to her hair.

# THE ANSWER IS "NO"

What answer maketh the crow?
Always "No."

Put several questions in a row
To a crow,
You will get "No, no, no,"
Or "No, no, no, no."

Sometimes, on being questioned,
The crow says "Naw"
Or "Caw."
But regardless of pronunciation,
There is never anything but opposition, denial,
And negation
In a crow.

In their assemblies at the edge of town,
Crows introduce resolutions, then vote them down.
How many times in summer, waked early by the mosquito,
Have I lain listening to the crow's loud veto!

Once, gunning, I wounded a thieving
Crow
And have not forgotten his terrible, disbelieving
"Oh, *no!*"

# WINDOW LEDGE IN THE ATOM AGE

I have a bowl of paper whites,
  Of paper-white narcissus;
Their fragrance my whole soul delights,
  They smell delissus.
      (They grow in pebbles in the sun
        And each is like a star.)

I sit and scan the news hard by
  My paper-white narcissus;
I read how fast a plane can fly,
  Against my wissus.
      (The course of speed is almost run,
        We know not where we are.)

They grow in pebbles in the sun,
  My beautiful narcissus,
Casting their subtle shade upon
  Tropical fissus.
      (No movement mars each tiny star;
        Speed has been left behind.)

I'd gladly trade the latest thing
  For paper-white narcissus;
Science, upon its airfoil wing,
  Now seems pernissus.
    (Who was it said to travel far
      Might dissipate the mind?)


I love this day, this hour, this room,
  This motionless narcissus;
I love the stillness of the home,
  I love the missus.
    (She grows in pebbles in my sun
      And she is like a star.)


And though the modern world be through
  With paper-white narcissus,
I shall arise and I shall do
  The breakfast dissus.
    (The tranquil heart may yet outrun
      The rocket and the car.)

# UNDER A STEAMER RUG

There's a horn on the play.
There's a haze in the dell.
Dakin will kick.
Hooper will hold.
The hills are in gray.
The air will turn cold.
Fumble.

There's a haze in the dell.
The ball's on the ten.
He got it away.
There's a horn on the play.
Hoogin will hold.
Caskey will kick.
Are your hands cold?
Your feet?

DeLoosey for Wrenn.
The year's at the close.
The ball's on the ten.
He fades, throws.
The pass is complete.
Goal.
The wind blows
And blows.

The hills are in gray.
Someone will kick.
Someone will hold.
The year has grown old
They made it.
A minute to play.
A gain of two yards.
The game has grown old.
An overcast day.
A sweet, sad day.
They're leaving the stands.
It's over.

# DISTURBERS OF THE PEACE

The cows lie sweetly by the pond,
　At ease, at peace (except for flies);
The glassy morning waves its wand
　And bids the summer day arise.

Arise, O pesky day, arise!
　The peaceful cow, with flies to bother,
The dog his worms, the hen her lice,
　And Man—Man his eternal brother.

# SPRINGTIME CROSSTOWN EPISODE
## IN FOUR-TIME

As I was crossing Chatham Bar
  In Fortywhich Street west of Lex,
An Eastern Doorman sprang from cover,
  Unmistakable as to sex:
A brilliant Doorman, adult male,
With flashpatch wings and rufous tail,
A piping Doorman whistling clear,
And oh, it was a song to hear!
  Chwee . . . whee,
  And a skyview taxi-taxi-taxi.

The morn was tied with Aprilstrings,
  The bar was warm, the air was sweet,
The Doorman danced and drooped his wings
  And circled bravely in the street.
And when his whistling drew no cab,
Out from the tangle, shy and drab,
A female crept—a little doxy,
Drawn more sure than any taxi.

The Eastern Doorman quit his questing,
Chirruped twice, and they went to nesting.
  Chwee . . . whee!

# SONG OF THE QUEEN BEE

"The breeding of the bee," says a United States Department of Agriculture
bulletin on artificial insemination, "has always been handicapped by the fact
that the queen mates in the air with whatever drone she encounters."

When the air is wine and the wind is free
And the morning sits on the lovely lea
And sunlight ripples on every tree,
Then love-in-air is the thing for me—
 I'm a bee,
 I'm a ravishing, rollicking, young queen bee,
 That's me.

I wish to state that I think it's great,
Oh, it's simply rare in the upper air,
 It's the place to pair
 With a bee.
Let old geneticists plot and plan,
They're stuffy people, to a man;
Let gossips whisper behind their fan.
 (Oh, she *does?*
 Buzz, buzz, buzz!)
My nuptial flight is sheer delight;
I'm a giddy girl who likes to swirl,
 To fly and soar

And fly some more,
   I'm a bee.
And I wish to state that I'll *always* mate
   With whatever drone I encounter.


There's a kind of a wild and glad elation
In the natural way of insemination;
Who thinks that love is a handicap
Is a fuddydud and a common sap,
For I am a queen and I am a bee,
I'm devil-may-care and I'm fancy-free,
The test tube doesn't appeal to me,
   Not me,
   I'm a bee.
And I'm here to state that I'll *always* mate
   With whatever drone I encounter.


Let mares and cows, by calculating,
Improve themselves with loveless mating,
Let groundlings breed in the modern fashion,
I'll stick to the air and the grand old passion;
I may be small and I'm just a bee
But I *won't* have Science improving *me*,
   Not me,
   I'm a bee.
On a day that's fair with a wind that's free,
Any old drone is the lad for me.


I have no flair for love *moderne*,
It's far too studied, far too stern,
I'm just a bee—I'm wild, I'm free,
   That's me.

I can't afford to be too choosy;
In every queen there's a touch of floozy,
   And it's simply rare
   In the upper air
   And I wish to state
   That I'll *always* mate
With whatever drone I encounter.

Man is a fool for the latest movement,
He broods and broods on race improvement;
What boots it to improve a bee
If it means the end of ecstasy?
   (He ought to be there
   On a day that's fair,
   Oh, it's simply rare
    For a bee.)
Man's so wise he is growing foolish,
Some of his schemes are downright ghoulish;
He owns a bomb that'll end creation
And he wants to change the sex relation,
He thinks that love is a handicap,
He's a fuddydud, he's a simple sap;
Man is a meddler, man's a boob,
He looks for love in the depths of a tube,
His restless mind is forever ranging,
He thinks he's advancing as long as he's changing,
He cracks the atom, he racks his skull,
Man is meddlesome, man is dull,
Man is busy instead of idle,
Man is alarmingly suicidal,
   Me, I'm a bee.

I am a bee and I simply love it,
I am a bee and I'm darned glad of it,
I am a bee, I know about love:
You go upstairs, you go above,
You do not pause to dine or sup,
The sky won't wait—it's a long trip up;
You rise, you soar, you take the blue,
It's you and me, kid, me and you,
It's everything, it's the nearest drone,
It's never a thing that you find alone.
  I'm a bee,
  I'm free.

If any old farmer can keep and hive me,
Then any old drone may catch and wive me;
I'm sorry for creatures who cannot pair
On a gorgeous day in the upper air,
I'm sorry for cows who have to boast
Of affairs they've had by parcel post,
I'm sorry for man with his plots and guile,
His test-tube manner, his test-tube smile;
I'll multiply and I'll increase
As I always have—by mere caprice;
For I am a queen and I am a bee,
I'm devil-may-care and I'm fancy-free,
Love-in-air is the thing for me,
  Oh, it's simply *rare*
  In the beautiful air,
    And I wish to state
    That I'll *always* mate
  With whatever drone I encounter.

# V.

## The City and the Land

# THE HOTEL

## OF THE TOTAL STRANGER

With the train having arrived and the blurred terminal having been safely passed through and the porter ahead with the bags and then the bags first into the cab and the question "Where to?" obediently and correctly answered, Mr. Volente settled back into the leather seat with one foot on his luggage and his head now resting back and his gaze fixed upward through the open skylight, the buildings crouching over him and sweeping by. There is no earliness, said Mr. Volente without saying anything, quite like the earliness of a city morning in the great heat of summer, the audible heat, the visible heat, odorous and vaporous and terrible and seductive. He could still feel against his toe the quick nudge of the metal plate at the top of the escalator, hitting his toe at the end of the ascent as though it (the stationary element) were actually the moving element, as though the terminal had slipped itself under his foot, he being rigid, still, quiescent, the terminal being fluent, restless, and suddenly buoyant and he suddenly floor-borne.

The Hotel of the Total Stranger, he had said to the driver, Max Weinraub, and the door had closed and the hand of Weinraub had, reaching back, lowered the flag on the meter and the yellow flight had begun toward the known destination, the predictable hotel room (although it might be almost any number, still always the same room—it might be 302, or it might be 907 on the ninth floor, or it might be Number 1411 which would be a hard number to remember and he would be always asking for the wrong key perhaps), but it would be the familiar room just the same with the, Mr. Volente was sure, same things in it, no matter what number. It would have first the airless abandoned feeling and then the windows flung up by the boy dropping the bags and instantly the infiltration of the noise and the heat and the life and the pigeon on the sill straightening its feathers. The walls would be apple green, the paneling (apple green) decorative on the wall being formed by strips of molding, also the same color. And the mirror would match the bureau because it would match, and would be suspended by a gold cord with a decorative gold button concealing the hook and a gold tassel as the crowning effect. Oh, beloved room, the steel girders structurally in place here overhead, neatly buried in their white cerements, giving Mr. Volente something to gaze upon while lying in bed; and the bathroom with the shower curtain on little roller-hooks, a single shake being enough (Oh, room!) to distribute the curtain the whole length of the tub, and the glass shelves of the medicine cabinet ready (and able) for the safe-keeping of the brush, the cream, the paste, the things. In the closet would be the paper bag to catch the soiled clothes which if sent before eight would be returned on the afternoon of the third day. It was a Biblical promise, the afternoon of the third day, almost.

New York lay stretched in midsummer languor under her trees in her thinnest dress, idly and beautifully to the eyes of Mr. Volente her lover. She lay this morning early in the arms of the heat, humorously and indulgently, as though, having bathed in night, she had emerged and not bothered to put anything on and had stretched out to let the air, what air there was, touch her along arms and legs and shoulders and forehead, he thought, admiringly.

The trucks and the sudden acceleration and the flippant horn and the rustle of countless affairs somewhat retarded by the middle-of-summer pause in everything, these were the sounds of her normal breathing (if you knew her well enough and had lived with her at this season in the long past) and her pulse, normal. It was the hour the earliest people were entering the buildings. Awnings were being cranked down already to spread the agreeable shade, the rectangles of relief sketched on the sidewalks. In every street the glimpse he caught of some door or some vestibule or some window would stir his memory and call up the recollection of something in his life that had once been.

"It was in this doorway . . .

"It was down that side street . . .

"It was in the back room of this café that . . ."

That was the thing about New York, it was always bringing up something out of your past, something ridiculous or lovely or glistening. Here all round him, he mused, was unquestionably the closest written page in the book of his life; here in the city in the streets and alleys and behind the walls and in the booths and beneath the roofs and under the marquees and canopies were the scenes of the story he remembered in tranquillity, however poorly constructed, however unconvincing when retold.

In the short space of time it took the cab to go from the Penn Station to the hotel Mr. Volente mentally made the long sentimental journey to the historical places of the past. He knew that in the flesh he would soon visit some of these spots, just in passing, when he got loose in the city—as he always did; the habit of revisitation was fixed in him, it was a date he kept with himself, unconsciously—the only date he regarded with complete seriousness in New York. It was always that way: when he got to town the first phone message he put through was to himself. Mr. Volente, calling Mr. Volente. Meanwhile, sitting in the cab, he piloted his thoughts swiftly to the ports they always called in. Here was Fifth Avenue and the Childs restaurant where the waitress had long ago spilled a bottle of buttermilk down his blue suit. A turning point, he liked to think. He often wondered where the girl was, this somehow invaluable and clumsy girl who had unwittingly shaped his life into a pattern from which it had not since departed. (Mr. Volente had written an account of the catastrophe at the time and had sold it to a young and inexperienced magazine, thus making for himself the enormously important discovery that the world would pay a man for setting down a simple, legible account of his own misfortunes. With the check in his pocket and trouble always at his elbow, the young Volente had faced life with fresh courage and had seen a long vista of profitable confession; and in fact he had stuck it out and done well enough.) I suppose I shall run out eventually, he thought dreamily, but I haven't yet. That poor girl—that waitress! Where is she? He should send her something, a large sum of money such as five dollars perhaps, or an autographed copy of his latest book, let's see, what was the name of it?

What is this we have here? A shop window. That's it. On University Place. It was while looking into this window that a small dog he had once loved (and a great window shopper) had been struck by a cab and killed. The very place. And the dog was a sort of symbol of something which was still alive, still very much alive, and must be kept forever safe against disaster and the badly driven cabs that there are in the world. University Place, corner of Eighth Street (careful about the car tracks that aren't there any more, Volente!) a stone's throw from the place—yes, there is the garden, visible through the iron gates, a comic pleasance surrounded by walls, the same pergolas, the same privet hedges, the brick paths, and the pinched and sooty symmetry. How infinitely refreshing it had seemed in those days and still seems now in memory, from the third-floor rear of the house where in the bedroom on the hot days the cool cross draft across the low rooftops of the Mews struck through, filtered of all devils by the coarse mesh of the fire escape, the peaceful ineradicable room! Farther west . . . it was in this block, it was here, in Washington Place, it was down these three steps, or is it four, in this now legitimate café once so lawless and hospitable, that they had dined the night they were married (only nobody knew) and had sipped the wine in joy. Here is the very lamp-post (next block, please) under which, in another chapter, in another vein, with equal wonder and intensity . . .

This statue in the Square—something familiar here, Volente! Of course! Subject of a sonnet. Sonnet twenty-nine, the one with the tired feet. Yet how tender and fine and wonderful it had seemed on the occasion of its troubled birth!

It was here on this stoop he had vomited, but we will not dwell on that. He was always vomiting, thought Volente with a sigh. Nausea and love, the twin convulsions, one of the stomach, the other of the entire system sometimes called the heart. O passionate and disturbing city to whose innumerable small rooms at whose uncountable tables he had committed the immediate problems of the soul, to have them clarified in the wine at evening and returned to him (as though by special messenger) on a tray the following morning—all those crazy little places, ennobled by the so many confidences. (In those days, he thought, there was no air-conditioning; the same air remained in the small rooms and moved about, distributed by a fan, from table to table with the drifting smoke, until the whole place gathered over a period of months and years an accumulation of ardor and love and adventure and hope, a fine natural patina on floors and walls, as a church accumulates piety and sorrow and holiness.)

Mr. Volente's cab moved swiftly but not so swiftly as his mind, which was in West Thirteenth Street in a remoter past, only the El was there and the shoe-shine hat-cleaning parlor on the corner. It was up two flights, he thought, and heard the clicking of the release latch on the outer door and saw the polished plates of the letter boxes and read the names. Two flights up, what lean and tortured years, with those other fellows—all gainfully employed except himself—those mornings alone in the apartment straightening up after the others had left for work, rinsing the dirty cereal-encrusted bowls, taking the percolator apart and putting it together again, and then sinking down on the lumpy old couch in the terrible loneliness of midmorning, sometimes giving way to tears of doubt and misgiving (his own salt rivers of doubt), and in the back room the compensatory window box with the brave and grimy seedlings struggling, and the view of the naked fat lady across the yard. It had always been a question then of how to get through the day, the innumerable aimless journeys to remote sections of the town, inspecting warehouses, docks, marshes, lumberyards, the interminable quest for the holy and unnamable grail, looking for it down every street and in every window and in every pair of eyes, following a star always obscured by mists. But there were also the noons in the restaurant in Waverly Place (it was through that door) studying the menu to get the biggest value for fifty cents including tip, studying the faces of the other lunchers and the answering grave look in the eyes of the girls and the constant and abiding riddle, and on fine warm June days in the back garden, the same food and ritual, in the ailanthus shade. And the healing night (Mr. Volente had glided swiftly down Sixth, turned right on West 4th, then left on Barrow and vanished down a rabbit hole where he was welcomed by an Italian, and there would be the same cheap table d'hôte that he liked and the same girl with him that he loved, together discovering the indispensable privacy of a dim and crowded room).

It was in this flower shop that I bought the . . . it was in the third booth from the door in the second restaurant from the corner that B. told me that . . . it was at this newsstand that I bought the Morning *World* that contained . . . here walked I under these great trees alone with my misery . . . it was from this drugstore that I phoned M. . . . it was up that narrow and deplorable stairway I ascended . . .

Mr. Volente's mind skipped again, downtown to a doorway in Park Row. It was late Saturday afternoon in the fall of the year and he was standing in the lobby slowly eating Tokay grapes and spitting out the seeds. He had just quit his first job in New York and he was moodily eating the grapes by way of celebrating, in one inclusive ritual, the failure of his first major maneuver in life and the renewal of his liberty. His inability to cope with the requirements of the job was a stone in his stomach, to which he was now adding ripe grapes; but the sense that his movements were no longer circumscribed by the hands of a clock, the sense of the return of footlooseness, the sense of again being a reporter receiving only the vaguest and most mysterious assignments, was oxygen in his lungs. He stood there a long time, having nowhere in particular to go any more. An important doorway, he had always thought. He had never eaten a red grape since without tasting again the sweet tonic of rededication.

Ah, me, thought Mr. Volente.

Doorways! Had he never been anywhere except in some doorway for God's sake? There was an almost furtive quality to his past. Fourth Avenue in the twenties, what are you doing here, Volente, in this doorway in this dreary section of Fourth Avenue? You know well enough—you know you are waiting, because you think if you wait cleverly enough, you will catch a glimpse of her as she gets out at five o'clock from her job in that woolen place unless it was a cotton place, anyway a glimpse being the only nourishment that this bitter day affords, and this waiting, like a hungry dog for a crust. I said hungry, Volente.

Gramercy is round the corner, the green Gramercy with the snobbish fence behind which the rich children ride the velocipedes from Schwarz's. It was in that park, keyless though I was at the time, said Mr. Volente . . .

Here is the house where I awoke after the ball was over and in the solemn dreadful noon put on the dinner jacket again, and the rumpled-bosomed formal shirt again, and traveled across town pretending I was a waiter or a musician on his way to keep an engagement. Here is the tower where my son was born, and the sound of the Sunday bells, and the angel of death in a starched uniform and the blood running slowly through the transfusing tubes.

The cab stopped at the Hotel of the Total Stranger, and Volente registered and was shown to his room, Number 704, the one with the mirror with the gold tassel. He unpacked, putting his razor and things in the medicine cabinet. After breakfast he walked out as he had known he would, and met the heat as he emerged into the street, and took the city in his arms affectionately and held her, with love and recognition. The people were moving slowly, the delivery boys in shirtsleeves with the half-moon of sweat under the armpit, the porter languidly shining the bronze standpipe with the creamy stuff from the old gin bottle, the cop in shirtsleeves, even his revolver wilting under the terrible blow from the sun. Mr. Volente strolled aimlessly over to Park Avenue and turned uptown. Presently he noticed a doorway that seemed familiar. He glanced at the number, then at the names on the plaque. Names of medical men. Volente smiled. It was in this building, on a May morning . . .

Volente sighed. Oh inscrutable and lovely town! oh citadel of love.

# NOTES ON THE CITY

## High Noon

We LUNCHED alone today, as is our wont. It has its peptic advantages and induces a disconsolate attitude which has some slight literary value. Looking about the room, though, at the tables of twos, threes, and fours, we realized how important a function lunch is in New York, how drastic and purposeful. There was a dark pall of gain hanging over every table—everyone there for some reason of business or intrigue: salesmen, applicants, supplicants, agents provocateurs, contact executives, actresses gaming with managers, writers taking the temperature of editors, lovers sparring for their strange vantage, everywhere a sprig of personal increase garnishing the cold salmon. Next to us a burlap-bag man was convincing a poultry-feed gentleman that his particular sack kept the vitamins alive longer than usual. As we watched the interplay, we envisioned millions of hens standing in caked hen-yards, uttering the dreamy summer sound that hens make, unaware of the new sack, the new retention of vitamins in the laying mash, the myriad other new things which arise from lunch in town.

With nothing much else to do, we complained of the fish, which stank. "You do not like the fish?" said the captain, after the waiter had whispered about the trouble at his table. "It stinks," we said, in our simplest vein. But the captain would not smell it, despite the nose being the most valuable of all organs in the appraisal of food. He would bring us, without charge, another dish —but he wouldn't be caught sniffing his own fish. Dogs are more forthright in these situations. They not only will sniff bad fish, they will stick up for it.

❦

Our waiter told us he felt surprisingly well, and thought this was because he always ate the skin of fishes. He strongly recommended fish skin as tonic. But we draw our strength not from admitting the rind of fish into our stomach but from holding the fish itself firmly in mind—the protein remembrance of the cool fish-in-being, the silver meteor, perfectly adapted to its environment. It is a mistake to underestimate the sustaining power of a thing in its natural, or undigested, form. Everyone must have his own secret source of vital strength. Some eat grapes to avoid cancer, and receive strength that way. Others knit in silence, and draw electric power directly from the needles. Recently we opened a box from the country and were restored by the sharp smell of fir balsam and the flash of alderberry, as though we had received a transfusion from the great blood bank of New England. It is important that everyone feel strong and recognize the sources of his strength.

### Transient

In the patchy little gardens of Turtle Bay, where half a dozen dry sycamore leaves constitute the pungent fall, a thrush appeared the other morning. We watched him from a window, exploring the tangle, dipping at the fountain, brown and unannounced. There is a special satisfaction to a city person in such a visitation; we took twice the pleasure in this thrush that we would have felt had we discovered him in the country. The city is the place for people who like life in tablet form, concentrated: a forest resolved into a single tree, a lake distilled into a fountain, and all the birds of the air embodied in one transient thrush in a small garden.

## Business Show

It was a soft afternoon with smoke rising in straws of light from the chimneys, and pink clouds the color of chrysanthemums folded gently against a pale sky. Even Eighth Avenue seemed to dwell in heavenly pallor when we left it to plunge into the Business Show and walk in the chattering aisles of calculators, addressographs, electric tabulation machines, where girls in purest white satin, enthroned on chromium chairs, their blonde hair gleaming like clouds, their nails shining pink the color of chrysanthemums, pushed the little shining keys—tick, tap, PULL, tick, tap, PULL— adding, subtracting, filing, assembling, addressing, dictaphoning, typing, silhouetted firmly against the pure walls of steel that was grained to look like wood, and the murmurous mysteries of business enlarged a hundred times, staggering the mind. Adoringly we paused before each machine, as a traveller before a shrine; and it all seemed more mechanistic than any play we had ever seen, even than the plays produced by the little groups who take the theatre seriously. But what we noticed was that the seeming dominance of the machines was an illusion of the senses, that the electric current was in fact impotent, for everywhere we saw men standing gravely talking to the girls in purest white satin, and always something passed between them, something a little extra in their look, the eyes of the girls returning the clear, desirous gaze of the builders of the incredible machines, giving back desire for desire, and that the current of this exchange (the exciting unfulfillment) was the thing in all the room, and not the chattering mysteries of the addition, tabulation, punctuation, subtraction, which were as nothing, which were as an accompaniment (tick, tap, PULL) to the loud, insistent, throbbing song of beauty unattainable, hair (like clouds) infinitely desirable (in a hall on Eighth Avenue), with smoke rising in straws of light from the chimneys.

## Quietude

The city's effort to quell noise turned out to be loudly characteristic. To the existing din the city added a large yellow truck, filled it with flashy newspaper reporters and decibel detectors, and hired two taxicabs to roar across its path, blowing their horns continuously. The heavens boomed with anti-sound.

We have never regarded the decibel as a particularly trustworthy index of sound. Sound is not easily measured. Some of the loudest sounds wouldn't give a decibel machine the faintest tremor: a hushed voice in a house where someone has died; or a child's finger on the latch of a door where a man is trying to work, timorously testing the lock to see if the man won't come out and play. The quality of sound is much more telling than the volume, and this is true in the city, where noise is inevitable. A country sawmill is rich in decibels, yet the ear adjusts easily to it, and it soon becomes as undisturbing as a cicada on a suburban afternoon. New York's noise, even in its low decibel range, has an irritating quality, full of sharp distemper. It is impatient, masochistic—unlike the noise of Paris, where the shrill popping of high-pitched horns spreads a gaiety and a slightly drunken good nature. Heat has an effect on sound, intensifying it. On a scorching morning, at breakfast in a café, one's china coffee cup explodes against its saucer with a fierce report. The great climaxes of sound in New York are achieved in side streets, as in West 44th Street, beneath our window, where occasionally an intestinal stoppage takes place, the entire block laden with undischarged vehicles, the pangs of congestion increasing till every horn is going—a united, delirious scream of hate, every decibel charged with a tiny drop of poison.

We are not fooled by the town's earnest, wistful quest for quietude. We have been all through things like this, including an anti-smoke campaign which choked us half to death. The vitality of our citizenry is too great to hope for silence. Even now, on our pointed ears, there comes the distant racking of a motor horn— unquestionably the horn of a member of the League for Less Noise, urging a pedestrian out of his path so he can get to an anti-noise meeting on time.

### Sadness of Parting

The barber was cutting our hair, and our eyes were closed—as they are so likely to be. We had passed into that deep and bountiful world of repose which one finds only at the end of the tonsorial trail. The scissors, stroking, had entered into the deliberate phase well behind the ears; our head was bowed; and peace had settled over the chair, with only the asthmatic inhalations of the barber marking life's beat. Deep in a world of our own, we heard, from far away, a voice saying goodbye. It was a customer of the shop, leaving. "Goodbye," he said to the barbers. "Goodbye," echoed the barbers. And without ever returning to consciousness, or opening our eyes, or thinking, we joined in. "Goodbye," we said, before we could catch ourself. Then, all at once, the sadness of the occasion struck us, the awful dolor of bidding farewell to someone we had never seen. We have since wondered what he looked like, and whether it was really goodbye.

### Rediscovery

Coming in from the country, we put up at a hotel in midtown for a few days recently, to give the moths free rein in our apartment. Our hotel bedroom was on an air shaft, and whenever anyone took a shower bath the sissing sound could be heard clearly. People took showers frequently, because of the heat and because a shower is one of the ways you can kill time in a hotel. Somebody would come in at five in the afternoon and take a shower, then in the evening people would be taking showers around eight or nine, then after the theatre they would come back and take one, and then the late people—the playboys and the playgirls—would return at three in the morning and cool off in a shower. One morning we woke at seven, or half woke, and lay in bed listening to the sissing. Everybody in the building seemed to be taking a shower. After a while we caught on. It was raining. Good for the crops at the bottom of the air shaft, probably.

Sometimes our affection for New York becomes dulled by familiarity. No building seems high, no subway miraculous, no avenue enchanted—all, all commonplace. Then, in a moment of rediscovery, it is as though we were meeting the city again for the first time. This happened a couple of days ago when we dropped into our abandoned apartment to retrieve a book. It was a shut place —a stagnant tomb of camphor, drawn shades, and green memories. No air had entered or left, no tap had been turned, no picture gazed upon. The furniture, under dust covers, seemed poised to receive the dead. A fashion magazine lay open where it had been tossed, the fashionable ladies poised in summer dresses, waiting for fall. There was no mouse in the trap, no sherry in the decanter. Silent in the middle of turmoil, a cube of heat and expectancy, the place felt exciting and we were visited by a fresh sense of the surrounding city: the salt pressure of its tides, the perfect tragedy of each of its eight million inmates—so many destinations, so many arrivals and departures, and the fares being given and received, the promises given and received, the lights being switched on and off in the innumerable chambers, the flow of electricity and blood, the arrangements, the meetings, the purposeful engagements, and the people sealed tightly in phone booths dialling Weather, the calamities, the dead ends, the air drill poised ready to open the pavement, the dentist's drill poised ready to open the tooth, the conductor's baton poised ready, the critic's pencil poised ready, the ferry chain winding on the windlass, the thieves and vegetarians in the parks —we saw them all in dazzling clarity, as though the curtain had just lifted on New York. And when we quit the apartment and walked up the street, as though out upon a stage, we saw clearly the lady in black fishing in a trash can, and the sportive bachelor leaving his pointed shoes with the shoe-shine man at the corner, and we were spellbound at the majesty of ginkgoes and the courtesy of hackmen. We hadn't had anything to drink, either. Just stopped in to get a book.

## Impasse in the Business World

While waiting in the antechamber of a business firm, where we had gone to seek our fortune, we overheard through a thin partition a brigadier general of industry trying to establish telephone communication with another brigadier general, and they reached, these two men, what seemed to us a most healthy impasse. The phone rang in Mr. Auchincloss's office, and we heard Mr. Auchincloss's secretary take the call. It was Mr. Birstein's secretary, saying that Mr. Birstein would like to speak to Mr. Auchincloss. "All right, put him on," said Mr. Auchincloss's well-drilled secretary, "and I'll give him Mr. Auchincloss." "No," the other girl apparently replied, "you put Mr. Auchincloss on, and *I'll* give *him* Mr. Birstein." "Not at all," countered the girl behind the partition. "I wouldn't dream of keeping Mr. Auchincloss waiting."

This battle of the Titans, conducted by their leftenants to determine which Titan's time was the more valuable, raged for five or ten minutes, during which interval the Titans themselves were presumably just sitting around picking their teeth. Finally one of the girls gave in, or was overpowered, but it might easily have ended in a draw. As we sat there ripening in the antechamber, this momentary paralysis of industry seemed rich in promise of a better day to come—a day when true equality enters the business life, and nobody can speak to anybody because all are equally busy.

### Security

"When the war ends," said an ad in the *Times*, "you will need to own a farm or plantation as never before." The advertiser suggested three thousand acres on the coast of Georgia, most of it formerly planted to rice, these days a haven for wild ducks. "Create now an estate that will stand as a bulwark of safety against the vicissitudes of the future . . ."

This may well be a matter that is occupying many people's thoughts, for men, like ducks, are always searching for a haven. But to sell country real estate on a safety appeal seems to us to misrepresent the case. Ownership of land is still a pioneering adventure of major proportions; an estate is the very pattern of dangerous living. A city man, when he becomes the owner of a farm or plantation, is faced with two alternatives: he can restore the land to cultivation, exposing himself to a thousand hidden booby traps he didn't know were there, or he can leave the land alone and live on the income from his investments and on wild duck—also a very hazardous sort of life. On the whole we approve of people rediscovering the land, if they are in earnest about it, and pitting themselves against the elements, but the new life should be presented for what it is, an adventure of incalculable danger. Anyone proposing to take on a plantation should go forewarned and with the full realization that he will find, in his run-out fields, as many vicissitudes as ducks.

## In an Elevator

In an elevator, ascending with strangers to familiar heights, the breath congeals, the body stiffens, the spirit marks time. These brief vertical journeys that we make in a common lift, from street level to office level, past the missing thirteenth floor—they afford moments of suspended animation, unique and probably beneficial. Passengers in an elevator, whether wedged tight or scattered with room to spare, achieve in their perpendicular passage a trancelike state: each person adhering to the unwritten code, a man descending at five in the afternoon with his nose buried in a strange woman's back hair, reducing his breath to an absolute minimum necessary to sustain life, willing to suffocate rather than allow a suggestion of his physical presence to impinge; a man coming home at one A.M., ascending with only one other occupant of the car, carefully avoiding any slight recognition of joint occupancy. What is there about elevator travel that induces this painstaking catalepsy? A sudden solemnity, perhaps, which seizes people when they feel gravity being tampered with—they hope successfully. Sometimes it seems to us as though everyone in the car were in silent prayer.

## Twins

On a warm, miserable morning last week we went up to the Bronx Zoo to see the moose calf and to break in a new pair of black shoes. We encountered better luck than we had bargained for. The cow moose and her young one were standing near the wall of the deer park below the monkey house, and in order to get a better view we strolled down to the lower end of the park, by the brook. The path there is not much travelled. As we approached the corner where the brook trickles under the wire fence, we noticed a red deer getting to her feet. Beside her, on legs that were just learning their business, was a spotted fawn, as small and perfect as a trinket seen through a reducing glass. They stood there, mother and child, under a gray beech whose trunk was engraved with dozens of hearts and initials. Stretched on the ground was another fawn, and we realized that the doe had just finished twinning. The second fawn was still wet, still unrisen. Here was a scene of rare sylvan splendor, in one of our five favorite boroughs, and we couldn't have asked for more. Even our new shoes seemed to be working out all right and weren't hurting much.

The doe was only a couple of feet from the wire, and we sat down on a rock at the edge of the footpath to see what sort of start young fawns get in the deep fastnesses of Mittel Bronx. The mother, mildly resentful of our presence and dazed from her labor, raised one forefoot and stamped primly. Then she lowered her head, picked up the afterbirth, and began dutifully to eat it, allowing it to swing crazily from her mouth, as though it were a bunch of withered beet greens. From the monkey house came the loud, insane hooting of some captious primate, filling the whole woodland with a wild hooroar. As we watched, the sun broke weakly through, brightened the rich red of the fawns, and kindled their white spots. Occasionally a sightseer would appear and wander aimlessly by, but of all who passed none was aware that anything extraordinary had occurred. "Looka the kangaroos!" a child cried. And he and his mother stared sullenly at the deer and then walked on.

In a few moments the second twin gathered all his legs and all his ingenuity and arose, to stand for the first time sniffing the mysteries of a park for captive deer. The doe, in recognition of his achievement, quit her other work and began to dry him, running her tongue against the grain and paying particular attention to the key points. Meanwhile the first fawn tiptoed toward the shallow brook, in little stops and goes, and started across. He paused midstream to make a slight contribution, as a child does in bathing. Then, while his mother watched, he continued across, gained the other side, selected a hiding place, and lay down under a skunk-cabbage leaf next to the fence, in perfect concealment, his legs folded neatly under him. Without actually going out of sight, he had managed to disappear completely in the shifting light and shade. From somewhere a long way off a twelve-o'clock whistle sounded. We hung around awhile, but he never budged. Before we left, we crossed the brook ourself, just outside the fence, knelt, reached through the wire, and tested the truth of what we had once heard: that you can scratch a new fawn between the ears without starting him. You can indeed.

### Life in Bomb Shadow

The Inquiring Fotographer of the *Daily News* stopped Harry Fox, Lucio Porrello, Mrs. Helen E. Kopp, Pvt. Lawrence M. Zamparelli, Joseph Zovich, and Pvt. Andrew L. Trano last week and asked them what they would like to buy if they could afford it.

Zovich wanted a television set, so he would stay home nights, Fox wanted real estate (because "it is real"), Mrs. Kopp wanted a mortgage-free home, Porrello wanted a college education for his children, and Zamparelli craved a red convertible for his girl. That left only Private Trano, of the Bronx. When the question was put to Trano, he replied, "A home in the country for my father and mother. There they would be free from any fear of atom bombs. I'd provide a cellar built of lead, too, in case of an accidental bombing or a near-miss. Please print this, because my folks are in bad shape and it might cheer them up."

We have been thinking about this couple in the Bronx who are in bad shape from fear of atom bombs, and about their dream home in the country with its cellar built of lead. The subject of New York as a target for bombs is not much discussed, it seems to us, except indirectly, through casual news items about air-raid shelters and schoolroom instruction in how to dodge when a light is seen in the sky.

Roughly, the city divides into three groups: first, those who, because of lack of money, have no choice whether they will move out of range; second, those who enjoy the luxury of free choice and have decided to leave; and third, those who are free to go but prefer to remain. The first and third groups are very large, the second is very small.

Private Trano's answer to the *News* illustrates not only the demoralization of fear but the futility of flight. For he no sooner gets his parents into the country than he builds them a lead cellar, so their fears can be perpetuated in an atmosphere of peril and apprehension.

We've been trying to analyze our own sensations and convictions in the matter of New York as a place to live in the mid-twentieth century. We belong to the privileged group that could, if it chose, flee the town to the less plausible areas of the open country. Perhaps, if we knew for a certainty that on such and such a day, at such and such an hour, the city would in fact be exploded, we would get out, following the compelling urge for self-preservation that is in all animals. But since we lack such knowledge, our tendency, as it is the tendency of so many, is to stick around and maintain a business-as-usual demeanor. "Why?" we sometimes ask ourself. Partly pride. Partly lethargy. Partly a sense of fatality. Partly a sense of duty and a feeling that even the smallest endeavor, if it absorbs a man, is a contribution to the strength of all men.

There is, of course, hardly a person of any age or either sex in New York who hasn't pondered these matters, and probably almost everyone has come up with some sort of personal credo or philosophy about urban life in bomb shadow. We find no great desire in people to compare notes, though. Each prefers to keep his ideas locked up inside him.

We would not try to argue that it is sensible of human beings to continue living in a big city during the atomic age, but we are fairly sure of one thing: the lead cellar of Private Trano indicates that if fear is part of a person's baggage, it doesn't make much difference where he dwells; he will carry his bomb with him. The only way to dwell in cities these days, whether it be wise or foolish, is in the conviction that the city itself is a monument of one's own making, to which each shall be faithful in his fashion.

### Little Green Shebang

For us, one of the excitements of New York in these racy times is living near enough to the United Nations headquarters so that we can wander in now and again and sit in the new chairs and listen to the old debates. For about eight years, we have followed the U.N. around the country, have sat with it in sadness in the queer dwellings where, for lack of any better place to go, it has parked its briefcase. Opera houses, hotel rooms, college gyms, skating rinks, gyroscope factories. And now the little green shebang on the East River. All its homes have been queer; all have had one quality in common—a kind of dreaminess compounded of modern interiors, ancient animosities, and the aching hopes of invisible millions.

We saw an article in a Texas paper not long ago about the U.N. —a warning by an educator that grade-school children are being indoctrinated with one-worldism. He felt that it is improper, or inadvisable, to introduce youngsters in their formative years to anything as mysterious and complex as this international forum, and to what he called "the false mirage of hope." His argument was that until children have become acquainted with their own America, and have attained maturity of judgment, it is dangerous to introduce them to the United Nations and to "bespeak its virtues." He wants school children to "see America first." He suspects a sinister motivation behind the attempt to teach school children about the U.N. His concern is a genuine concern, obviously, and his argument is a familiar one, for the question of the United Nations has bothered many a board of education.

It seems to us that the answer is rather simple. Of course children should see America first; they are bound to see it first anyway, as it is what they see when they look out the window, or at the blackboard, or into the faces of their teachers and their contemporaries. But one of the many visible facts about America today is that it is, for better or for worse, participating in the United Nations. It would be indefensible to tell school children that the United Nations is working well, but we think it's equally indefensible to pretend that it doesn't exist, or that we're not involved deeply in it. The writer of the article in the paper describes the

U.N. as "ill-sired and begotten." Well, we were there at the birth, and we came away with the impression that the U.N. had indeed a very odd parentage: its dam was hope, its sire was fear. The result was a weak constitution. The infant is, we admit, unpromising. But the desires and passions that brought nations and peoples together in 1945 are by no means unpromising. There was something about that affair eight years ago that was inevitable, and shaky though it be today, it is a fact. No Texas educator should try to conceal the facts of life. Kids have always been quick to pick them up, despite the prudish attempts of their elders to prettify things.

We were thinking of these matters the other day as we sat moodily watching a meeting of the Political and Security Committee of the General Assembly. We wondered whether the Texas educator had ever wandered around much inside the U.N., as we do from time to time. We wondered whether he'd actually experienced the strange atmosphere of the place—the atmosphere he wants to keep secret from children. It is, we agree, a hall of fantasy. The fantasy is partly physical: the interiors always a little too good, the doors transparent, not really separating one area from another, the carpets too soft and deep, the words too hard and shallow, the corridors lonely, the chairs and facilities luxurious far beyond the facts of international harmony. Everywhere a sense of modernity, of elegance, of unreality. And over all a brooding excitement. Here under this roof are gathered every tension, every dream, every trick, every philosophy, every tongue. In many respects, when added all together, it is without meaning. There are days when it seems wholly without meaning. Yet in one respect it is the most significant place of all, and to keep a child from experiencing this side of it seems to us to misjudge the power of children to know and to understand. Any reasonably intelligent child of seven is capable of realizing that he has an opposite number somewhere in the world—some other seven-year-old, who is endowed with essentially the same properties and desires, if not the same opportunities and protections, and who is estranged because of distance and estranged because of language, and who is about to grow up into either an enemy or a friend.

The U.N. is a home that hasn't been lived in; the rooms are the work of a decorator, not of a wife. There is no more chilling sight than the spectacle of the preliminaries: the delegates standing around the periphery, talking in low tones, each in his own tongue; the wise smiles on the wise faces; the strategy of the day being plotted—the strategy that plays with the lives of millions all over the globe, including, we must sadly add, the lives of school children in Texas. This is the chilliest sight we ever saw. And the photographers closing in on Vishinsky as though he were the last man on earth, as though he had some special meaning that could be revealed to the world through the power of the lens.

The place often reminds us of a hospital. Recently we walked in and the public-address system was paging the delegate from Iran (as in a hospital you hear a doctor being called, and you shudder with the feeling that somewhere a patient has taken a turn for the worse). In the U.N. you hear them calling, calling, "The delegate from Iran," hear it sound importantly in the corridors, and you wonder if something in the Middle East has taken a turn for the worse. The U.N. is that kind of place—a chamber of horrors, but not anything you can keep from children. Even the building itself leaks; it has weep-holes in the spandrels, and is open to the rains and the winds of the world. Confronted with its unsuccess, confronted with its frauds and its trickeries and its interminable debates, we yet stand inside the place and feel the winds of the world weeping into our own body, feel the force underlying the United Nations, the force that is beyond question and beyond compare and not beyond the understanding of children. It will be their task (as it is ours) to plug the weep-holes in the spandrels.

# THE HEN

## (An Appreciation)*

CHICKENS do not always enjoy an honorable position among city-bred people, although the egg, I notice, goes on and on. Right now the hen is in favor. The war has deified her and she is the darling of the home front, feted at conference tables, praised in every smoking car, her girlish ways and curious habits the topic of many an excited husbandryman to whom yesterday she was a stranger without honor or allure.

My own attachment to the hen dates from 1907, and I have been faithful to her in good times and bad. Ours has not always been an easy relationship to maintain. At first, as a boy in a carefully zoned suburb, I had neighbors and police to reckon with; my chickens had to be as closely guarded as an underground newspaper. Later, as a man in the country, I had my old friends in town to reckon with, most of whom regarded the hen as a comic prop straight out of vaudeville. When I would return to city haunts for a visit, these friends would greet me with a patronizing little smile and the withering question: "How are all the chickens?" Their scorn only increased my devotion to the hen. I remained loyal, as a man would to a bride whom his family received with open ridicule. Now it is my turn to wear the smile, as I listen to the enthusiastic cackling of urbanites, who have suddenly taken up the hen socially and who fill the air with their newfound ecstasy and knowledge and the relative charms of the New Hampshire

* Preface to "A Basic Chicken Guide for the Small Flock Owner," by Roy E. Jones (William Morrow, 1944).

Red and the Laced Wyandotte. You would think, from their nervous cries of wonder and praise, that the hen was hatched yesterday in the suburbs of New York, instead of in the remote past in the jungles of India.

I am writing these preliminary remarks without having had the opportunity of reading what Mr. Jones, the author, has to say by way of instruction. To a man who keeps hens, all poultry lore is exciting and endlessly fascinating. I must have read millions of words of it, over the years, and I am not tired yet. The subject seems to improve by much repetition. Every spring I settle down with my farm journal and read, with the same glazed expression on my face, the age-old story of how to prepare a brooder house —as a housemaid might read, with utter absorption, an article on how to make a bed.

Since this book is a guide, I feel I should instruct the reader, and should not only praise the hen but bury her. Luckily I can squeeze everything I know about chickens into a single paragraph, and it is presumably my duty to do so without further delay. Here, then, is my Basic Chicken Guide:

Be tidy. Be brave. Elevate all laying house feeders and waterers twenty-two inches off the floor. Use U-shaped rather than V-shaped feeders, fill them half full, and don't refill till they are empty. Walk, don't run. Never carry any strange object into the henhouse with you. Don't try to convey your enthusiasm for chickens to anyone else. Electricity is easier than coal, but an electric brooder should be equipped with a small fan in its apex to provide a down-draft. Keep Rocks if you are a nervous man, Reds if you are a quiet one. Don't drop shingle nails on a brooder house floor. Never give day-old chicks starter mash for the first couple of days—give them chick feed, which is finely cracked grain. Don't start three hundred chicks if all you want is eight eggs a day for your own table. Don't brood with electricity unless you are willing to get out of

bed at 3 A.M. for a thunderstorm and a blown fuse. Do all your
thinking and planning backwards, starting with a sold egg, ending
with a boughten starter. Don't keep chickens if you don't like
chickens, or even if you don't like chicken manure. Always count
your chickens before they are hatched. If you haven't got three
hundred dollars and don't expect to have, don't buy three hundred day-old chicks, because you will soon need three hundred
dollars. Use clean sawdust for nest material and renew it often.
Never use straw for litter unless it is chopped. Tie your shoelaces
in a double knot in the morning when you get dressed, since hens
are under the impression that shoelaces are worms. When you
move birds from a brooder house to a range shelter, keep them
locked up in the shelter for two nights and one day before letting
them out to play.

That is my basic guide. I have no doubt Mr. Jones should be
consulted also.

A common charge made against the hen is that she is a silly
creature. It is a false charge. A hen is an alarmist but she is not
silly. She has a strong sense of disaster, but many of her fears
seem to me well founded: I have seen inexperienced people doing
things around hens which, if I were a hen, would alarm me, too.
Of course, the hen is intensely feminine. She is what the farmer
calls "flighty," and this is particularly true of young pullets who
are adjusting themselves to the severe strain of ovulation in the
intoxicating days of early fall. Although I refuse to believe that
she is a silly creature, I will admit that the hen is a rather
unpredictable one and sometimes manages to surprise even an old
friend and admirer like myself. Last December, after about sixteen
weeks of collecting eggs in my laying house without causing any
undue alarm among the birds, I went in one morning wearing a
wrist watch my wife had given me for Christmas. I opened
the first deck of nests and thrust my hand in under a hen to pull

the eggs out. The hen took one look at the watch and shrieked, "A time bomb!" Instantly the whole house was in an uproar, with hens trampling each other in a mad rush for the corners. This sort of panicky behavior causes some people to regard the hen as a silly creature.

Countless persons have had disastrous experiences with chickens —city persons who have imagined they could retire to the country and, with no previous training and no particular aptitude, make a nice living with hens. They might better have chosen dancing bears. The countryside is strewn with the crumbling ruins of their once golden adventure. Few people have any idea how much it costs to maintain chickens in the style to which they have been accustomed, how much and how varied the equipment required, how insatiable their appetite for grain, how many stages there are to the growth and development of a laying fowl, how easily the flock can be wiped out, how much labor is involved. It seems to me that anyone who proposes to go in for chickens should start slowly and cautiously—not with a lot of new buildings and shiny fountains but with a few ready-made pullets from good stock. If chickens are to be merely a luxury or a fad, and you have money in your pants and want to erect a dream palace for hens and hire a governess to look after their wants and button them up, then that is a different story; but I am sure it is not sensible to keep hens extravagantly, or ineptly, or at too great cost in materials and time.

In one matter I may be at variance with the author and publishers of this book, namely, the definition of a "small flock." My idea of a small flock is a flock of twelve. Or at the most, eighteen. Anything over eighteen is not a small flock, in my opinion, but a big one. I know that a flock of two or three hundred birds is often spoken of as a small flock, and maybe it is, but I will let the reader answer for himself on the night in late spring when he comes in to bed after having transferred his three hundred young birds from their brooder houses to the range, picking each bird up in the darkness, loading it into a truck or wheelbarrow, transporting the living cargo to its destination, and then picking each bird up again and placing it darkly on the roosts. If after performing this nocturnal bit of husbandry he still thinks three hundred is a small flock, he is entitled to his opinion.

Keeping chickens, like any other year-round work, loses some of its original luster after long periods of it. But a man who really gets on close terms with hens is not apt to want escape. There are moments and days of discouragement: a hen on a sad morning making her sad noise and undoing your cleverest devices can take the stuffing out of a man about as fast as anything I know. There are other moments and days which are richly rewarding and exhilarating. The feeling I had as a boy for the miracle of incubation, my respect for the strange calm of broodiness, and my awe at an egg pipped from within after twenty-one days of meditation and prayer—these have diminished but slightly. It was a city man, Clarence Day, who wrote:

> Oh who that ever lived and loved
> Can look upon an egg unmoved?

Surely that is the gentlest tribute and most exhausting sentiment ever written on this inexhaustible subject. Reader, if you can look upon an egg unmoved, stay away from hens!

# PASTURE MANAGEMENT

Down below the pasture pond,
　O'er the lovely lea,
I went spraying bushes
　With 2, 4-D.

*(For young, susceptible annual weeds, apply one to two pints
per acre.)*

I had read my bulletins,
　I was in the know.
The two young heifers
　Came and watched the show.

*(Along ditches and fence rows, use 2, 4-D when weeds are in a
succulent stage. Won't harm livestock.)*

Rank grew the pasture weeds,
　The thistle and the bay;
A quiet, still morning,
　A good time to spray.

*(Control weeds the easy way with Agricultural Weed-No-More—
not by chemical burn but by hormone action.)*

Suddenly I looked and saw
　What my spray had found:
The wild, shy strawberry
　Was everywhere around.

(*An alkyl ester of 2, 4-D is produced by reacting an alcohol with the raw 2, 4-D acid. The result is an oily liquid that sticks to weed leaves.*)

What sort of madness,
　Little man, is this?
What sort of answer to
　The wild berry's kiss?

(*Any 3- or 4-gallon garden pump-up sprayer can be used, after the standard nozzle has been replaced with a new precision nozzle.*)

It seemed to me incredible
　That I'd begun the day
By rendering inedible
　A meal that came my way.
All across the pasture in
　The strip I'd completed
Lay wild, ripe berries
　With hormones treated.

(*The booklet gives you the complete story.*)

I stared at the heifers,
　An idiot child;
I stared at the berries
　That I had defiled.

I stared at the lambkill,
The juniper and bay.
I walked home slowly
And put my pump away.
Weed-No-More, my lady,
O weed no more today.

(*Available in quarts, 1-gallon and 5-gallon cans, and 55-gallon drums.*)

# DEATH OF A PIG

I SPENT several days and nights in mid-September with an ailing pig and I feel driven to account for this stretch of time, more particularly since the pig died at last, and I lived, and things might easily have gone the other way round and none left to do the accounting. Even now, so close to the event, I cannot recall the hours sharply and am not ready to say whether death came on the third night or the fourth night. This uncertainty afflicts me with a sense of personal deterioration; if I were in decent health I would know how many nights I had sat up with a pig.

The scheme of buying a spring pig in blossomtime, feeding it through summer and fall, and butchering it when the solid cold weather arrives, is a familiar scheme to me and follows an antique pattern. It is a tragedy enacted on most farms with perfect fidelity to the original script. The murder, being premeditated, is in the first degree but is quick and skillful, and the smoked bacon and ham provide a ceremonial ending whose fitness is seldom questioned.

Once in a while something slips—one of the actors goes up in his lines and the whole performance stumbles and halts. My pig simply failed to show up for a meal. The alarm spread rapidly. The classic outline of the tragedy was lost. I found myself cast suddenly in the role of pig's friend and physician—a farcical character with an enema bag for a prop. I had a presentiment, the very first afternoon, that the play would never regain its balance and that my sympathies were now wholly with the pig. This was slapstick—the sort of dramatic treatment that instantly appealed to my old dachshund, Fred, who joined the vigil, held the bag, and, when all was over, presided at the interment. When we slid the body into the grave, we both were shaken to the core. The loss we felt was not the loss of ham but the loss of pig. He had evidently become precious to me, not that he represented a distant nourishment in a hungry time, but that he had suffered in a suffering world. But I'm running ahead of my story and shall have to go back.

My pigpen is at the bottom of an old orchard below the house. The pigs I have raised have lived in a faded building that once was an icehouse. There is a pleasant yard to move about in, shaded by an apple tree that overhangs the low rail fence. A pig couldn't ask for anything better—or none has, at any rate. The sawdust in the icehouse makes a comfortable bottom in which to root, and a warm bed. This sawdust, however, came under suspicion when the pig took sick. One of my neighbors said he thought the pig would have done better on new ground—the same principle that applies in planting potatoes. He said there might be something unhealthy about that sawdust, that he never thought well of sawdust.

It was about four o'clock in the afternoon when I first noticed that there was something wrong with the pig. He failed to appear at the trough for his supper, and when a pig (or a child) refuses supper a chill wave of fear runs through any household, or icehousehold. After examining my pig, who was stretched out in the sawdust inside the building, I went to the phone and cranked it four times. Mr. Dameron answered. "What's good for a sick pig?" I asked. (There is never any identification needed on a country phone; the person on the other end knows who is talking by the sound of the voice and by the character of the question.)

"I don't know, I never had a sick pig," said Mr. Dameron, "but I can find out quick enough. You hang up and I'll call Henry." Mr. Dameron was back on the line again in five minutes. "Henry says roll him over on his back and give him two ounces of castor oil or sweet oil, and if that doesn't do the trick give him an injection of soapy water. He says he's almost sure the pig's plugged up, and even if he's wrong, it can't do any harm."

I thanked Mr. Dameron. I didn't go right down to the pig, though. I sank into a chair and sat still for a few minutes to think about my troubles, and then I got up and went to the barn, catching up on some odds and ends that needed tending to. Unconsciously I held off, for an hour, the deed by which I would officially recognize the collapse of the performance of raising a pig; I wanted no interruption in the regularity of feeding, the steadiness of growth, the even succession of days. I wanted no interruption, wanted no oil, no deviation. I just wanted to keep on raising a pig, full meal after full meal, spring into summer into fall. I didn't even know whether there were two ounces of castor oil on the place.

Shortly after five o'clock I remembered that we had been invited out to dinner that night and realized that if I were to dose a pig there was no time to lose. The dinner date seemed a familiar conflict: I move in a desultory society and often a week or two will roll by without my going to anybody's house to dinner or anyone's coming to mine, but when an occasion does arise, and I am summoned, something usually turns up (an hour or two in advance) to make all human intercourse seem vastly inappropriate. I have come to believe that there is in hostesses a special power of divination, and that they deliberately arrange dinners to coincide with pig failure or some other sort of failure. At any rate, it was after five o'clock and I knew I could put off no longer the evil hour.

When my son and I arrived at the pigyard, armed with a small bottle of castor oil and a length of clothesline, the pig had emerged from his house and was standing in the middle of his yard, listlessly. He gave us a slim greeting. I could see that he felt uncomfortable and uncertain. I had brought the clothesline thinking I'd have to tie him (the pig weighed more than a hundred pounds) but we never used it. My son reached down, grabbed both front legs, upset him quickly, and when he opened his mouth to scream I turned the oil into his throat—a pink, corrugated area I had never seen before. I had just time to read the label while the neck of the bottle was in his mouth. It said Puretest. The screams, slightly muffled by oil, were pitched in the hysterically high range of pig-sound, as though torture were being carried out, but they didn't last long: it was all over rather suddenly, and, his legs released, the pig righted himself.

In the upset position the corners of his mouth had been turned down, giving him a frowning expression. Back on his feet again, he regained the set smile that a pig wears even in sickness. He stood his ground, sucking slightly at the residue of oil; a few drops leaked out of his lips while his wicked eyes, shaded by their coy little lashes, turned on me in disgust and hatred. I scratched him gently with oily fingers and he remained quiet, as though trying to recall the satisfaction of being scratched when in health, and seeming to rehearse in his mind the indignity to which he had just been subjected. I noticed, as I stood there, four or five small dark spots on his back near the tail end, reddish brown in color, each about the size of a housefly. I could not make out what they were. They did not look troublesome but at the same time they did not look like mere surface bruises or chafe marks. Rather they seemed blemishes of internal origin. His stiff white bristles almost completely hid them and I had to part the bristles with my fingers to get a good look.

Several hours later, a few minutes before midnight, having dined well and at someone else's expense, I returned to the pighouse with a flashlight. The patient was asleep. Kneeling, I felt his ears (as you might put your hand on the forehead of a child) and they seemed cool, and then with the light made a careful examination of the yard and the house for sign that the oil had worked. I found none and went to bed.

We had been having an unseasonable spell of weather—hot, close days, with the fog shutting in every night, scaling for a few hours in midday, then creeping back again at dark, drifting in first over the trees on the point, then suddenly blowing across the fields, blotting out the world and taking possession of houses, men, and animals. Everyone kept hoping for a break, but the break failed to come. Next day was another hot one. I visited the pig before breakfast and tried to tempt him with a little milk in his trough. He just stared at it, while I made a sucking sound through my teeth to remind him of past pleasures of the feast. With very small, timid pigs, weanlings, this ruse is often quite successful and will encourage them to eat; but with a large, sick pig the ruse is senseless and the sound I made must have made him feel, if anything, more miserable. He not only did not crave food, he felt a positive revulsion to it. I found a place under the apple tree where he had vomited in the night.

At this point, although a depression had settled over me, I didn't suppose that I was going to lose my pig. From the lustiness of a healthy pig a man derives a feeling of personal lustiness; the stuff that goes into the trough and is received with such enthusiasm is an earnest of some later feast of his own, and when this suddenly comes to an end and the food lies stale and untouched, souring in the sun, the pig's imbalance becomes the man's, vicariously, and life seems insecure, displaced, transitory.

As my own spirits declined, along with the pig's, the spirits of my vile old dachshund rose. The frequency of our trips down the footpath through the orchard to the pigyard delighted him, although he suffers greatly from arthritis, moves with difficulty, and would be bedridden if he could find anyone willing to serve him meals on a tray.

He never missed a chance to visit the pig with me, and he made many professional calls on his own. You could see him down there at all hours, his white face parting the grass along the fence as he wobbled and stumbled about, his stethoscope dangling—a happy quack, writing his villainous prescriptions and grinning his corrosive grin. When the enema bag appeared, and the bucket of warm suds, his happiness was complete, and he managed to squeeze his enormous body between the two lowest rails of the yard and then assumed full charge of the irrigation. Once, when I lowered the bag to check the flow, he reached in and hurriedly drank a few mouthfuls of the suds to test their potency. I have noticed that Fred will feverishly consume any substance that is associated with trouble—the bitter flavor is to his liking. When the bag was above reach, he concentrated on the pig and was everywhere at once, a tower of strength and inconvenience. The pig, curiously enough, stood rather quietly through this colonic carnival, and the enema, though ineffective, was not as difficult as I had anticipated.

I discovered, though, that once having given a pig an enema there is no turning back, no chance of resuming one of life's more stereotyped roles. The pig's lot and mine were inextricably bound now, as though the rubber tube were the silver cord. From then until the time of his death I held the pig steadily in the bowl of my mind; the task of trying to deliver him from his misery became a strong obsession. His suffering soon became the embodiment of all earthly wretchedness. Along toward the end of the afternoon, defeated in physicking, I phoned the veterinary twenty miles away and placed the case formally in his hands. He was full of questions, and when I casually mentioned the dark spots on the pig's back, his voice changed its tone.

"I don't want to scare you," he said, "but when there are spots, erysipelas has to be considered."

Together we considered erysipelas, with frequent interruptions from the telephone operator, who wasn't sure the connection had been established.

"If a pig has erysipelas can he give it to a person?" I asked.

"Yes, he can," replied the vet.

"Have they answered?" asked the operator.

"Yes, they have," I said. Then I addressed the vet again. "You better come over here and examine this pig right away."

"I can't come myself," said the vet, "but McFarland can come this evening if that's all right. Mac knows more about pigs than I do anyway. You needn't worry too much about the spots. To indicate erysipelas they would have to be deep hemorrhagic infarcts."

"Deep hemorrhagic what?" I asked.

"Infarcts," said the vet.

"Have they answered?" asked the operator.

"Well," I said, "I don't know what you'd call these spots, except they're about the size of a housefly. If the pig has erysipelas I guess I have it, too, by this time, because we've been very close lately."

"McFarland will be over," said the vet.

I hung up. My throat felt dry and I went to the cupboard and got a bottle of whiskey. Deep hemorrhagic infarcts—the phrase began fastening its hooks in my head. I had assumed that there could be nothing much wrong with a pig during the months it was being groomed for murder; my confidence in the essential health and endurance of pigs had been strong and deep, particularly in the health of pigs that belonged to me and that were part of my proud scheme. The awakening had been violent and I minded it all the more because I knew that what could be true of my pig could be true also of the rest of my tidy world. I tried to put this distasteful idea from me, but it kept recurring. I took a short drink of the whiskey and then, although I wanted to go down to the yard and look for fresh signs, I was scared to. I was certain I had erysipelas.

It was long after dark and the supper dishes had been put away when a car drove in and McFarland got out. He had a girl with him. I could just make her out in the darkness—she seemed young and pretty. "This is Miss Owen," he said. "We've been having a picnic supper on the shore, that's why I'm late."

McFarland stood in the driveway and stripped off his jacket, then his shirt. His stocky arms and capable hands showed up in my flashlight's gleam as I helped him find his coverall and get zipped up. The rear seat of his car contained an astonishing amount of paraphernalia, which he soon overhauled, selecting a chain, a syringe, a bottle of oil, a rubber tube, and some other things I couldn't identify. Miss Owen said she's go along with us and see the pig. I led the way down the warm slope of the orchard, my light picking out the path for them, and we all three climbed the fence, entered the pighouse, and squatted by the pig while McFarland took a rectal reading. My flashlight picked up the glitter of an engagement ring on the girl's hand.

"No elevation," said McFarland, twisting the thermometer in the light. "You needn't worry about erysipelas." He ran his hand slowly over the pig's stomach and at one point the pig cried out in pain.

"Poor piggledy-wiggledy!" said Miss Owen.

The treatment I had been giving the pig for two days was then repeated, somewhat more expertly, by the doctor, Miss Owen and I handing him things as he needed them—holding the chain that he had looped around the pig's upper jaw, holding the syringe, holding the bottle stopper, the end of the tube, all of us working in darkness and in comfort, working with the instinctive teamwork induced by emergency conditions, the pig unprotesting, the house shadowy, protecting, intimate. I went to bed tired but with a feeling of relief that I had turned over part of the responsibility of the case to a licensed doctor. I was beginning to think, though, that the pig was not going to live.

He died twenty-four hours later, or it might have been forty-eight—there is a blur in time here, and I may have lost or picked up a day in the telling and the pig one in the dying. At intervals during the last day I took cool fresh water down to him and at such times as he found the strength to get to his feet he would stand with head in the pail and snuffle his snout around. He drank a few sips but no more; yet it seemed to comfort him to dip his nose in water and bobble it about, sucking in and blowing out through his teeth. Much of the time, now, he lay indoors half buried in sawdust. Once, near the last, while I was attending him I saw him try to make a bed for himself but he lacked the strength, and when he set his snout into the dust he was unable to plow even the little furrow he needed to lie down in.

He came out of the house to die. When I went down, before going to bed, he lay stretched in the yard a few feet from the door. I knelt, saw that he was dead, and left him there: his face had a mild look, expressive neither of deep peace nor of deep suffering, although I think he had suffered a good deal. I went back up to the house and to bed, and cried internally—deep hemorrhagic intears. I didn't wake till nearly eight the next morning, and when I looked out the open window the grave was already being dug, down beyond the dump under a wild apple. I could hear the spade strike against the small rocks that blocked the way. Never send to know for whom the grave is dug, I said to myself, it's dug for thee. Fred, I well knew, was supervising the work of digging, so I ate breakfast slowly.

It was a Saturday morning. The thicket in which I found the

gravediggers at work was dark and warm, the sky overcast. Here, among alders and young hackmatacks, at the foot of the apple tree, Lennie had dug a beautiful hole, five feet long, three feet wide, three feet deep. He was standing in it, removing the last spadefuls of earth while Fred patrolled the brink in simple but impressive circles, disturbing the loose earth of the mound so that it trickled back in. There had been no rain in weeks and the soil, even three feet down, was dry and powdery. As I stood and stared, an enormous earthworm which had been partially exposed by the spade at the bottom dug itself deeper and made a slow withdrawal, seeking even remoter moistures at even lonelier depths. And just as Lennie stepped out and rested his spade against the tree and lit a cigarette, a small green apple separated itself from a branch overhead and fell into the hole. Everything about this last scene seemed overwritten—the dismal sky, the shabby woods, the imminence of rain, the worm (legendary bedfellow of the dead), the apple (conventional garnish of a pig).

But even so, there was a directness and dispatch about animal burial, I thought, that made it a more decent affair than human burial: there was no stopover in the undertaker's foul parlor, no wreath nor spray; and when we hitched a line to the pig's hind legs and dragged him swiftly from his yard, throwing our weight into the harness and leaving a wake of crushed grass and smoothed rubble over the dump, ours was a businesslike procession, with Fred, the dishonorable pallbearer, staggering along in the rear, his perverse bereavement showing in every seam in his face; and the post mortem performed handily and swiftly right at the edge of the grave, so that the inwards that had caused the pig's death preceded him into the ground and he lay at last resting squarely on the cause of his own undoing.

I threw in the first shovelful, and then we worked rapidly and without talk, until the job was complete. I picked up the rope, made it fast to Fred's collar (he is a notorious ghoul), and we all three filed back up the path to the house, Fred bringing up the rear and holding back every inch of the way, feigning unusual stiffness. I noticed that although he weighed far less than the pig, he was harder to drag, being possessed of the vital spark.

The news of the death of my pig travelled fast and far, and I received many expressions of sympathy from friends and neighbors, for no one took the event lightly and the premature expiration of a pig is, I soon discovered, a departure which the community marks solemnly on its calendar, a sorrow in which it feels fully involved. I have written this account in penitence and in grief, as a man who failed to raise his pig, and to explain my deviation from the classic course of so many raised pigs. The grave in the woods is unmarked, but Fred can direct the mourner to it unerringly and with immense good will, and I know he and I shall often revisit it, singly and together, in seasons of reflection and despair, on flagless memorial days of our own choosing.